JUSTIFIABLE RISK

Praise for the novels of
VK Powell

Fever

"VK Powell has given her fans an exciting read. The plot of *Fever* is filled with twists, turns, and 'seat of your pants' danger...*Fever* gives readers both great characters and erotic scenes along with insight into life in the African bush."—*Just About Write*

Suspect Passions

"From the first chapter of *Suspect Passions* Powell builds erotic scenes which sear the page. She definitely takes her readers for a walk on the wild side! Her characters, however, are also women we care about. They are bright, witty, and strong. The combination of great sex and great characters make *Suspect Passions* a must read."—*Just About Write*

To Protect and Serve

"If you like cop novels, or even television cop shows with women as full partners with male officers…this is the book for you. It's got drama, excitement, conflict, and even some fairly hot lesbian sex. The writer is a retired cop, so she really writes from a place of authenticity. As a result, you have a realistic quality to the writing that puts me in mind of early Joseph Wambaugh, before his writing became formulaic."—*Lesbian News*

"*To Protect and Serve* drew me in from the very first page with characters that captivated in their complexity. Powell writes with authority using the lingo and capturing the thoughts of the law enforcers who make the ultimate sacrifice in the fight against crime. What's more impressive is the command this debut author has of portraying a full gamut of emotion, from angst to elation, through dialogue and narrative. The images are vivid, the action is believable, and the police procedurals are authentic…VK Powell had me invested in the story of these women, heart, mind, body and soul. Along with danger and tension, Powell's well-developed erotic scenes sizzle and sate."—*Story Circle Book Reviews*

"VK Powell has a surefire winner with her first novel, *To Protect and Serve*. It is well-written, balancing an enchanting romance with a stimulating police procedural… Lust and love fill the novel, and the story touches us viscerally. We feel the characters' emotions, and are exposed to the intimacy that they crave… Powell has a wonderful future ahead of her as an author if *To Protect and Serve* is any indication."—*Just About Write*

Visit us at www.boldstrokesbooks.com

By the Author

To Protect and Serve

Suspect Passions

Fever

Justifiable Risk

JUSTIFIABLE RISK

by

VK Powell

2011

This Trade Paperback Original Is Published By
Bold Strokes Books, Inc.
P.O. Box 249
Valley Falls, NY 12185

First Edition: January 2011

Credits
Editor: Shelley Thrasher
Production Design: Stacia Seaman
Cover Design by Sheri (graphicartist2020@hotmail.com)

Acknowledgments

It would not be possible to do the work I love without the support and encouragement of incredible friends. Each of you brings a special gift to my life, and I am grateful.

To Len Barot, deep appreciation for allowing me to be a "writer." And to each person in the amazing Bold Strokes family who reads, tweaks, massages, and improves my imperfect product, I say thank you.

To Gill and Jove, thank you for making my first experience with beta readers a rewarding and painless one. This book is better for all your efforts.

My deepest gratitude to Dr. Shelley Thrasher for your guidance (subtle and otherwise), suggestions, and kindness. You help me view my work through fresh eyes.

To all the readers who support and encourage my writing, thank you for buying my work, visiting my website (www.powellvk.com), sending e-mails, and showing up for signings. You make my "job" so much fun!

PROLOGUE

A gun barrel was pressed against his temple. Cold shivered down his spine. His heart drummed, his body stinking of fear-sweat.

"Do it or I'll blow your fucking brains out. Bad sight for your family—body with no fucking head." The stranger motioned to the thin white lines of cocaine on the coffee table.

"Please, why are you doing this? I don't even know you."

"Just ain't your day."

"What do you want? Money?" His voice trembled and tears stung his eyes. What was happening? He couldn't think—was trying to survive. "Please."

"Nice big inhale. You'll like it." The gunman laughed—cold, like he was forcing it.

He shook his head, then looked around for an escape. The man stood between him and the door—trapped.

"Fucking snort. Do it. I don't have all night." The stranger jabbed the gun barrel against his temple again.

"Can I take off my shoes?"

The gunman's forehead wrinkled. "Sure, but make it quick."

He slid his Kenneth Cole oxfords off without untying them and tossed them toward a chair. Then he removed his socks and threw them on either side of the room. How freeing—to be careless and sloppy in the face of death. His captor shifted impatiently from side to side.

"Okay, you've had your fun. Snort."

Shaking, he picked up the straw and inhaled, trying to remember the last time he'd spoken with his family. If he'd only told someone where he was going today. If only…

"Now the other one." He repeated the process. "Excellent. Just sit back and enjoy the ride."

His heart pounded erratically. Energy surged in his brain. He gasped for air. Not enough air. Sweat trickled into his eyes, and he wiped at it, lethargic. "Please." A series of pictures flashed through his mind: his parents, brothers, sister, the woman he loved. Scenes from his life, good and bad. He tried to hold on to the images.

Everything around him blurred. He reached out for help. The coffee table rose toward him. His vision dimmed. He fell.

CHAPTER ONE

"Clare!" Greer Ellis's own horrified voice echoed in her ears, her throat dry and raw from screaming. Perspiration soaked the bedsheet, and she was hot and sticky. She threw off the wet covers and slowed her rapid breathing. The pulse pounding in her temples eased, and she slid her hand to the opposite side of the bed—still empty. The nightmare continued even after she woke. She'd had it less often during the past two years, but it remained as vivid.

Greer rose and crossed to the barn-style doors in her second-story garage apartment. They overlooked a stream-fed pond, and after she slid them apart she listened to the melodic trickling of water over rock. Gradually it reconnected her with the present. The gray dawn light bathed her cooling nude body in soft shadows, and the brisk fall air licked and tingled her clammy skin.

She grabbed the old kaleidoscopic throw that Clare had knitted, hugged it around her, and relaxed into its warmth. The wool-blend material was faded, its corners fraying. She inhaled deeply, hoping some remnant of Clare's scent remained. But it had vanished, like Clare had. Greer had refused to wash the afghan, or even use it very often, but that hadn't helped. She sat in the open doorway, swinging her legs and staring across at the deciduous trees. They had been stripped of their colorful leaves like she had been stripped of her lover.

A loud clanging from the main house announced that the morning's first pot of coffee was ready. Bessie had started using this method of notification when Greer moved from the house to the apartment two years ago. No matter how early the ghosts arrived in Greer's dreams, Bessie was awake first, like a sentinel keeping watch.

Greer walked through the back door ten minutes later fully dressed and ready for work. The beautiful log home that Bessie had built with her lover, Ruth, still held too many memories of their happy foursome. She'd hoped she wouldn't have to live in the apartment long, but each time she entered this space, she saw and heard Clare. She kissed her sixty-three-year-old aunt lightly on the cheek. "How you feeling, Aunt Bessie?"

"Next to perfect, as always." Bessie pinned her with sharp blue eyes that dared her to be untruthful. "Bad dream?"

"The usual." Her aunt was capable of peeling away her defensive layers like an orange. Greer busied herself pouring coffee to avoid prolonged exposure to the look that always left her feeling too vulnerable.

"When you're ready to talk, I'm here."

"I know. Thanks."

They slid into their morning breakfast routine with eggs, bacon, and grits, salted by the latest hospital gossip. As head nurse, Bessie knew all the rumors, which she shared—*in confidence.*

When they finished cleaning up and headed to their vehicles for work, Bessie said, "And one more thing. Stop trying to test your mortality with these stupid stunts you've been pulling." She tilted her head toward the new Harley-Davidson Fat Boy that Greer straddled. "Hospital gossip isn't the only scoop I'm privy to."

Greer throttled Icarus and shot out of the driveway around Bessie's old truck. In the side mirror, she saw her aunt mouth the words "slow down" before she disappeared in a cloud of gray dust. Greer twisted the grip again, laying a long stretch of rubber and popping a wheelie as she hit the road toward downtown New Hope. She had to completely concentrate and carefully control her body to perform the maneuver. She loved the power that pulsed between her legs and the way the bike teetered on its rear wheel. Riding Icarus flat-out made her enjoy life in a way that she hadn't for too long.

But her exhilaration vanished when the bike's front wheel reconnected with the pavement. Only the cool fall air, the vibrating machine, and memories of Clare remained. She could almost feel Clare's slender body pressed against her back, thighs cupping her butt, hands caressing her crotch until wetness seeped through her jeans. She often arrived at work horny and happy. During the day, the edginess kept her sharp and focused in her job as a beat cop. And at night Clare held her again and satisfied her need.

But Clare wasn't here. Reality sliced through her like the crisp morning wind stinging her face. She wouldn't hold Clare again. A stranger had made sure of that. Greer gunned Icarus and wished she could ride into the sun and burn away the loss and guilt. But no one answered her prayer. She couldn't soothe the ache permanently. She found relief only when she flirted with death.

She gripped the throttle tighter and buried the speedometer needle in the red zone. The bike burst into top speed and the frame vibrated with power. When her pain eased, she was entering the no-passing zone leading into town behind a very slow-moving vehicle. Greer pumped the brakes and cursed. Slowing, she followed the sightseer on Elm Street through downtown toward the police department.

"Get back," Eva Saldana said to the impatient motorcyclist who zoomed up behind her. She flashed to her assignment in Jakarta last year when two cyclists rode her bumper, then whizzed past with automatic weapons strapped to their sides. She shivered and tapped her brakes.

As the tailgater slowed, Eva again focused on the pleasant scene before her. Breakfast patrons chatted under rainbow-colored umbrellas lining the sidewalks of the cozy downtown avenue. The tires on her rented BMW thumped over the brick-paved street with the steady cadence of a carriage on cobblestones. As she gazed at the quaint small-town setting, several people waved as she passed.

But older warehouse buildings towered behind the colorful awnings and smiling faces. They reminded her of two movie sets quickly constructed with no time to clear the lot. The worn and crumbling façades looked ominous, as if waiting to consume the inviting foreground. If this scene was the norm in New Hope, North Carolina, population 55,000, her time here would be an experience in contrasts.

She nodded to the waving people and returned her attention to the street ahead. Hopefully the directions the pimple-faced gas-station attendant had given her were accurate. He'd said, "The police department's straight ahead about two miles on Elm. You can't miss it." So far he'd been wrong. She drummed the steering wheel impatiently, wishing she'd had more than a double espresso for breakfast.

Eva refused to be late for her meeting with Police Chief Sam Bryant. It was too important and, besides, she had lost control over too many things in her life. This wouldn't be one of them. She'd taken time from her job as an investigative journalist to come here and correct a terrible injustice. She would send the wrong message if she was even one minute tardy.

In spite of her anxiety, something about New Hope resonated with her. She lowered her window and breathed in the fresh fall air. Eating utensils clanked against dishes, and the low murmur of conversation wafted through her open window. The charcoal smell of burned wood mingled with the aroma of strong coffee and the sweet yeast of freshly baked pastries. A memory of home swept through her.

Her mother held a woven blue and brown basket filled with fresh bread and muffins in one hand and Eva's tiny fingers in the other. They walked toward the beach at Lagos, carrying breakfast to her father and brothers working at the fisheries. Along the white sandy path, neighbors and friends called out greetings. She was warm, happy, and safe.

That had been the last time Eva felt a complete sense of family. Her father's journalism career had taken off shortly afterward, and so had he. One assignment followed another until her memories of him dimmed. His brief visits made Eva want to cling to him and persuade him to stay in Portugal. But he also told wonderful stories that excited Eva and stirred her own wanderlust. Now she understood how addictive excitement and acclaim were. She had chosen the capricious lifestyle of a reporter too. Would he have understood why she had decided to put her family before her career right now, when she was so successful?

The impatient motorcyclist behind Eva tapped his horn twice. Eva was stopped at a green light staring at the New Hope Police

Department with its scroll-top Ionic columns and long, wide stairs. If she hadn't spotted the sign on the front lawn, she might have thought it was a historic antebellum home. She pulled behind the two-story structure with five minutes to spare and reached for the door handle.

As she swung the car door open, a rumble like an oversized lawn mower assaulted the air, and the motorcyclist who had screeched up behind her appeared. She barely had time to shut her door before the noisemaker skidded to a stop too close to her vehicle, rattling the entire car.

She watched from the safety of the BMW. The rider kicked down the stand on the white Harley-Davidson and swung his right leg over to dismount. Only an anatomically challenged male would wield such a loud, aggressive vehicle. Her temper sparked.

She shouldered the door wide and braced her leg against it to keep it open only inches from the resting motorcycle. Then she jumped out and prepared for her first fight of the day. "Didn't you see me here?" She gestured to the space between their vehicles.

The rider shucked off his helmet, raking his hand through a mop of thick blond hair. "Sorry, got a little close, didn't I?"

The simple gesture made Eva's anger fade into something as intense but even more uncomfortable. She thought of her father's favorite American Western, *Butch Cassidy and the Sundance Kid*. The woman who stood before her had the same wild-eyed look of unrest that Robert Redford did when he stood on a cliff before he and Paul Newman dove into a raging river. Her father had worn that type of restlessness like a cloak, and their family had been constantly in turmoil because of it.

"You lost?" The woman's husky voice rumbled through Eva as completely as the vibrations from her Harley had.

The motorcyclist stared at her with aqua eyes the hue of the Atlantic as it washed into the Bay of Lagos. A small scar bisected her left brow and stopped close to her eye, giving her a dangerous yet vulnerable air. Her blond hair fell into place as the woman raked it again with her hand, sunlight bouncing off a silver band on her left ring finger. What type of person would take on this roguish specimen?

Eva returned to the woman's question about being lost, scanning her feelings and recent behavior. If she answered honestly, she would have to say, "Very." Instead, she said, "I'm here for a meeting."

"Okay, then, gotta go."

Before the woman turned, her shameless gaze roamed over Eva's body once again like that of a hungry animal. The look left Eva disturbed. The rider's lips parted slightly into what Eva interpreted as a smirk. Reckless *and* rude. Pivoting on her calf-length riding boots, the woman sprinted toward the building with the same energy Eva imagined must accompany her every breath. Eva wanted to absorb some of that essence to recharge her own dwindling reserves. She needed to feel grounded but vibrant again.

As the woman retreated, her long, lean legs were outlined by clinging, threadbare jeans. When she took off her tattered leather jacket and whipped it over her shoulder, her back muscles appeared firm under her body-hugging T-shirt. Eva caught a whiff of soap and water without fragrance. Reckless, rude, and *attractive*, she thought as the stranger disappeared around the corner of the building.

Greer rushed through the police department entrance with only two minutes until lineup. She couldn't handle another lecture from Sergeant Fluharty about punctuality and responsibility.

"You're late again," Donna Burke, the chief's secretary, stated. "You and Bessie get into it over something this morning?"

"Just behind, as usual." Greer loved her aunt dearly, but sometimes she could be a pain to live with. Hell, sometimes the entire city of New Hope wasn't big enough for the two of them.

Greer waved as she passed Donna's desk. "Incoming hot chick. Looked vaguely familiar. See you."

"So she's attractive, huh?"

"Didn't notice," she answered, flashing Donna a grin. But Greer remembered the woman's full lips and sexy dimples as she spoke. Every carefully pronounced word flowed with a hint of a foreign accent and was punctuated by hand gestures. She was a bit high-strung, the kind of woman who cultivated attention like royalty. And she'd certainly gotten Greer's, an unusual occurrence for the past months.

"Must've been a looker for you to call her hot, but you wouldn't know because you didn't notice," Donna teased her.

Greer looked back over her shoulder, rolled her eyes, and hurried down the hallway toward the lineup room as the front door opened again.

Eva paused in the huge entry and glanced at photos that hung against the portico's rock walls. Plaques dedicated to officers for acts of professional excellence surrounded a picture of Chief Sam Bryant. One plaque contained the picture of the rude woman she'd encountered in the parking lot, and the engraved nameplate read *Greer Ellis*. Reckless, rude, attractive, and heroic.

"Good morning, ma'am, I'm Donna Burke. May I help you?"

"Yes, please, my name is Eva Saldana. I have an appointment with Chief Bryant."

"Of course, he's been expecting you. Welcome to New Hope."

"Thank you."

"Vaguely familiar. She wouldn't know a celebrity if one bit her on the nose," Donna muttered. "Sorry. One of our detectives thought you looked *familiar*. Obviously she doesn't watch CNN or she'd know who you are, Ms. Saldana." Without waiting for a response, she said, "The chief is on a conference call right now, but he'll be with you in a few minutes. Could I offer you something to drink while you wait?"

"No, thank you."

How much about Eva's visit had the chief relayed to his secretary? Did she know the reason for their meeting this morning? If so, would she be as cordial? Donna motioned to one of the red-cushioned armchairs in front of her desk and Eva sat down.

"If you don't mind my asking, how long will you be in New Hope, Ms. Saldana?"

Eva searched Donna's face and found only sincerity. "I'm not sure yet."

"Have you found a place to stay? I could recommend something."

"I've made arrangements in Hurley at an extended-stay facility."

"That's a shame. Hurley's a thirty-minute drive, and it's not nearly as welcoming as New Hope. I think you'll like our town."

Eva relaxed a little. Why was she accepting Donna's questions without reservation? Her voice, which had a slightly Southern accent, genuine and hospitable, helped make some of Eva's stress about her meeting evaporate.

Donna smiled conspiratorially. "Well, if you change your mind, I might be able to help with a place much closer and cheaper. A private home with more of a personal touch."

"You're very kind." Why did small-town residents try to assimilate anyone who crossed their borders? Eva thought of Lagos, grimaced, and decided she wouldn't be staying long enough to find out.

The door to Chief Bryant's office opened and a tall, silver-haired man strode toward her. Weather-etched skin crinkled around his eyes and mouth when he smiled. He extended his hand. "Ms. Saldana, I'm Sam Bryant. It's a pleasure to meet you, though I'm sorry it's under such unfortunate circumstances." His deep voice was soft and soothing. "I was a big fan of your father's work and of yours as well."

"Thank you, sir."

Chief Bryant released her hand and motioned her into his office. "We can talk inside. Donna, hold my calls, please."

As Eva walked by, Bryant's lanky frame loomed at least six inches above her, foreshadowing the enormity of her task. What happened here today would determine what she would be doing in the immediate future. Would she be on assignment in yet another foreign location or stay in this quaint little town? Either the police department would grant her request or she'd have her next assignment right here.

Bryant crossed to a corner fireplace, repositioned the logs with a poker, and pointed to a mahogany-colored leather chair near the heat. "Have a seat, Ms. Saldana, and we'll get started." Bryant pulled a matching chair alongside and joined her.

Eva began her rehearsed speech. "Chief Bryant, I'm very concerned about the investigation of my brother's death, which was ruled an overdose. Paul was a very stable and socially connected person. He didn't even use over-the-counter medications. He believed in natural alternatives. I believe your detectives missed something and I'm requesting that they reexamine his death. I can't accept their conclusion. It simply isn't possible. You don't know Paul as I do—did." She released a sigh at having finally said the words she had repeated over and over in her head for weeks. She couldn't say any more. Tears burned behind her eyes but she maintained her composure.

"I'm sorry about your brother, and I understand that you have concerns. I've asked Sergeant Fluharty of the homicide squad to review the case to make sure we didn't miss anything. He's in the best position to do that."

"Thank you. I appreciate his time and yours."

Chief Bryant's gaze never left Eva's. "I not only want you to think that we did our best, but I also want you to *know* that we did. And I apologize for having to ask this, but you're sure your brother wasn't into recreational drug use?"

The question made her shudder. She'd asked herself that many times in the four months since his death, and the answer was always the same. Paul was the straightest arrow in their family, focused and completely above reproach, as far as she was aware. But you never truly know another human being, especially someone in your family. She couldn't say that to the chief of police. She had to go with her gut. "My brother wouldn't defile his body with drugs."

Bryant silently studied her, offering, it seemed, an opportunity to reconsider her answer. "You evidently have astute investigative skills, Ms. Saldana, so we have our work cut out for us. If Sergeant Fluharty doesn't clear things up, feel free to call." He pulled a business card from his pocket and handed it to her. "All my numbers are on there. In a small town, it's a requirement to be available twenty-four seven."

Something in Sam Bryant's eyes reassured Eva that he and his staff would hear her concerns and take them seriously. "I'm willing to listen."

"Thank you for that. Fluharty runs a tight ship. I'll have Donna call the evidence room. Someone will bring your brother's personal effects to you shortly." Bryant preceded her to the door and held it open. "To the right."

When they approached the door marked Homicide Squad, Eva stopped and drew a ragged breath. She silently promised her baby brother again that she would uncover the truth about his death. Then she promised herself that when this was over, she would settle down and have a real life. Her nomadic lifestyle didn't satisfy her any longer, though the work defined her in so many ways. Paul's death had proved that no one is guaranteed tomorrow.

Bryant opened the door and waved her inside.

When Eva stepped into the room with the homicide detectives, her game face slipped on and her posture tightened. This was about her loved one, not an anonymous face in some third-world country. This small group of strangers had already judged the events in the most important story of her life and she wanted to try to reverse that decision. At least she didn't know any of these people, so it should be easier to be objective. But as she gazed at the woman holding center stage in the room, something else became clear. Greer Ellis, friend or foe, would be an issue.

CHAPTER TWO

Eva walked into the narrow room crowded with battered metal desks. A patchwork of bulletin boards, wanted posters, and phone numbers covered the faded beige walls, riddled with nail holes. The room smelled of scorched coffee and fresh donuts. Eva smiled at the old cliché but focused on Greer Ellis.

As she and Chief Bryant entered unnoticed, everyone was staring at Greer, who stood in the center of the room, hands raised. She debated a dark-haired, middle-aged man with no neck and a football-player build. His checked shirt needed ironing, and he strummed his fingers on the desk as she spoke.

"Come on, Sarge. I wasn't even a minute late. Besides, I was helping some lost woman in the parking lot. Really, when I came in, she was—"

"Sit down, Greer. We've had this discussion before. I don't like to repeat myself." The man's tone was calm and fatherly.

"Jeez, Sarge. I promise, I was helping a lady."

Chief Bryant whispered into Eva's ear, "Greer obviously had too much caffeine this morning."

The comment implied a level of familiarity that Eva didn't share with her own staff or colleagues.

"And another thing, Greer. What do you mean pulling that stunt yesterday? You know we don't make any kind of arrest, especially felonies, without backup. You need to be more careful. We have rules for a reason. I don't want to be the one to tell your Aunt Bessie..." The man shuffled some papers uncomfortably.

Greer straightened and the muscles along her shoulders twitched. "I'll do better." The statement sounded obligatory but not binding. Greer Ellis obviously found it easier to get forgiveness than permission.

The sergeant started to speak again, but glanced at Eva and Chief Bryant at the back of the room and sprang from his seat. "Good morning, Chief."

The detectives swiveled, then straightened in their chairs. Maybe because of the chief, or maybe because of her. Greer pivoted on her heel and swept her piercing stare over Eva again, making her uneasy.

Chief Bryant grinned, shaking his head as Greer sat down. "Good morning, folks. This is Ms. Eva Saldana, CNN investigative journalist. She's here in an unofficial capacity, inquiring about the death of her brother, Paul Saldana. I believe JJ handled the case."

A fortysomething man with a buzz cut, blue eyes, and pale crow's-feet offered his hand. "Jake Johnston at your service. Call me JJ. I'll be glad to answer any questions." JJ was moderately handsome with his bronze skin and flashy smile, but a bit too eager.

Sergeant Fluharty elbowed JJ aside and shook Eva's hand. "It's good to meet you, Ms. Saldana. I'm Sergeant Fred Fluharty, welcome to NHPD." Fluharty, as tall as Chief Bryant, was heavier, with a small potbelly. His oval face glowed when he smiled, sending a blush up to his retreating hairline. "JJ's our most experienced detective. We'll try to address your concerns."

Chief Bryant headed for the door. "I see you're in good hands, so I'll leave you to it, Ms. Saldana. Let me know if you need anything else."

Sergeant Fluharty relaxed his posture when the door closed behind the chief. "Let me introduce you to our other three detectives." He motioned toward the others in the room. "Since our squad is so small, everybody usually works on the major cases."

He pointed to a young, dark-skinned man with an inscrutable expression. The Fu Manchu–style facial hair that encircled his mouth and chin made him appear serious. His body was muscular, his bearing militaristic. "This is Detective Derrick Bastile. We call him Breeze."

The man nodded. "Welcome, Ms. Saldana." His rich baritone voice suggested confidence and authority.

"Breeze?" she asked.

"As in cool, I would imagine. You'll probably get a nickname if you're here longer than an hour or two."

Eva turned her attention to the other male. "This is Craig Myrick," Fluharty said, "our resident computer guy and an excellent detective."

Myrick glanced up from his laptop long enough to mumble, "Hey, I like your stuff on CNN," and returned to his work. His pale skin contrasted to his jet black swept-back hair and droopy eyebrows.

"Thank you." Eva's pulse hiked as she and the sergeant approached the final officer, who had been so rude earlier. She breathed deeply to control her response, but this woman made her wary and excited.

"And this is Greer Ellis." Fluharty gave Greer his best be-nice stare.

The vibrant blue of Greer's eyes churned like the depths of the ocean, briefly emitting pleasure, pain, and confusion. Eva stared at the mysterious scar that carved a clean path through the woman's brow and clung to the strong hand that covered hers. Strangely familiar warmth crawled down her spine and grounded her. Eva couldn't force herself from the overwhelming visceral sensations until Greer's full lips moved.

"Eva Saldana. Now I know why you looked familiar." Greer radiated mischief and rebellion like a neon warning sign on the roadway.

Eva struggled to maintain her equilibrium as sensation flooded her. She hadn't responded to a woman this strongly or quickly… ever, not even with her recently increased appetites. But she needed to control her overactive libido right now.

JJ cleared his throat and announced, "Hey, Greer, shouldn't you let the lead detective take the lead?"

When Eva realized they still held hands and locked eyes, she stepped away.

Sergeant Fluharty said, "Ms. Saldana, if you'll follow me, we'll get started. JJ has court this morning, but we won't need him." The detective looked disappointed as he gathered his briefcase and headed out.

Fluharty closed the door to his office and motioned for Eva to take a seat. Then he poured a cup of coffee and loaded it with sugar. "Care for some?"

"No, thank you." Fluharty's office seemed like a closet full of filing cabinets.

"I'm sorry we had to meet under these circumstances. It isn't easy to lose a loved one especially unexpectedly." He sat down and spread his huge hands across a file folder on his desk. "Now, how can I help you, Ms. Saldana?"

Fluharty's eyes looked tired and bloodshot. Eva hoped he hadn't been up all night on a case, because she needed his full attention. "That should be obvious. I don't believe my brother overdosed."

"What do you base that on?"

"He didn't take drugs of any kind."

"To your knowledge." Fluharty's statement sounded like an accusation.

"I'm in a better position to know what my brother would do than a group of strangers. No disrespect intended, Sergeant."

"So you saw your brother often and spent long periods of time with him?"

"No. We have separate lives, like most siblings."

"He lived in Lagos, Portugal. Is that your home as well?"

"My work requires a great deal of travel, but what does that have to do with Paul's death?"

"I'm trying to understand your relationship better."

Fluharty's professional tone contained no hint of compassion for her situation. He seemed to be trying to paint an ugly picture of her brother's life. "Sergeant, my brother didn't have a complete personality change. I know what he is—was—like."

"How many deaths have you investigated during your career?"

"That's not the point." Eva's skin prickled.

"It is certainly *a* point. Jake Johnston has investigated death cases for ten years. Nothing gets by him. If he says your brother died of an overdose and the autopsy shows nothing to the contrary, that's how he died. I know how difficult this is for you."

The warmth in Eva's veins turned hot. "I'm sorry, but I don't share your confidence. Is your idea of a case review to simply defend your decision?"

"Hardly, Ms. Saldana. The chief told me three days ago that you were coming, so I've studied every detail of the case numerous times. JJ followed every lead, considered every angle, and explored every possible scenario. I wish I could tell you that I have questions, but I don't." Almost apologetic, he showed the first signs of emotion.

Despite his warmth, Eva clenched her hands into tight fists and struggled to contain her anger. A man in Fluharty's position would probably use her volatile emotions to justify his point. "But *I* have questions, Sergeant. I just want your detectives to review the case once more."

"We don't have the manpower to revisit cases every time a family member asks. That's why I went over this one again personally. Unfortunately, drug deaths are a fact of life here, and we get more every day. I can't spare an officer to look into a closed case."

Eva willed her voice to remain calm. "Then give me access to your files and I'll investigate it myself."

"I can't release departmental files to a civilian. Besides, that would hardly be an objective third-party review."

"What about a compromise, a joint review? I'll study the facts with one of your men supervising."

Fluharty blew out a long breath. "That's against policy too. I wish I could do more, but my hands are tied."

"Change the policy. Nothing is carved in stone." *Except your rules and regulations, apparently.*

"That's not how we do business, Ms. Saldana. This isn't one of your CNN cover stories. We have departmental guidelines for a reason. If we make one exception, the whole system comes under scrutiny."

Fluharty threw up roadblocks to every suggestion, and Eva slipped into panic mode, an uncommon state for her. She'd faced far more dangerous opponents on assignments throughout the world, but this one was personal. This man's decision threatened to dislodge one certainty in her life—Paul's basic goodness. "Please, Sergeant, I know my brother. Consider another possibility."

"I'm sorry, ma'am, there *is* no other possibility. People lie. Evidence doesn't. We found a half ounce of cocaine in your brother's room. His nasal cavity looked like upstate New York during a blizzard." He stopped, as if reconsidering his comment. "I'm sorry, that was unkind. But he had enough drugs in his system to kill him twice. Nothing in his room or on his person pointed to foul play." Fluharty waved the file in front of her like a red flag. "Everything we have points to an overdose. I know this isn't what you want to hear, but these are the *facts*." His final statement rang with genuine regret.

Eva was standing over Fluharty's desk with her fists clenched at her sides before she realized that she'd risen. "My brother did not do drugs. Are you listening?" Her voice sounded strained and foreign, its pitch higher and shaking with emotion. "You must believe me." Fluharty's expression told her she was wasting her breath. To him, she was just another bereaved relative incapable of objectivity.

The beige folder on his desk with her brother's name scribbled across it looked blurry through her tears, but she refused to let them fall. This man had no idea how much this case meant to her or how far she would go to uncover the truth. She straightened and locked stares with him. "I'm sorry to have wasted your time. I'll continue this conversation with the chief."

It took every ounce of her willpower to walk slowly out of his office and into the parking lot. All she saw was the red of her anger and the dark abyss of her situation.

Greer tried to complete her paperwork without eavesdropping on the low, intense mumbles from Fluharty's office. Would the sergeant reopen the Saldana case?

She had thought the initial investigation four months ago was a bit hasty, but all evidence pointed to an overdose. She had been taught to look beyond the obvious, and in this instance her training officer, JJ, had done exactly the opposite. He wrapped the scene in a matter of hours, accepted the coroner's preliminary cause of death, and filed the jacket. When she'd asked him about it, he'd quipped something about a duck being a duck.

He'd done his job properly, though. JJ was the best detective in the squad, and she'd learned a lot from him. Without his friendship, especially the way he covered for her during her grief, the last two years wouldn't have made much sense.

But why was JJ in court instead of meeting with Ms. Saldana and the sergeant? Breeze and Craig were out trying to locate a witness, and right now Greer would rather be anywhere but here. The intensity in Sergeant Fluharty's voice increased, and she flinched. It wasn't going well. She'd heard Fluharty's logical, fatherly sermons many times. She didn't want to think about how that poor woman was feeling right now.

She was the first person who'd stirred any real interest in her since Clare. Guilt, immediate and brutal, seized her. She slumped in her chair as sensual memories invaded. She shouldn't feel attracted to Eva, but she ached for physical attention. Sex was different from love, she told herself, and she knew her limits.

Eva was nothing like Clare, but her expressiveness mesmerized Greer. When they met, Greer wanted to say something genuine, but she hadn't wanted to show how much Eva attracted her. More beautiful than a model, Eva seemed innocent, passionate, and determined. Uneasy, Greer took a deep breath as the voices from Fluharty's office grew more urgent.

Eva Saldana sounded increasingly distressed and desperate. Situations like this made Greer uncomfortable. She understood grief over the loss of a loved one, but she couldn't identify with someone who expressed it so earnestly. Suddenly the door to Fluharty's office opened and Eva walked slowly but deliberately toward the parking lot, gazing straight ahead, her lips pursed in a tight line. She looked only seconds from tears. Greer ran after her, compelled to help.

As Greer exited the squad room, an evidence tech waved a brown box. "Saldana's property." She stopped long enough to sign the obligatory form, grabbed the box, and ran after Eva.

"Ms. Saldana." Eva sat in her car gripping the steering wheel, her eyes closed. She didn't acknowledge Greer. "Ms. Saldana, please. I have these—"

Eva opened her eyes and rolled down the window, staring at Greer through a mask of controlled grief. "You have what? My brother's personal effects?" She snatched the box and shook it at Greer. "You want to pass this off and wash your hands of him entirely? Are police officers supposed to be unfeeling and inflexible, or is it an option?" She waited as if expecting Greer to answer.

The pain reflected in Eva's eyes and in her trembling voice disturbed Greer. She felt totally inadequate to help this woman, yet she wanted to. "I'm sorry."

Eva gestured more slowly yet more intensely. "You're sorry? Could you be more specific? Are you sorry because you and your fellow conspirators have desecrated the name of an honest, respectable man? Or are you sorry because you did a poor job and lack the integrity to admit it and make it right? Perhaps you're sorry that you had to deliver this box and confront the hysterical woman. What *exactly* makes you sorry, Detective Ellis?"

Greer was tempted to say nothing, but something inside her prevented it. "I'm sorry for your loss." Though heartfelt, the statement sounded so clichéd.

"You're sorry for my loss? You know *nothing* of loss."

Greer twirled the wedding band on her finger. Eva stared at her, but Greer couldn't look up. She'd already revealed too much.

"What do you know of my pain?"

"You're not the first person to lose somebody." Greer noted the unintended bite in her tone.

The reply quieted Eva momentarily before she asked, "And your loss made you like this?" It sounded more like an observation than a question.

Greer straightened and forced a smile she didn't feel. She wasn't sure what Eva meant and wasn't sure she wanted to know. This woman was prying into her private thoughts and feelings. Time to take a giant step back. "Nah. I blame genes and an overindulgent guardian."

"You use professional bravado well—to bury your loss and keep you prisoner."

The truth in the words surprised Greer. Eva sounded like Bessie, wise and empathic. Greer couldn't respond. It had taken her months to build a façade around her loss—months of denial and avoidance. She refused to let this stranger with pinball emotions rattle her bubble of protection. "Ms. Saldana, I'm also sorry the sergeant won't reopen your brother's case." Then, to her surprise, she said, "But if it'll help, I'm willing to listen."

Hope replaced the sadness in Eva's eyes. "You'll review the case?"

What the hell had she done? "That's not what I meant. I don't have the authority to reopen a closed case, but I can hear what you have to say. Meet me for coffee later at the diner on Elm? I'm off at three."

Greer would at least listen to her. She wasn't part of this investigation, but she took pride in her squad's work. She was a professional and wanted everyone to think of her and the department in that way. She'd try to convince Eva that the squad had done its job properly. She owed it to herself and her coworkers.

"I'll meet you. And thank you, Detective." Her gaze held Greer's a moment longer. "I'm sorry for my outburst. I'm overly emotional and a bit raw right now but—"

"No problem." Greer doubted seriously that Eva ever repressed her emotions. She headed back inside the station as Eva pulled out of the parking lot.

Where had this woman come from and how had she insinuated herself into Greer's life? With her soft, rhythmic voice she molded her words into an English-foreign hybrid that oozed sensuality. But beyond her obvious appeal, she was in pain and looking for answers. As Greer walked back to the office, her thoughts strayed from her lengthy to-do list to Eva and her own questions about Paul Saldana's death four months earlier.

That afternoon, on her way to meet Eva, Greer considered how she could possibly help. She wouldn't go against her fellow officers, so she refused to intervene professionally. She'd failed to find peace in her own life since Clare's death, so how could she mitigate anyone else's suffering? What the hell was she doing?

The fifties retro eatery was full of downtown workers taking a midafternoon coffee break. Their conversations hummed in the background of clanking dishes and whirring espresso machines. The aroma of the morning's bacon and onion-laden hash browns still filled the air. Greer waved and nodded as she walked over to the only outsider in the place.

Eva already sat at a booth in the back and waved as Greer entered. "I was afraid you'd change your mind." Several empty espresso cups and a barely touched muffin littered the table. Greer inhaled the aromatic fragrances of mingled coffee concoctions and signaled for a waitress.

Janice Johnston, JJ's wife, sauntered over to their table and pulled a pencil from behind her ear. "Your usual, Greer?" When Greer nodded, Janice asked Eva, "Another double espresso?" She scribbled their orders and started back to the counter.

"Thanks, Janice." Greer returned her attention to Eva. "How long have you been here?"

"Since this morning. Where else would I go?" Eva looked at her like the answer made perfect sense.

"Where were you before? I mean, you just arrived in New Hope from Portugal?"

"Yes. I came from Lagos, my childhood home. Vincent and Lucio, my twin brothers, and I arranged for Paul's burial. We remained there to settle his estate and to grieve."

"That was four months ago."

"Yes. Grieving is a long and sacred process in my family. We mourn the dead by celebrating their lives. We stay together until everyone feels a little more comfortable with the loss. Some heal faster than others. Some never release the pain."

She gazed at Greer, seeming to wait for a reaction to her point. Her stare was as invasive as it was welcoming. Surprisingly, Greer wanted to respond to the statement, but opted to let Eva open their professional discussion at her own pace.

After Janice placed their drinks on the table and walked away, Eva began her story. "My brothers and I were very close after my parents died. We called ourselves the quad and talked every month, sometimes more, in person or on conference calls. Paul and I were especially close, only a year between us. Vincent and Lucio are seven years older. We spoke the week before Paul's—before this happened. He was excited about a real-estate discovery here in New Hope."

"Any more details?"

Eva shook her head. "He usually e-mailed all the information. I hadn't received the latest project details." Her voice dropped and a pained expression shadowed her lovely features. "I didn't ask enough questions the last time we talked. My father would've been ashamed of my amateurishness. He was a perfectionist and encouraged us to be as well. But my investigative work hasn't been this personal before."

The comment about her father seemed to cause Eva more pain. Greer didn't understand fathers, but she'd had experience disappointing people. Bessie's expectant face flashed through her mind. "You didn't hear from Paul again?"

"No." Eva brushed a strand of wavy brown hair from her face and looked at her apologetically.

"What about your other brothers, any contact?"

"No."

"Tell me about Paul."

Eva's hand trembled as she took a sip of espresso. "Paul was a wonderful man, compassionate and loyal. He was engaged to his college love, and they were planning to marry next year and raise a family. He wouldn't put impurities in his body, especially not drugs. If an organic or alternative medicine was available, he used that instead."

"Did he have any enemies or any disagreements over recent business deals? Past lovers who might have been a problem? Anything?" Greer asked all the questions that might suggest motive, suspicion, or grounds for a review. So far all she had was a grieving woman who couldn't accept her brother's death.

"Nothing. Everyone loved Paul. He was a good man, established in his career as an international-realty specialist, had a zest for life. How does such a man end up dead in a motel room with drugs he didn't use? I can't understand it." Eva seemed to search Greer's face for answers. "Can you do anything, Detective?"

"Please call me Greer. I didn't work on your brother's case directly, but JJ is the best. He assured me he handled everything properly."

Eva's eyes sparked with interest. "You had questions, Greer. Why?"

The way Eva spoke her name, the *r*'s rolling softly off her tongue like a whisper, stalled Greer's next thought. Damn. She'd inadvertently revealed more than she intended. In a botched effort to be sympathetic, she'd hinted at her uncertainty. That was all Eva Saldana needed.

"Not exactly. Detectives often look over each other's cases." Her answer sounded lame and unlikely to derail this intuitive woman.

"Still, you speak with dubiety. Would you be so cautious if this was your loved one?" She pointed to the ring on Greer's finger. "Wouldn't you listen to your instincts? Wouldn't you want to illuminate even the smallest shadow of doubt?"

Her question struck at the very heart of the issue. Clare's killer had been immediately sentenced—to death. The shoot-out in front of the police station left two people dead, Sergeant Fluharty a hero, and Greer a widow. No need to second-guess the judicial process. How would she feel if the killer was still free or even still alive? She tightened her grip on her coffee cup as anger boiled in her veins.

"Or has your loss robbed you of compassion? I don't believe that's true. The pain on your face says otherwise. Will you help me, Greer?"

"Eva, I—" She *had* questioned why they had settled Paul's case so quickly, then accepted this death as an overdose, like so many others. If she doubted the results now, she would be questioning her mentor and all he'd taught her. If she denied her instincts again, she would add another layer of denial to her slowly atrophying emotions. Greer didn't like either option.

Eva took Greer's hands and smiled for the first time, deep dimples punctuating the corners of her mouth. The grieving woman suddenly looked very young and innocent.

She drew a card from her purse, scribbled her number on the back, and placed it on the table between them. "You're conflicted, and I don't want to cause you trouble. But I'm not going away. With or without your help, I'll get to the bottom of Paul's death. Search your heart, and if you have *any* doubt, please let it serve my brother's memory. I'm at the Sunset Motel in Hurley."

CHAPTER THREE

Eva thought about Greer Ellis's mesmerizing blue eyes repeatedly as she drove toward her motel. Who had Greer lost? Had that caused her guarded behavior? She seemed profoundly sad, but tried to hide behind her cop's demeanor and recklessness, if the way she rode that monstrous motorcycle was any indication. Greer had been the only person even mildly concerned about her situation today. However, with her libido running amok, it was dangerous and distracting to be curious about her. But, if Greer was also attracted to her, that might be useful in her own investigation of Paul's death.

The brown evidence box on the car seat made a pang of sorrow rip through her. She couldn't open it until she was safely off the street and behind closed doors. Handling personal items that Paul had last touched would be painful, and she wanted to give the process all the reverence it deserved.

How could something so terrible happen to her baby brother? He was the most alive, totally present individual she had ever known. He loved every minute of his existence and encouraged her to do the same. She hadn't followed his example, choosing to let work instead of people stimulate her.

Eva stifled an urge to cry as she entered her drab motel room and placed the box on the bed. She changed into a bathrobe and returned to the unpleasant task. As she reached for the tape-wrapped container with trembling hands, her cell phone rang. Unenthusiastically, she answered.

"Eva, darling, it's so good to hear your voice. I've been worried witless."

"Constance?" The woman she'd most recently bedded sounded relieved and a bit accusatory.

"Of course it's Constance. You left so suddenly. I had to bribe someone at CNN to get your new phone number. Is all this secrecy necessary? We *are* lovers, after all."

"Were." She hated to have to restate the sad truth about her life. Relationships had become like an addendum to her assignments, and they ended simultaneously. Through the years she'd wondered if the pain of leaving wasn't as bad as that of being left. Either way, she effectively avoided the possibility of real intimacy.

"Sorry?"

"We *were* lovers, and I told you I was leaving. I finished my job there and another was waiting. I can't put down roots whenever I want. I thought you understood." The long pause confirmed that Constance had probably dismissed Eva's early warnings about her lifestyle. When they became involved, she chose to believe that she could change Eva.

"But I thought…"

Their last dinner together had left little doubt about what Constance thought. When Eva told her about her new assignment, Constance had been visibly upset and caused a scene in the restaurant. In retrospect, she had possessed potential as a long-term partner, if Eva had been so inclined. But her childhood memories prevented it. Her life of wanderlust and uncertainty wouldn't translate easily into domesticity.

"I'm truly sorry, Constance. I didn't intend to hurt you." How many times had she said those same words and sincerely meant them? She tried many times to establish a connection deeper than the flesh, but she was like her father after all. Her profession defined yet limited her. "Forgive me."

"Will you be in Madrid again—soon, I mean?" The hope in Constance's voice only added to Eva's guilt.

"I don't know. Constance, I realize this isn't what you wanted. It's simply all I can manage."

"What if I come visit?"

"That wouldn't be a good idea. This isn't a vacation, and I wouldn't be very good company."

Silence on the other end cued Eva that Constance didn't like her answer. "Did you ever love me, Eva?"

Oh, God. How could she possibly answer that question without causing more pain? "We had a wonderful time, but we were together only a short while."

"Because you left."

"We've been over this, Constance. It's my job."

"Bullshit, Eva. It's your excuse. CNN has been trying for months to get you off the investigative track and into your own show. You like this nomadic lifestyle. It's an easy out for having a real life, taking responsibility and making a commitment."

Eva was at a loss. Was the statement false or was it too close to the truth? She stuck to the facts. "Who told you I'd been offered my own show? No one's supposed to know about that."

"You're not the only one with friends around the globe, dear."

"Constance, I can't deal with this right now. I'm sorry you're upset, and I apologize again for hurting you. Give me time to straighten things out here, and we'll talk more."

A long sigh preceded Constance's last comment. "I guess that's all I'll get, isn't it?"

Another round of self-recrimination hit Eva as she disconnected. She stared at the evidence box like it was a serpent waiting to strike. Without her brother, who had been her closest friend and staunchest supporter, she felt helpless and lonely. Tears filled her eyes. Now, in the privacy of this stale environment away from the judgment of others, she allowed the frustrations and disappointments of the day to rise and the tears to fall.

As she cried, she ripped the container open, determined not to let her grief interfere with her mission. The scent of Paul's cologne spilled from the box and she sobbed. She emptied the box on the bedspread and checked the contents against the inventory receipt: Paul's BlackBerry, an Italian leather wallet, Rolex Submariner watch, gold St. Francis de Sales medal. But she didn't find his compact Nikon camera. He usually kept it close for quick shots of the properties he was researching.

Four articles and a slip of useless paper—neither the definition nor the essence of her brother's life. She held the necklace in her palm and stared at the patron saint of writers and journalists. The face was barely visible, eroded by time and contact. Paul had worn it since early adulthood in honor of their father, and later for her. If her life had been as full as Paul's, perhaps she wouldn't be so cynical.

She opened the wallet and thumbed through Paul's collection of credit cards. Tucked behind two of them were spare camera cards. He liked to be prepared. Opposite the credit cards was a picture of the woman he'd loved since college and, under that, several family photos. *We were never far from his thoughts.* She clutched the necklace to her chest and wept.

When she couldn't cry any more, she put Paul's necklace on and placed the other items in her bedside table. Nothing in his belongings indicated what happened to him. Later she would check his BlackBerry, but right now she ached inside and out.

Maybe a shower would flush out some of her pain, her guilt about Constance, and the memories of this unproductive day. Fred Fluharty's stubborn indifference to her attempts to clear Paul's name made his death seem even more senseless. How could anyone dismiss her brother so callously? Her father had believed in persevering until he uncovered the entire story. As she turned on the shower, she thought, *I will not fail.*

The stinging cold-water spray shook Fred Fluharty's mechanical tone and inflexibility from her mind. She recalled his doubts about Paul one final time as she washed them away. Then she adjusted the tap for a warmer flow, determined again to uncover the truth about Paul's death. No stranger knew her brother better than she did. Even though detectives dissected people's lives as a career and discovered their flaws, they weren't always right. She turned up the hot water and waited for the heat to consume her, envisioning Greer Ellis with a surge of sexual desire.

Eva acknowledged the emotional ache that moved from her heart and became a physical throb between her legs. Her roller-coaster emotions over the past four months had elevated her desire for sexual interaction. What was wrong with her? Statistically, sexual activity usually declined during bereavement. Was she trying in some twisted way to honor Paul's memory by squeezing the vitality out of every second? Or maybe she needed to prove she was still alive and capable of feeling.

But her recent encounters hadn't salved the wound. Maybe a loss so deep required mind-blowing sex that purged thought completely. But she couldn't pursue her need for human contact in this small town. She had to stay on point. She brushed her hand across her tender flesh, but masturbation couldn't appease the impulses coiled in her. She turned the cold water off and stood under the hot stream until her skin burned. When she couldn't take the pain any longer, she closed the tap and sank to the tiled floor exhausted, as if her life spiraled down the drain too.

Eva had no idea how long she'd crouched in the tiny shower enclosure when she became aware of heavy pounding outside her room. She pulled the terry-cloth robe around her, trudged to the door, and opened it. Greer Ellis stood outside looking roguish in a breast-hugging T-shirt, a bomber jacket, and well-worn leather pants, her thumbs hooked through her belt loops.

"Yes?" Eva asked, confused. Her throat was raw, her eyes burned, and she could barely breathe through her nose. She remembered sliding to the tiled shower floor but nothing else. "I'm sorry. Did I forget an appointment? I have…it's been—"

"No. I should've called. I'm sorry. I'll go." The compassion in Greer's eyes validated her statement.

Eva moved aside and waved her in. "That's okay. I'm fine."

Greer scanned the room like a typical cop. "Would you believe I was in the neighborhood?"

"No, but you don't owe me an explanation." Pulling the robe tighter, Eva wiped her face on the sleeve. She didn't want Greer to see her like this. She couldn't afford to appear weak when so much was at stake. But she *felt* weak and needy. She shivered from the closeness of a woman who exuded confidence and was so alive with suppressed energy that she seemed to radiate warmth. Eva swayed toward Greer and stumbled forward.

"Are you all right?" Greer's arms slid around Eva's waist just before she slumped to the floor. She lifted Eva easily, placed her on the bed, and sat beside her. "What's wrong? Do you need a doctor? I can—"

The words froze on Greer's lips and Eva realized that her robe had fallen open. The blue of Greer's eyes turned midnight, and she moistened her lips with the tip of her tongue. Something in Greer's eyes told Eva that this woman could give her what she needed with no regrets and no expectations. Right now she just wanted to find out. She craved the temporary relief that pure sex provided. As the dizziness receded, she reached for Greer.

"Don't. I shouldn't have come here." Greer pulled the edges of Eva's robe together across her naked body, then skimmed the tender skin at her waist and neckline and held the contact momentarily.

Eva shivered. "It's just sex. Nothing more." But *should* she sleep with the only person who could possibly help with her brother's case? Would sex help or hurt her cause? Torn, she sat up and edged closer to Greer.

"If you weren't, you know, business—"

"I see." Eva withdrew, crossing her arms over her aching breasts. "Sorry about the drama. I took a hot shower. I guess it made me light-headed." Greer was the first woman to refuse her advances in many years. Her ego stung as urgent need pulsed between her legs.

"No problem." Greer rose and paced near the door like she was afraid to be near Eva. She shoved her hands in her front pockets as if to restrict any further chance of touching.

"Why are you here, Detective?"

"You asked if I would help you. I wanted to give you my answer, in person. You deserve that after all that's happened."

At least Greer had the courage to face Eva with her decision. It would have been easier to say and do nothing. "Let me guess. You're sorry, once again, but the answer is still no." Eva tried to distinguish the jumble of emotions that churned inside. As if the sexual rejection wasn't enough, now Greer added another insult.

"JJ did a thorough investigation. And the sergeant reviewed it. We're a small department, but we're not amateurs. Besides, I owe them both more than my professional loyalty."

Eva listened to the commitment in Greer's words and wished she understood how to earn such devotion. "Things aren't always as they seem."

"And sometimes they are." Greer opened the door. "I know you're disappointed, but I can't help you."

As the door closed behind Greer, Eva fell back on the bed in frustration. This day had been full of emotional highs and lows, and now she felt only disappointment. She couldn't believe she'd allowed this small-town cop to see her need, even her sexual need. But Eva refused to let her momentary lapse in judgment interfere with her goal. If nobody wanted to help, she would launch her own investigation into Paul's death. It would be easier if the police cooperated, but she wouldn't let their stonewalling deter her.

Eva pulled Chief Bryant's business card out of her purse and made the phone call she had hoped wouldn't be necessary. Perhaps a little nudge from above would produce the cooperation she needed. The chief was cordial and promised he'd handle the situation first thing in the morning. In the meantime, she had one more possible source of information.

Eva powered up Paul's BlackBerry and searched the recent files for a lead on the property he was researching in New Hope. She retrieved a Listingbook real-estate page from Paul's favorites, clicked it open, and read the particulars of the warehouse for sale. This had to be the reason Paul had come to town. She scribbled down the address, 247 Lewis Street, and closed the page. Next she checked his calendar and found the same address entered on the day he died. Other than a Google Maps directional file to New Hope, she found nothing else of interest. She turned the BlackBerry off, replaced it in the nightstand drawer, and rolled her aching shoulders.

The relaxation from her earlier shower had evaporated. Her insides hummed with anger at Greer's refusal to help and the arousal she sparked. She yearned to sleep, long and deep, but she wouldn't be able to.

She ripped her bathrobe open and slid her hand into the wetness between her legs. At first touch, she gasped aloud. The memory of Greer's fingers lightly skimming her flesh filled her with heat. Those fingers would be skillful and strong, and she wanted to feel them on her and inside her so badly that the ache echoed through her body. She would have to make do with her own hands until Greer Ellis physically claimed her.

She visualized the two of them naked astride her rumbling Harley, power from the engine and the proximity to Greer pulsing through her clit. The vibrations soaked into her nerves and muscles like a current as Eva rubbed herself faster. She cupped a breast and raked the puckering nipple with her thumbnail, imagining Greer's teeth scraping across it.

Pressure built inside Eva as she stroked the sides of her rigid clit, and it elongated. Wetness soaked her fingers and the inside of her thighs. She captured the pulsing length of flesh between her fingers and lowered her other hand to her opening. Replaying the feel of Greer's hand on her again, Eva thrust her fingers inside and wailed with the rush of release that rippled through her. She bucked and quivered until she lay exhausted and drenched.

As the last wave of orgasm subsided, Eva pictured Greer's deep blue eyes staring down at her full of passion and the promise of much more. This self-flagellation couldn't compare to the pleasure Greer Ellis would eventually provide, but maybe she could sleep.

Greer closed the motel room door and breathed a lungful of brisk autumn air. The coolness chilled her body, too aroused by a single, inadvertent touch. When Eva's robe fell open, Greer had acted like a shell-shocked teenager. But her olive-skinned body was so damn gorgeous, full yet perfectly toned. She smelled of citrus and something Greer couldn't distinguish, almost tasty. Her breasts stood erect, darker areolae puckered and waiting like a tempting chocolate treat. The curly patch of pubic hair at the V of Eva's thighs called to Greer's basal instincts. Fire pulsed in her veins and she nearly succumbed. But Eva Saldana would want more than she was prepared to give, physically and professionally.

Greer could see in the depths of Eva's chocolate brown eyes when she reached for her that Eva wanted her. For a moment, Greer had welcomed their interaction. But loyalty to her coworkers and to Clare stopped her, barely. She hadn't experienced such a strong burst of desire since Clare died. Something about Eva Saldana was dangerous, potentially explosive. The heat and softness of Eva's skin still burned on her fingertips. She shouldn't have come here.

What had she been thinking? She could have phoned. But after their introductory handshake at the station and Eva's touch earlier at the diner, Greer had thought of little else as she careered along the back roads to Hurley.

The first touch had surprised her, the second mesmerized her, and this last one urged her to behave unprofessionally. The ease with which Eva expressed her needs tapped on an emotional door that Greer had sealed off two years ago. And as a result, she'd nearly compromised her loyalty. She walked through the parking lot toward her Harley and vowed to stay as far away from Eva as possible. She would get discouraged soon and leave.

"A little late-night booty call, Greer?"

She instinctively reached for her concealed service weapon and squinted in the dim lights to make out the figure approaching her. "JJ?"

He stepped from behind his restored canary yellow '66 Chevy truck with his hands up. "Don't shoot. I come in peace...or maybe I should say, I come for a piece." He laughed at his joke and craned his neck back the way Greer had come, probably trying to determine which room she'd just left. "Anybody I know?"

"Maybe I should ask you that question. Does Janice know you're carousing tonight?"

"No, and she better not hear it from you."

"Not mine to tell. But everybody within three counties knows your truck. Not exactly sneaking around in that thing." They stood in silence for a few minutes, Greer pondering her next question and JJ seemingly unwilling to let her see which room he'd be visiting. "Why weren't you in that meeting with the sergeant and Eva Saldana this morning?"

JJ swiped his boot across a rough patch in the asphalt. "I had court."

"But it's your case." Detectives were usually included when their cases were questioned or up for review. Greer waited for JJ to respond, but decided to drop it. Eva Saldana was making her question the dedication of her coworkers, their integrity, and her own boundaries between work and play.

"Come on, Greer, I got better things to do than talk shop on my off time. Got a little something-something waiting, if you get my drift. Let this go, partner." He walked toward the row of rooms at the end of the lot and called over his shoulder. "And remember, not a word about this to Janice."

CHAPTER FOUR

There might've been an easier way, you know." Eva looked up from her morning espresso and bagel into the boyish face of Jake Johnston. His normally pleasant features scrunched together in an expression of displeasure, like he smelled something foul. Every patron in the diner turned toward them, eyes wide and ears undoubtedly open for fresh gossip.

"I beg your pardon?"

He sat down at her table uninvited. "As we say in the South, sometimes it's easier to catch flies with honey than vinegar."

Eva hoped this wasn't a culture lesson. After her embarrassing night with Greer and the phone call she'd made afterward, she wasn't in the mood for games. "JJ, if you have something to say, say it. It's too early for riddles."

"We all heard the good news this morning. You didn't get the answers you wanted, so you went to the chief." He traced a finger along the back of her hand. "I'm saying we might've been able to work something out if you'd come to me. I can be pretty obliging."

She pulled her hand away as the meaning behind his words registered. "I simply need more information. The meeting with your sergeant wasted my time."

"Yeah, well, Fluharty can be that way. But I could probably help considerably—if you decide to come around."

His gaze roamed over her body and Eva cringed. He didn't even undress her with his eyes, but went straight to leering. "Your offer is tempting," she lied.

"Don't worry, you don't have to ask. The sergeant will

assign one of us to review the case, probably me, since it was my investigation. I can hardly wait to get better acquainted."

Eva finished her coffee and prepared to leave. "This isn't a social event, JJ. It's a very serious matter, and I'd appreciate it if you'd treat it that way."

"I understand. You think we're a small-town bunch of hicks who don't know how to do our jobs. But I worked for ten years in Boston before relocating here. I've seen more, been involved in more, and investigated more violent incidents than you'll ever report. So I'm trying not to take it personally that you've questioned my abilities and my integrity."

As JJ's voice grew louder, a waitress came out of the back of the diner and moved in their direction. JJ shot her a cautionary stare as she got closer. "Stay out of this, Janice. It's not your business."

Janice Johnston stopped with her hands on her hips and returned his stare. "Well, excuse me for living. I kind of thought you were my business since you're my husband."

"This is work. Back off."

"Then take it to the office, not in here where everybody can hear your *business*."

From her tone, Eva surmised that JJ's wife considered her one of his dalliances. She started to object but decided that would only create a bigger scene. Janice held his gaze with a challenge of her own before she turned and disappeared into the kitchen.

Eva sat quietly for a few minutes while JJ took a couple of deep breaths. Why would any woman put up with a man she so obviously couldn't trust and who blatantly disrespected her? And why would a cop, if he was any good, leave Boston for a small department like New Hope? Maybe she'd make a few phone calls and find out. But right now she needed his cooperation. This man knew more about her brother's case than anyone.

"I'm sorry to upset you. I'm not questioning your methods, only the outcome. As you point out, I don't investigate violent crimes. You have all that experience. Would you object to walking me through the facts?"

The corners of JJ's mouth twitched into a smirk. "You're good. I understand how you get all those tough interviews on CNN now.

But our relationship won't be like that. No animosity here, just a little quid pro quo. When the sergeant officially gives me the case later today, I'll call you." He stood to leave.

"I understand but—"

Before she could object, a group of older women, some dressed in nurses' uniforms, approached the checkout station near Eva's table.One of them, a tall, distinguished-looking woman with grayish blond hair and sharp blue eyes, walked over to them. "Have a problem, JJ?"

His look would have sent a less confident person running in the opposite direction, but his tone softened noticeably. "No problem, Bessie. I was giving our visitor a friendly lesson on how we do things in the South."

"And that's a good thing?" The woman's voice teased with equal parts levity and sarcasm. "It didn't sound too friendly from where I was sitting. How about conducting your lessons in a more private setting? The whole town doesn't need to hear."

JJ started to respond, but turned and stalked out of the coffee shop. The room immediately buzzed with whispers. Customers stared and pointed as Eva rose to pay her bill.

The older woman waved good-bye to her nurse friends, escorted Eva to the cash register, and followed her outside. Something about her seemed familiar, though Eva was certain they hadn't met. Her frankly inquisitive stare swept over Eva's body and back to her face. Those eyes. Greer Ellis. The two women had the same piercing stare and high cheekbones—disarming and attractive.

"I'm sorry for butting into your conversation in there, but JJ can get a little ornery when his testosterone kicks in." The woman smiled and offered her hand. "Where are my manners? I'm Bessie Ellis, lifelong resident of New Hope and head nurse at the hospital." She pointed across the street to the three-story structure.

"Eva Saldana. It's a pleasure." And she meant it. Bessie epitomized small-town hospitality, her smile warm, her demeanor friendly. She'd actually helped Eva, the first person to do so since she arrived. Not that she needed anyone to rescue her from JJ, but it reassured her that someone else considered his behavior a little odd and not simply a juicy piece of gossip.

"You're Portuguese, right?" Eva nodded. "I spent some time in Portugal during my younger days as a military nurse. I love the language. It has such a romantic rhythm."

"You said Bessie *Ellis*?"

"Yes, and I'm guessing you've already encountered my niece, Greer. If you've met JJ, it makes sense that you've met her. They're a bit like a wrestling tag team—bonded by the work and just as subtle."

Eva hesitated, unsure how to respond. Her encounters with Greer Ellis invigorated, disturbed, and disappointed, unlike this pleasant encounter with her aunt.

"It's okay. She can be a bit hard to take at times. I only hope she didn't put you off permanently. And I'm sorry about your brother, Ms. Saldana." Eva's face must have shown her confusion. "Small town. News travels quickly and not necessarily accurately, unlike CNN."

"Thank you, Ms. Ellis. You're very kind." She started to excuse herself, but if Bessie had lived in New Hope all her life and worked at the hospital, she was bound to know the history of everybody in town. Maybe she could hang out with her and listen for a while. "Are you on your way to work now?"

"No, honey. And please call me Bessie. This is my day off. I met the girls for breakfast after their night shift, and now I'm going back to the house to pick up Greer. She isn't much of a morning person, so she's sleeping in. We're headed to the farmers' market. Hey, why don't you join us?"

Seeing Greer so soon after her sexual rejection didn't entirely appeal to Eva, but getting to know her better did. This might be her only opportunity to glimpse Greer's private world. It could help her learn how to get Greer on her side. "I don't want to intrude. Besides, she might not want to see me, especially at her home."

"Don't worry about her. She's used to me bringing strangers home. I'm sort of a magnet for strays, animal or human. Besides, I'll have a chance to show off the house and entice you to stick around a while. Every visitor to New Hope is a potential resident. That's my philosophy, and I'm the self-appointed Welcome Wagon. Say you'll come. We seldom get guests, and one of your stature, even less often." Bessie's smile faded a bit and her exuberance waned. "I'm being too pushy, aren't I? Greer says I can be terribly pushy at times. Forgive me. I'm sure you have other things to do."

Bessie's obvious disappointment made Eva's decision easier. She didn't even know this woman, but she didn't want to disappoint her. And she did want to explain why she'd phoned the chief last night before Greer heard it from someone else. It was often best to deliver bad news in person. Though, if JJ's reaction this morning was an indication, it might already be too late. "If you're sure, I'll visit for a while."

As Eva followed Bessie's pickup into the country, she wondered about the reception awaiting her. Surely they could put aside a momentary attraction and concentrate on professional matters. But Eva acknowledged the subtle sting to her ego as she turned onto an asphalt drive leading through a stand of beautifully colored fall foliage.

They stopped in front of a large two-story log home with a green metal roof and wraparound porch that looked like a cover shot for *Log Home Living*. Off to one side, a matching three-car garage sat beside a small body of water. Nestled among the trees, the place screamed warmth, serenity, and stability. Two wildly enthusiastic dogs bounded off the porch and loped in their direction. Eva had imagined a home like this to share with someone she loved, a place of dreams and possibilities. Wiping a tear from her cheek, she opened the car door and walked toward Bessie.

"Meet Straw Dog and Frisky, my two most recent wards." Bessie scratched each dog behind the ears, then looked back toward the house. "Quite a sight, isn't it? Would you believe my partner and I built this? Both floors have the same square footage, but arranged a little differently. It's sort of like a stacked duplex. I thought when Greer got older she'd want a place of her own. And that worked fine until... Sorry, I'm rambling. Come on in. I'll give you the nickel tour. And don't panic if you see a big fluffy ball of black fur skitter by. That's Nina, our resident cat, and not very sociable, kind of like Greer."

Eva followed Bessie inside and listened as she proudly pointed out details of her amazing home with its open floor plan. Large master bedroom suites occupied either end of the common space. A library, half bath, and expansive deck completed the first-floor living area. Every room housed large, comfortable furnishings that made Eva want to sink into them and rest.

She stood in the center of the great room, staring at the second-floor railing and the bank of windows overlooking the lake. "How did you get the same space up there with a vaulted ceiling down here?"

"Ruth, my partner, took care of that. She was architecturally gifted."

The sadness in Bessie's eyes broadcast her pain. "And she's—"

"Passed, yes, several years ago. But she's still with me, everywhere I look." Bessie spread her arms as if to embrace the spirit of her departed lover. "How about a cup of coffee?"

"If it's not any trouble, that would be perfect, Bessie. This is a beautiful home, open and welcoming."

"Thank you. For Ruth and me, our life was our family. You can't raise a kid in a museum. Speaking of Greer, I better go light a fire under her."

"Why don't I go while you make the coffee?" Eva offered.

"If you're sure you don't mind. She'll be out back or in her apartment over the garage."

Eva followed the rock-lined path toward the garage. Maybe she'd take this chance to talk privately with Greer. If the rest of the day turned out like the morning, Bessie would amuse them with nonstop chatter. A relaxing break sounded good after the events of yesterday. But, first, she needed to tell Greer about her phone call to the chief.

As she rounded the corner of the garage and started toward the steps, Eva froze. Greer stepped from an outside shower enclosure completely naked. Eva imagined her hands replacing the water that slid down Greer's belly. Sunlight reflected off the moisture that covered her body and she seemed to glow.

Eva could only stare, mesmerized, at the boyishly thin figure with feminine attributes. Tight, perky breasts accented strong shoulders and a slender waist. Narrow hips sloped into a golden, neatly trimmed triangle at the apex of her thighs. Heat bubbled up inside Eva as Greer bent to retrieve her towel and her tight ass mooned her. Eva's tiny gasp echoed between them like a bullhorn.

Greer whipped around, wrapping the bath sheet around her as she moved. "What the—"

Eva didn't wait to hear the rest. She ran back toward the house, unable to see anything except Greer Ellis's body in all its naked glory. She paused on the deck to catch her breath and compose her rampant libido before telling Bessie she needed to leave. When she entered the kitchen, Bessie was preparing the table for coffee.

"I think I should go, Bessie. This suddenly doesn't seem like such a good idea."

"You look a little rosy, darling. What's the matter? Catch Greer in the buff? I've told her a hundred times about that—and in this weather. She's lucky she hasn't caught pneumonia."

"She didn't look too happy." In truth, she'd received friendlier looks from the murderers and terrorists she'd interviewed.

"She'll get over it. After all, you're my guest and she'll act accordingly. I didn't raise her to act like a heathen."

"I don't want to cause any trouble."

"Honey, this house without trouble is like summer without heat. It doesn't happen."

Eva started to object again, but Greer entered through the French doors from the deck, fully dressed. Her blue eyes still sparked with anger, but Bessie didn't give her a chance to attack.

"Look who I dragged in from town. I believe you two have met, officially and otherwise." A grin tugged at the corners of her mouth. Greer started to speak. "Be nice, girl," Bessie warned her.

"Yes, we met at *work*," she said as if that explained everything. "What are you doing here?"

"I told you I invited her," Bessie said.

Eva smiled at Bessie in appreciation and finally met Greer's stare. "Yes, your aunt is a wonderful hostess. But I also need to talk to you before—" The cell phone clipped to Greer's side rang.

"Excuse me." Greer turned away from her to answer the call. "Detective Ellis."

Bessie motioned for Eva to have a seat at the table and poured everyone a cup of coffee. "Yes, sir, I'm on second shift. No, sir, I can come in now." Eva scooped sugar and poured cream into her cup and tried not to eavesdrop. "She *what*?" Greer whirled back toward Eva, her face flushed except for the white scar bisecting her left eyebrow. "I'll be there in ten minutes."

Greer slid the phone back into its case with slow deliberation. The anger that burned in her eyes earlier flared again and her pupils darkened. "What have you done?"

Eva rose and reached toward Greer. "That's why I'm here. I wanted to explain before you heard it from someone else."

"Too late. What do you hope to get out of this?"

"Answers. I need answers, and no one wants to give me any. Can't you understand that?" Eva tried to control her breathing. When she got too emotional, her accent thickened.

Greer grabbed her leather jacket off the back of a chair and started toward the door. "I understand that you've opened a can of worms. I hope I don't end up in the middle of it."

"Greer, I'm sorry but—"

"Save it." She slammed the door after her, and seconds later the Harley roared to life and spun out of the driveway.

Eva started to apologize to Bessie, but didn't get the chance. "You go, honey. We can talk another time."

"Thank you." She was already halfway out the door but Greer had left. Why did her search for answers in Paul's death place her at odds with Greer? And why did it bother her so much?

❖

Greer paced in front of Donna Burke's desk while she waited to see Chief Bryant. Donna had tried teasing, picking, sparring, even outright flirting, but Greer wasn't in the mood for idle conversation. She didn't look forward to this meeting.

The chief opened his office door and waved her in. "Thanks for coming, Greer."

"Sure, Chief. What's up?"

"I won't beat around the bush. I don't like to micromanage, but this is an unusual situation. Eva Saldana called me last night very displeased after meeting with Sergeant Fluharty. I know how victims' families can be, but this woman can bring down a boatload of negative publicity on the department. I have to make sure that doesn't happen."

Greer shifted in her chair, wondering when he would get to the part that involved her. Had Eva complained about her showing up at her motel room? Had she spun the failed seduction attempt into a complaint against her?

"I asked Fluharty to assign a detective to review the Saldana case and to read Eva Saldana into that review—completely."

"I'm sure JJ will do a great job."

"Fluharty chose you."

Greer felt like someone had punched her in the gut. A personal misunderstanding was turning into a professional nightmare. This reeked of disaster on so many levels. She stared at the chief, waiting for the punch line. When he didn't smile and didn't attempt to continue, she had to ask. "Is this a joke?"

"I'm afraid not. Like I said, I don't dictate how a sergeant runs his squad, but you need to know exactly what I expect. The investigation's all yours. Run it through Fluharty like any other case. But I expect full disclosure with this woman and, of course, keep me in the loop because of the potential publicity."

"But, Chief, this is JJ's case. He knows it better than anybody else."

"Fluharty wants fresh eyes on this. That makes perfect sense to me. I trust you to do what's right." Bryant rose and started toward the door. "You clear on what I expect?"

Hell, no, but she'd straighten it out with Sergeant Fluharty shortly. "Yes, sir."

"Good. Do us proud."

Greer walked toward the homicide squad like a zombie. She didn't want to second-guess a fellow officer's investigation, especially not her mentor's. This resembled an Internal Affairs assignment—policing the police, not her thing. And the guys would treat her like a pariah. She could count on Sergeant Fluharty to make this right.

When she plopped into the chair in front of Fluharty's desk, he immediately stated, "I know what you're about to say, so don't. You've got the review and that's final."

"But, Sarge." The walls of his tiny office closed in on her. This job carried an unhealthy dose of professional suicide topped with a heaping scoop of personal complications. How was she supposed to work side by side with Eva Saldana after they'd seen each other naked? Not at the same time, but that was a technicality. The replay of Eva lying nude on her motel bed made Greer tingle with arousal.

Fluharty raised his hand. "Listen to me, Greer. I need you to do this. I know you don't want to. I know you're the junior detective. It's JJ's case. He'll be pissed. I know all of it. But he handled the investigation initially, and if I give it to him it'll look like a whitewash. Besides, he'd try to get in that woman's pants. We can't afford that. You'll do a good job. Look the case over, check for any obvious errors, walk Ms. Saldana through it, and close it again."

"What can I find that you and JJ didn't?"

"Nothing. But we have to look. Can you do that—*for me?*"

Sergeant Fluharty had never even vaguely referenced that day and the tremendous debt she owed him. He wouldn't ask for anything directly. Her guilt tasted like a wave of nausea. Against her better judgment and every gut instinct, she said, "Okay, Sarge. But JJ will go ballistic."

Sergeant Fluharty sighed in visible relief, and the worry lines around his eyes relaxed. He hadn't looked well lately. Was he sick? She couldn't ask now. Besides, they weren't exactly friends and he might think she was meddling.

"Let me worry about JJ. I'll keep him too busy to complain. You'll work only this case until it's closed. Set your schedule and check in with me for periodic updates. I'm depending on you, and so are the chief, JJ, and the department. We can't have this reporter make us look incompetent."

Greer nodded, rose from her chair, and walked back into the squad room feeling like she was facing a firing squad.

JJ took one look at her and jumped up from his desk. "Oh, *hell*, no!"

CHAPTER FIVE

"JJ, this wasn't my idea." Greer wanted desperately to explain.

"This isn't right." She'd never seen him so upset. His tanned skin darkened as anger flooded his face.

"What's that supposed to mean?" Greer started to defend herself but wasn't sure what JJ meant. Did he think she wanted to one-up him for some reason? Could he possibly think she *wanted* him to be wrong to prove herself? Or had he picked up on the sexual tension between her and Eva that first day? Maybe she'd bruised his male pride and ego. Things didn't look good for her and this investigation.

Sergeant Fluharty exited his office with a case file in his hand. "She didn't want this assignment, JJ. I didn't give her a choice. What's the matter, don't trust your training?"

"It's not about that and you damn well know it, Sarge. You shouldn't put Greer in this position. It's not right for her to review the work of a senior detective."

Fluharty dropped the folder on Greer's desk. "Listen up, everybody." He raised his voice so Breeze and Craig could hear him clearly. "Nobody likes to have an outsider review their work, but the chief gave us orders. Greer's doing her job, so don't give her any crap. If you're worried about her inexperience, give her a hand and let's get this over with."

When Fluharty returned to his office, Breeze said, just loud enough for Greer to hear, "Well, that sucks."

Craig didn't look up from his computer screen but added, "Yeah, off-the-rails sucks."

JJ nodded and continued to glare. *Was* something wrong with the investigation? Maybe JJ *had* cut some corners or missed something important. Or maybe everyone just thought she was too green to review JJ's work.

These people depended on each other. She hated being at odds with them. Greer sat down at her old scarred desk and opened Paul Saldana's file, determined to end this nightmare as soon as possible. Slowly the hum of the workday resumed around her, but tension still hung in the air.

Greer reviewed the crime-scene photos first, starting with the victim. Paul Saldana's general appearance resembled his sister's—dark hair, striking features, and classic good looks. He wore a pair of suit pants and a dress shirt. Highly polished oxfords and dark socks littered the corners of the room. He'd apparently settled in for the night, draping his necktie and suit jacket over the back of the only chair. A small suitcase rested at the foot of the bed, clothes neatly folded inside. His wallet partially protruded from his back trousers pocket, and his BlackBerry hung on his side. Specks of white powder inside Paul's nostrils provided the only incongruities in the photos. Greer turned her attention to the other pictures.

She hadn't responded to the scene the night of the incident so these helped her visualize the setting. They also allowed her to check for anything out of the ordinary in the room. Other than the drugs and paraphernalia, the space looked like any other businessman's layover. The powder cocaine and sniffing straw on the coffee table supported an overdose scenario. They had found only Paul's fingerprints in the room and no other trace evidence. The absence of a suicide note lent credibility to the accidental-overdose theory.

But Greer had to view the evidence, or absence thereof, as she would a fresh case. The most significant clue often revealed itself in the tiniest detail, and she had to be thorough. On one side stood her fellow officers and on the other a woman who knew the victim and believed completely that someone had killed him. If she simply rubber-stamped JJ's conclusion, she wouldn't do them or herself justice.

She pulled the autopsy report out of the file next. The cause of death: inhalation of cocaine hydrochloride resulting in massive cerebral hemorrhage. The cocaine in Paul's system tested ninety-seven percent pure, unusual for street-level merchandise in this area. Normal purity levels hovered at fifty percent this far from a main source city. So either Paul had been very unlucky or someone intended for him to die. Greer started to read the rest of the medical examiner's report but the room had suddenly gone too quiet. She looked up and saw Eva Saldana walking toward her.

Like the day before, she looked as if she'd stepped off the pages of a fashion magazine. Brown wool-blend slacks seemed to wear her instead of the other way around; they hugged her curves beautifully and tapered at the ankles. A copper-colored turtleneck accentuated highlights in her unfettered hair and clung to her generous breasts. Eva seemed to glide across the room in a pair of gold-toned stiletto heels that would've caused her serious ankle damage.

Craig barely acknowledged Eva, returning to his computer when she entered. Breeze nodded in greeting, but didn't speak. JJ swiveled in his chair and followed her movements from the door to Greer's desk. From the corner of her eye, Greer saw Sergeant Fluharty coming out of his office. He had that oh-shit-there's-going-to-be-trouble look in his eyes.

JJ bolted from his desk and planted himself between Eva and Greer, circling Eva like a coyote tormenting his next meal. "I told you we could do things an easier way, but you wouldn't listen. Now you've put this girl," he nodded in Greer's direction, "in a bad place."

Greer didn't like JJ's inference or having him use her as an excuse for his agenda. "Hey, I don't appreciate—"

"I fail to see how a search for the truth puts anybody in a bad place, Detective. I thought we were all on the same side." Eva stared at JJ with unflinching certainty.

Eva wouldn't back down until she had the answers she needed about her brother's death. Greer admired that quality, which probably served Eva well as an investigative journalist. But right now she was only pissing JJ off.

"You already have the truth. You just don't want to accept it."

Sergeant Fluharty stepped between JJ and Eva. "Back off, Jake. I warned you about this. Let it go and get back to work."

JJ glared at Eva and Greer once more, picked up his briefcase, and stalked out of the squad room. This assignment was barely an hour old and her entire squad wanted to disown her. And a dangerously attractive woman, with no problem using her body to get what she wanted, had already tried to seduce her. In the past her professional life provided stability when her personal life fell apart. She couldn't afford another disconnect between her instincts and her job. Number-one priority, keep her emotions in check and wrap up the review ASAP.

Fluharty said to Eva, "I'm sorry about that. JJ is touchy about someone second-guessing him."

"That's only an issue if he's wrong," Eva said, then focused on Greer and the papers feathered across her desk. "Is that Paul's file?"

Greer swept the pages together and stuffed them back in the folder. Grabbing her jacket, she lowered her voice as she guided Eva toward the exit. "You shouldn't have come here."

"You have a lot of those."

"Lot of what?"

"Shoulds."

"Let's go somewhere we can talk." Greer heard the tension in her voice and wanted to be out of earshot before she let loose. "Follow me back to the house. At least we can avoid the town gossips there."

Greer used the drive back home to corral her irritation. When they arrived, she motioned Eva inside, placed the file on the kitchen table, and put on a pot of coffee. While it brewed, she gave Straw Dog and Frisky a quick treat and tried to decide where to start. Her furry pals acted content to let her pet them and avoid the conversation altogether. In the corner, Nina curled beside the stove and stared at her as if waiting to see what magic trick she pulled out of her hat. Cats were harder to impress than their canine counterparts. Greer couldn't launch into an angry tirade. She needed to lay some ground rules, establish boundaries with Eva before this went any further.

"You said you wanted to talk. So far, I haven't heard anything except silence and heavy sighs. What is it, Greer?"

She finally faced Eva, hoping to avoid that probing stare long enough to state her case. "Do you understand what you've done?"

"Why don't you enlighten me?"

"You've threatened the reputation of a decorated detective and our entire department. And put me in a touchy position with my squad. I recognize a citizen's right to question the police. It's vital to our justice system. But we've already given your brother's case more attention than most. When will you let this go?"

Eva stared at her for a few seconds before she spoke. "I'm impressed. I'd begun to think you uttered only single-line quips. But to answer your question, I'll let this go when *someone* has *heard* my concerns. And I couldn't care less who's uncomfortable with my questions. I'm interested in the truth—and you should be as well."

Eva looked totally determined. Her red lips turned deep crimson and glistened when she moistened them with the tip of her tongue. For a moment, Greer lost herself in those lips and the hypnotic strength of Eva's stare. A ripple of sensation forced her to look away.

"I'm a police officer. Of course I care about the truth."

"But one doesn't necessarily guarantee the other. Did it ever occur to you that one day you might have to choose?"

The unflattering inference annoyed Greer. "Did it ever occur to you that you might be wrong?" She sounded like a ten-year-old firing insults back at her opponent. "Can we just agree to disagree? I have a job to do, and since you're now in the loop, we need some ground rules."

Eva settled at the table and waited as Greer poured coffee and sat down across from her. "This should be good."

"First, I need time to review the full case file. I also need to see the personal items that you have. Then I'll reinterview witnesses." Eva started to speak, but Greer held up her hand. "And, in the meantime, I'd appreciate it if you would wait."

Eva gripped her coffee cup tighter and the muscles around her jaw tensed. "Wait?"

"Yes, please." Greer watched some of the fire drain from Eva's eyes. "I know that's probably the hardest thing for you to do, but I need to get up to speed on everything. Can you give me that? I didn't want this job, but now that I have it, I intend to give it my best." In the end she also fully expected to validate JJ's findings.

Eva nodded. "In the interest of full disclosure and cooperation,

I found an address when I went through Paul's belongings. I believe it's the warehouse he was scouting for another film studio. 247 Lewis Street. Do you know it?"

"Yeah, it's off Main in the strip of old sewing factories. I'll check it out. Thanks."

Eva stared into her coffee, appearing sad now. "When we were children, Paul feared any kind of creepy thing. Vincent, Lucio, and I constantly tormented him with worms and bugs. It's a miracle he grew to be so well-adjusted. We'll probably all burn in hell for it." She looked at Greer with pain-filled eyes. "I don't know why I thought of that. I'll try to be patient, but I can't promise. I tend more toward action."

"Thank you." Greer marveled at the easy way Eva Saldana let her emotions flow to the surface. How would it feel to let her emotions out without worrying about what people might think or if she'd be able to put herself back together? But Greer had spent years practicing self-control and emotional containment. That's who she was, especially now.

"Can I at least see the file?" Eva asked.

"Not right now. Let me review everything first." Greer didn't want to tell Eva the pictures might disturb her too much. And she didn't want anyone to handle the file until she was certain exactly what it contained. Grieving relatives sometimes removed or planted information to encourage a specific outcome.

"You don't make many concessions, do you, Detective? Any more rules I should know about? I wouldn't want to cross any invisible barriers."

Greer considered addressing the incident in Eva's motel room, decided it had been an irrational one-time thing, and let it go. "I've covered the important stuff. If anything else comes up, I'll let you know."

"Fair enough. What now?"

"I need more background information on Paul."

Greer took notes while Eva talked about her brother's life and business. Her attention occasionally slipped as Eva's lips formed the words or as she followed her sweeping hand gestures. Greer struggled to focus on work, content to listen as Eva strummed and tweaked ordinary-sounding words into auditory masterpieces. It was late afternoon when Greer realized Eva had stopped talking.

"Are you all right?" Eva squeezed Greer's forearm.

The touch was light but increased her heart rate. "Uh, yeah, sure." Greer rose from the table and cleared their coffee cups. "I guess we're finished for today. I'll talk to you when I have news." She turned back to speak to Eva, but bumped into her instead. "Oh."

Eva hugged Greer, close and tight. "Thank you for everything. I know you'll do your best." Her hot breath against Greer's ear infused her with sexual heat. She started to hug Eva back, but the dogs barked just before the front door opened.

A few seconds later Bessie stood propped against the doorway wearing a Cheshire-cat grin. "Am I interrupting something? I hope so."

Eva released Greer and walked toward the door. "Not at all. I was thanking Greer for her help. I'm on my way out. Nice to see you again, Bessie." She gave Bessie a quick hug, patted each dog on the head, and was gone.

Greer turned back to the sink and heard Bessie scrape a chair across the hardwood floor, a sign she was settling in—not good.

"Sit." Bessie spoke with authority and concern, and Greer didn't question her. "I've put this off long enough. I'd like you to *really* listen for a change."

"Please, Aunt Bessie." But Greer knew better than to argue with her when she got an idea in her head. And Greer had been avoiding these talks for months.

"Do me the courtesy of listening." When she nodded in resignation, Bessie said. "You need to move on, honey. Your life didn't end two years ago—as hard as that may be to accept. And you *did not* cause what happened to Clare."

Her aunt didn't believe in beating around the bush. Brief and blunt, that's how they related best. Greer tried to swallow Bessie's words without the bitter taste of guilt and loss that swelled up inside. "I've moved on, Bessie."

"Maybe you have, judging from what I just saw. But up till now you've been going through the motions. I did the same things after

Ruth died—moved into the apartment out back because I couldn't bear to be in this house we'd shared, threw myself into my job, avoided my friends and any connection to her, and refused to date again."

"I'm dating, and, for the record, you didn't see anything because nothing happened."

Bessie's right eyebrow arched toward her grayish-blond hairline. "Whatever you say. And *for your record*, I wouldn't exactly call what you're doing *dating*. I'm talking about something meaningful, something that makes you feel alive. Sex only feeds the body, not the heart and soul."

Her aunt's words crashed into her, and she choked out her response. "I'm not sure I *can*." Clare had been her heart, the living, feeling part of her. Now she was empty.

Bessie scooted her chair closer and hugged Greer. "Clare gave you exactly what you needed at the time, and you're stronger because of it. But she wouldn't want this half-life for you. It insults your love. Look at opportunities, like the one you just had in your arms, with a little more enthusiasm. I want to see you happy again."

Greer swallowed the sizable lump in her throat. "I'll try, Bessie, but it's hard."

"I know, baby. I know. Ellis women don't heal painlessly or quickly, but we come back stronger." She gave Greer a big squeeze and kissed her cheeks. "Now, how about something to eat? I'm starving."

Sometimes Greer swore that her aunt plugged directly into the universal hotline. Her advice and opinions often forecast the future. Bessie decided it was time for Greer to move on and, presto, Eva Saldana showed up—the first woman to spark her interest in two years. Poppycock, just coincidence pure and simple.

And when Eva got the answers she wanted, she'd be gone. The sooner the better. Then Greer could return to her own normal life. But the thought depressed more than comforted her. For the past two years, "normal" had equaled a series of sexual liaisons devoid of love or intimacy.

❖

Eva drove out of Greer's driveway like a rocket. Her knees still trembled from the proximity to Greer and her calculated hug. She'd meant to reassure Greer that she was on board with all her rules and prohibitions, though she had formulated her own plan. But the embrace became entirely too enjoyable and she lingered longer than she intended.

Greer's firm breasts against hers dimpled her nipples into concentrated pleasure points. The contact reignited her memory of Greer's touch the night before. Heat poured between her thighs and she fought not to fuse their pelvises as they hugged. At that moment she wanted relief, everything else be damned, and Greer Ellis could provide it. The passion between them pulsed with reciprocated energy. Sparks flashed in Greer's ocean blue eyes and her breath came in short spurts. Eva wanted to grab fistfuls of her thick hair, climb her lean frame, and ride her hips until she begged to come.

But when Greer reached to return her embrace, she tensed. She'd obviously heard Bessie come in, whereas Eva was too involved to notice. Depending on how Eva prioritized her needs, Bessie's timing either cursed or saved her. If she hoped to keep Greer on her side by using her considerable sex appeal, she'd have to do a better job of handling her attraction. She behaved like a novice.

By the time Eva reached downtown New Hope, she'd reined in her hunger and refocused on the case. Why hadn't she told Greer about Paul's missing camera? Maybe he hadn't brought it with him, but that possibility didn't ring true. She'd promised Greer she'd be patient with her investigation, but she hadn't promised to sit idly by. Maybe she could uncover things the police couldn't access. At the very least she needed some basic information on these people who had such a significant effect on her family's life. She should have put background checks on the top of her list as an investigator. She drove past the historic police station and pulled into the parking lot of the modest single-story *New Hope Tribune*.

Eva entered the building with a wave of nostalgia for her early days as a cub reporter. Many newspaper offices she'd visited seemed comfortably similar to every other, a lot of them still located in old construction downtown near the hub of activity in earlier days. Some still housed antique, and environmentally hazardous, presses that were cost-prohibitive to dismantle and move. Every time she entered one of these buildings, she breathed deeply, hoping for the faintest scent of printing ink, and listened in vain for the rhythmic roll of press cylinders. Instead she smelled the mustiness of disuse and the cacophony of computers versus people. Eva sighed as she experienced the disappointment again.

The large, open *Tribune* building housed two glass-enclosed offices and a large area of partitioned cubicles. She introduced herself to the editor of the paper and explained what she needed. Fortunately he watched CNN and her reputation held some sway. He was more than willing to help and even assigned one of his reporters to assist with research. She followed his directions through the maze of half-walled workstations and knocked on the side of a cubicle.

"Yeah, what is it now?" A redheaded man sat hunched over a desktop covered with papers. On either side, piles of newspapers and magazines threatened to topple over with the slightest breeze and bury him. A chair, two bookcases, and more periodicals stacked on every flat surface, including the floor, cluttered the rest of the small space.

"I'm sorry to disturb you, but your editor sent me back."

The man's head popped up like that of a surfacing groundhog. He craned his neck around the stacks of papers, did a polite assessment, and met her gaze. "I'm sorry for being snappish. It's hard to get any work done around here." He stood and offered his hand. "Tom Merritt, Mrs.— Hey, wait. I know who you are. Eva Saldana."

Tom's attention made her a little self-conscious and he appeared a bit awestruck. "Yes."

"Wow. I mean, excuse me for staring, but television doesn't do you justice. Though I'm sure you've heard that before." Tom's face flushed as red as his curly hair. He finally stepped from behind the mound of papers, his neatly pressed jeans and button-collar shirt quite a contrast to the disarray in his office. He looked young, but the editor had indicated Tom had been with the paper for ten years. "How can I help you? Whatever it is, ask."

Tom was obviously curious and maybe suffering a tiny case of hero worship. Her father had taught her to use whatever resource or advantage presented itself. In Greer's case her body provided the leverage; in Tom's, her star power. Whatever worked.

"I'm interested in some history on the police department,

specifically the homicide squad. Things like significant past cases, anything controversial or newsworthy. You know what I mean. You've been around a while, Tom."

Eva could swear the man's chest puffed out. "Yeah, I get your drift. Any *body* you're particularly interested in?"

"You're very astute. In fact, focus your efforts on Detectives Johnston and Ellis. Cases they've handled or incidents they've been involved in. I'm not trying to discredit anyone, so the facts will do nicely."

Tom stretched against the side of his cubicle and the flimsy panel swayed, nearly dumping him to the floor. He recovered quickly, trying to mask his embarrassment. "I understand what you need, but it could take some time to get all this together. JJ has been with the department several years. Greer moved over to homicide a couple of years ago after—"

Eva was immediately more attentive. "After what?"

"Well." He lowered his voice as if about to reveal the location of the Holy Grail. "It's a long, involved story. I'd be glad to fill in the small details, but you need to get the facts down first."

"Will I read about it in your research?" Eva wanted to know what made Greer tick, especially in her personal life. That's where her vulnerability would lie.

"Definitely."

"Then you might as well tell me."

Tom shuffled his loafer-clad feet. "Hey, I got no problem sharing what I know, after you've read the official version. Greer and I went to school together and I like her, but news is news. So, if we can reach an agreement, I'll be glad to cooperate."

The mystery intrigued her. Greer seemed overprotective of her fellow officers and refused to view them in a bad light. But the law-enforcement community in general guarded its secrets fiercely. If you didn't know the secret handshake, you didn't get in. Now Tom was waxing cautiously about Greer.

"What kind of agreement are you talking about?"

"I know how you TV types are, no offense intended. You waltz into a small town like ours and think you can snatch a story from under our noses and we'll be grateful for your crumbs. So, if you find something newsworthy, about your brother's case or the police department, we put a double byline on it. That would be a real coup for me. Agreed?"

Eva liked to know exactly what she was dealing with, and ambitious people seldom showed all their cards. "Absolutely, agreed." She stuck out her hand and they shook. "Now, what's your take on Detective Greer Ellis?"

"A good person—honest, loyal, committed, and works practically nonstop. Outgoing in school, but she's become a bit more closed. You couldn't want a better friend than Greer. I hope your investigation won't hurt her."

"I hope not too, Tom." As she spoke, Eva realized that she sincerely meant it. "When can you have something for me?"

Tom rubbed the back of his neck and shrugged apologetically. "A day or two. Is that good?"

"That's fine." She placed her hand on his arm and the muscle relaxed into her touch. "I appreciate this. It'll save me so much time." She scribbled her cell number on the back of her business card and handed it to him. "Call me, any time."

"I should be thanking you." As she walked away, he added, "Pleasure to meet you, Ms. Saldana. This could be my ticket out of Podunk, North Carolina."

"Eva, call me Eva," she said. Tom seemed like a nice man, who knew exactly what he wanted and took advantage of opportunities. Maybe she'd finally found one ally in this town. Two reporters against an entire police department. Not great odds, but she'd played worse.

CHAPTER SIX

After eight cups of the potent motel-room coffee, Eva paced her tiny space like a gerbil on steroids. She hadn't spoken with Greer or Tom in two days. At this point, neither of them seemed sincere about helping her. Another search of Paul's BlackBerry and wallet and a round of casual questions in town turned up no solid leads.

She hit the usual hotbeds of gossip in a small town: the diner, post office, quick-stop market, and the hair salon. Folks eagerly chatted about any topic she chose, as long as she kept it "confidential." According to local opinion, the New Hope Police Department was the best if you were on the right side of the law and the worst if you weren't. That was how it should be. Chief Bryant got high marks for running an honest force with limited resources. When Greer's name came up, the comments usually echoed Tom's: loyal, committed, honest, but nothing personal. In a town that loved to gossip, people remained tight-lipped on the subject of Greer Ellis the person. For a reporter that spelled story.

By midmorning Eva's patience had run out. She'd promised Greer time to go through the investigation, but she refused to wait any longer. Reporters sniffed out stories, they didn't wait for them to drop in their laps. Eva grabbed her purse and the local map she'd picked up at the post office and drove back to New Hope. She could follow up at least one lead that didn't require police assistance.

The rows of old warehouses on Lewis Street all looked the same: run down, windowless, and abandoned. This dismal picture of New Hope conflicted with the upbeat staging of colorful umbrellas and bright storefronts on Elm Street. These back streets represented a seedier side of the little town, and Eva wondered if her decision to come here alone was prudent. She slowed and searched for the address. When she found 247, she parked on the street in front and approached the precarious-looking entrance.

Rusty hinges barely held the weathered door upright. Eva nudged it with her shoulder and stepped back. It creaked open enough for her to scoot inside between the edge and the frame. Minimal light filtered in from above and shrouded the interior of the structure in a gray haze. Large crates and boxes stacked precariously on the floor sported a thick layer of dust and a spider commune. The floors buckled in places from the elements, and in spots tiny vegetation peeked through.

Eva edged around the hazards and walked toward the center of the space. Not even the dust had been disturbed. What had Paul seen in this place that made it worth considering as a film studio? But he had been the visionary in the family, which made him very successful in his job. However, nothing here helped explain what happened to him, so she turned to leave. As she moved toward the exit, the floor beneath her dipped slightly, pitching her forward. She grabbed at a stack of crates that gave way under her grasp. Groping for anything solid to hold on to, she fell backward and the boxes crashed down on top of her.

She lay stunned in the rubble with her head pounding like a weeklong hangover. She wiggled her arms and legs and was relieved that nothing felt broken. No sticky patches that might signal blood loss. Covering her head with her hands, Eva crouched and then stood, forcing the empty crates off her. She opened her eyes and tried to focus as pain shot through her temples. When her vision cleared, she was staring down the barrel of a very large gun.

"*Merda santamente,*" she swore.

"What in the hell are you doing here, Eva?" Greer lowered and holstered her weapon, but it looked like she was swaying from side to side.

"The same thing you are, I imagine—investigating." She grabbed her head to stop the dancing vision of Greer. "Can the sermon wait a while?"

"Are you hurt? You're a little unsteady. What happened?" Greer pulled Eva against her and wrapped an arm around her waist.

The light-headedness increased. Greer stood very close and Eva fought not to cling to her just for the contact. "Boxes fell on me, but I'll be okay."

Greer led her outside and toward her unmarked police car. "I'll drive you to the hospital. You might have a mild concussion."

Eva felt foolish for not being more careful. She didn't want Greer treating her like an invalid. "Don't need a hospital. I'll go back to the room and rest."

They stopped beside Greer's vehicle and she fixed Eva with her azure stare. "You're either going to the hospital or I'll stay with you until I'm sure you're okay. You decide."

As tempting as the option of having Greer with her sounded, nurse was not the role she had in mind. Besides, she wanted Greer working on Paul's case, not wasting time babysitting her. "Fine, hospital it is."

Fortunately, New Hope General wasn't busy and they settled Eva into an exam room quickly. Before the nurse could take her temperature, Bessie was standing at the door.

"Are you all right, honey?"

"I'll be fine, Bessie. Don't worry. Your niece insisted I come in."

"What happened, Greer?"

"I found her under a pile of boxes. Ask her what happened. Does the emergency room have you on speed dial when I come in?"

"We care about you, that's all. What happened to Eva?" Bessie wasn't giving up.

"She was snooping around the old warehouse district and a pallet of empty crates fell on her. She's a little woozy. I couldn't let her drive. But now that she's here, I can go."

Eva watched the interaction between Greer and her aunt with interest, finding it strange that they spoke about her as if she wasn't in the room. Was this how cops and medical folk discussed victims—as if they weren't really present? Or maybe this was simply Bessie and Greer's method of communicating—third-person cryptic.

"You certainly cannot go, young lady. You wait right here until she's finished, then take her to her motel. She doesn't have anybody in town."

"That won't be necessary, Bessie," Eva said. "I'll call a cab when I'm ready. I'm sure Greer has more important things to do."

Greer nodded and started for the door, but Bessie ended the discussion. "She can wait outside if she wants, but she *will* take you back to your motel when we finish."

Two hours later, Bessie rolled Eva's wheelchair to the hospital exit where Greer paced the concrete drive. Her posture was rigid, her gait long and purposeful, and her expression totally blank. Why did this place make her so uncomfortable?

As they approached her, Greer stopped. "Finally. I'll get the car."

"Is she okay?" Eva asked Bessie.

"She'll be fine. This isn't her favorite place anymore."

Bessie helped Eva into Greer's car, then walked around to the driver's side. "She has a mild concussion. Stay with her and watch her for a few hours."

"But, Bessie—"

"You heard me. Don't leave her alone for at least four hours. Understand?"

Greer put the car in gear and, without answering Bessie, drove out of the lot. "Why did I get the most meddlesome aunt in the history of the world?"

"She's trying to help, but you can drop me off. The headache meds are working." At this point Eva wasn't eager to spend alone time with Greer either. The combination of their attraction and a concussion could be dangerous. And now that Greer was finally working Paul's case, she didn't want to jeopardize their cooperative efforts.

"Afraid not. If I don't follow the general's orders, there'll be hell to pay." She clearly wasn't happy about the forced caretaking. "And what were you doing in that warehouse? You promised me some time."

"But I didn't agree to infinity. Why were you there, alone? Isn't that a violation of police protocol?" The day she and Greer met, Sergeant Fluharty had cautioned Greer about handling a dangerous situation without backup.

"I was doing my job."

"You like that, don't you? The risky part?" When Greer didn't answer, Eva pushed a bit more. "Taking down felons without assistance, riding your motorcycle like a maniac, showering outside in near-freezing water, searching buildings alone—it all appeals to you, doesn't it?"

"Help isn't always available. The guys have their own stuff to do and now that—" Greer stared too intently at the road ahead.

Eva mentally completed the statement: you've alienated me from my squad. "If you're taking unnecessary risks because of me, please don't."

"It's not about you. I enjoy my work, and I don't have anything to lose."

The certainty of Greer's comment struck Eva as heartbreaking. It sounded like a death wish. Eva had never grieved so deeply that it threatened to suck the life out of her. But this woman, shrouded in silence and mystery, personified a wounded soul.

When they arrived at the motel, Eva took a quick shower while Greer made phone calls. Eva walked out of the bathroom with the terry-cloth robe tied around her and Greer's gaze swept slowly up her body. The look was like a caress as she remembered Greer's fingers skimming the surface of her skin. She shivered as tiny shocks of arousal fanned through her.

All her earlier good intentions, all the mental discouragement evaporated with the flood of desire that drenched the inside of her thighs. The attraction overwhelmed her as she fought the urge to strip bare and press herself against Greer. She grabbed the edge of the bed for support and settled onto it.

When she looked up, Greer stood in front of her. "Are you dizzy again? What do you need?" Her normally husky voice softened, and the tenderness of it ripped away the last of Eva's restraint.

She pulled Greer into her, resting her face against Greer's breasts. "I'm sorry. It must be the head injury." Eva didn't usually blame outside forces for her desires. If she wanted someone, she went after her without excuse or explanation. But that approach probably wouldn't be as effective with Greer Ellis. "I can't help myself. I'm really attracted to you." At least that part was true. What she didn't add was, "In a purely sexual sense."

Greer tried to step back but Eva hugged her tighter. "I know this doesn't sound logical. I'm here to find out what happened to my brother. But it stirs up so many emotions. I can't seem to separate the grief from the need to connect. Please. I see how you look at me."

"But that doesn't mean we should—"

"For God's sake, enough with the *shoulds* already. Do what you feel for once." The tension in Greer's body relaxed slightly and Eva tugged her down on top of her on the bed. "Don't think. Don't talk. Just kiss me."

Greer tensed again. "No kissing." Her eyes said more about the comment than her words.

"Fine, fuck me, then." Eva shrugged out of the bathrobe and rolled over on all fours. "Is this impersonal enough for you?" She rubbed her ass against Greer's abdomen as she fondled her own breasts for stimulation. "Take me. You don't need to be gentle."

When Greer hesitated, seemingly uncertain what to do, disappointment settled over Eva. Did she misread this woman's abilities and her blatant sexuality? How much more explicit did she have to be about what she wanted?

She guided Greer's hand to her breast and squeezed hard. Her nipple instantly puckered. "Again." Greer's fingers pinched her erect flesh and sensation coursed through her. "Yes," she encouraged her, "yes." She rocked her hips back, desperate for contact. Her voice strained and quivered with need as she begged, "Please go inside me."

Greer crouched over Eva's body and slowly rimmed her sensitive opening with the tip of her finger, too tentative, too gentle. "Harder, I need to *feel* it."

Her words finally registered as Greer's touch became more purposeful. She twisted Eva's nipple and her other hand orchestrated a similar rhythm on her clit. Alternating jolts of pleasure and pain rifled Eva's insides. Jabs of electricity sparked through her body and her temperature spiked. It wouldn't take much for her to come, to experience that ultimate expression of life.

"Do it now."

Greer released Eva's pulsing clit and thrust her fingers deep inside. The entry was rough, and Eva buried her face in the pillow to muffle a scream. She pounded her ass against Greer's hand, urging her to go deeper. "More." Faster and harder—exactly what she needed.

Eva turned to watch the woman who had arrived like manna from heaven as her sexual savior in this godforsaken town. Greer's eyes were tightly closed and she humped her own driving hand as she thrust in and out of Eva. Her well-formed thighs bulged beneath tight jeans, and Eva ached to see her naked, her head thrown back as she climaxed. The thought of this confident, controlled woman in the throes of orgasm made Eva's abdomen clench with the first tremors of release. "Yes. Faster."

Greer slid her hand from Eva's breast and stroked her clit in time with her deep penetrations. Eva covered Greer's hand with hers and clamped down on her swollen tissue. The pain and pleasure coalesced at once in her groin and she surrendered, vibrantly alive, as the climax consumed her. It temporarily obliterated anything but the physical sensations of touch, relief, and satisfaction. She savored the last shudders of orgasm, waited while the soft moaning of Greer's release subsided, then rolled over.

Greer knelt beside her, still fully clothed, and for a second Eva glimpsed a faraway expression in her eyes. She'd seen that look many times, the sightless stare of an emotionally absent lover, physically present but mentally somewhere else. Then it disappeared.

"Jesus, I feel like I stumbled into the rabbit hole." Greer wiped a hand across her sweaty forehead and through her short hair. "This *shouldn't* have happened."

"I believe you went through the rabbit hole and directly into Dante's second circle of hell, whether you should or not." A stab of her headache returned as Eva calmed her breathing.

"I don't know what that means, but it won't be pretty if anybody finds out about this. You aren't planning to—"

"To what? Report you to the chief, blackmail you, or write it up in the *New York Times*? I need your help, but I do have limits." The thought about bedding Greer to secure her assistance skidded through her mind. As if to chastise herself, she added, "You don't need to worry, Detective, this was just sex."

Greer gave her a skeptical look as she stood and headed for the door. "Good. Sex I can handle. If you want anything else, I can't help you." With her hand on the doorknob, Greer turned back. "But thanks for this. It was…different."

Eva couldn't resist teasing Greer a little. "But what about my concussion and my car? We left it at the warehouse, remember?"

"I think you're fine. I'll drop your car off later and leave the keys under the mat." She opened the door and came face-to-face with JJ.

His gaze shot from Greer to Eva's naked body stretched across the bed. "I thought I smelled pussy coming from this room."

Greer tried to step outside and take JJ with her, but he pushed his way past. Eva pulled her robe around her and sat up on the bed. She wasn't about to let his insult or his arrogance get the better of her. "What can I do for you, Detective Johnston?"

"I could use some of what you gave her." The strong odor of alcohol spewed from him like raw sewage.

From the corner of her eye, Eva saw Greer's body tense and her fists clench. "We need to take this outside, JJ." Greer reached for his arm, but he jerked away.

"I like the view in here better." He stared at Greer with a look that made Eva fear for her safety. "Damn, that must be some good stuff if she's already got you pussy whipped."

Greer stood toe-to-toe with JJ and matched his angry glare. "You need to shut up right now and get out of here before one of us does something we'll both regret."

JJ didn't budge. "Has she told you what she's been doing the past couple of days? Maybe she was saving that for the pillow-talk segment of the performance."

"I'm warning you, JJ. Being drunk isn't an excuse for disrespect."

"Jesus, Greer, the woman's been bad-mouthing us all over town. She's hit about every place on Elm Street asking questions about the department and us. It sounds like she's trying to dig up dirt."

Greer stood very still as though listening to what JJ was saying.

"She's even got the newspaper going through their files to find shit. *And* she was asking questions about you personally. Did she tell you *that* before she rubbed it all over you?"

That got Greer's attention. She turned toward Eva with slow deliberation. "Is there something you want to tell me?"

Eva could see the anger in Greer's eyes. She had agreed to be patient while Greer worked the case, but she couldn't wait forever. The last thing she wanted was to have this conversation in front of a drunk Jake Johnston. Her chances of explaining to Greer were higher without his interference. "Maybe we could talk privately?"

"I'd advise against that, partner. It's a slippery slope between those thighs and into that honey pot of hers."

"One more nasty word out of your mouth and I swear I'll hit you, JJ."

"I've finished here anyway." He looked at Eva, shook his head, and staggered toward the exit. "Now I know why you brushed me off so fast. I wasn't the right flavor." He opened the door, stabbed his index finger in Greer's direction, and said, "Clare wouldn't approve of you thinking with your clit."

Greer bolted for the door so fast that it startled Eva. But it slammed in her face and she pounded on it with both fists. "You son of a bitch!"

Eva watched the uncharacteristic loss of control in stunned silence. This was the first time she'd seen Greer Ellis show such raw emotion. JJ knew exactly where to stick the knife to get a reaction from her. Clare was obviously Greer's Achilles' heel.

Eva waited until Greer stopped pounding and slumped forward. With her head against the door, she thumbed the wedding ring on her hand as if drawing strength from it. Eva walked up behind her and tentatively placed a hand on her shoulder. "Are you all right?"

"Fine." She didn't turn around.

"Why don't you sit down?"

"I should go."

"Would you like to talk?" Eva waited, interpreting Greer's reticence as a sign that she might actually want to share her feelings. "About Clare?"

Greer spun around and Eva stepped back to avoid being shoved away. "She's none of your damn business. Stay out of things that don't concern you." Before Eva could apologize, Greer opened the door and jogged across the parking lot toward her car.

❖

Greer slapped the alarm clock off the bedside table as its annoying beep rousted her from the only thirty minutes of sleep she'd gotten all night. She'd thought about JJ, this case, and Eva until they all blended together and made no sense. How had her life become so complicated in such a short time? JJ had turned into a major prick with an unknown agenda. He'd even brought Clare into his drunken tirade. He'd answer for that one. The review of the Saldana case was affecting everything in her life, and not in a good way.

And how had she gotten sexually involved with the family member of a victim? Even a rookie knew that was a no-no. She'd been attracted to Eva since the day they met. Her long wavy hair and dark eyes were like a siren call. Those luscious lips and cute dimples made it hard to concentrate. Eva's body curved in all the right places with a tight ass and ample, suckable breasts. Being in Eva's presence made her horny and skittish as a mustang. When Greer accidentally touched her the first time, she thought she might cry out. Eva's skin was so silky and soft that she wanted to nuzzle against it and feel it bond to her own. It had been a long time since she responded to anyone so viscerally.

And last night when Eva appeared wearing only her bathrobe, Greer couldn't think of anything but getting her out of it. Eva's vulnerability tinged with assertiveness had surprised her, especially when she pulled her into an embrace that quickly led to sex. When she said, "Fuck me, then," Greer's clit twitched in response. The accented cadence of Eva's voice sounded like a polite invitation instead of a cry for release. And Eva left no doubt that she only wanted sex: hard, fast, and *not* gentle—an outlet for her rampant emotions.

Eva's body responded to her like blown glass to the master's breath. She'd been desperate for contact and receptive to every manipulation. Greer fingered Eva's long mane as passion rode her like a stallion, bareback, exciting and dangerous. The moisture and heat Eva exuded blinded Greer to anything but her thundering release. It had taken all her willpower not to scream as she came, hard and wild against Eva's rounded ass.

But Eva had seen something Greer would've preferred to keep hidden. Somehow she understood that Greer needed the impersonality of taking her from behind. Once she knew she didn't have to kiss or look at Eva, Greer's appetites took over. She'd screwed women since Clare and knew her limitations. Sex was fine, as long as no one asked for anything more.

Maybe they could enjoy each other physically during Eva's time here without any complications. Normally Greer wouldn't mix business with pleasure, but this pleasure wasn't local and couldn't come back to haunt her. No matter how the review turned out, Eva Saldana would return to her life as a reporter.

The only possible complication—if Eva got too attached. Greer decided to talk with her and make sure they were on the same page. If they agreed on the terms and the sex didn't totally disrupt their business dealings, she'd have an enjoyable few days with the fiery brunette. But Eva absolutely couldn't mention Clare. She didn't talk about her lover to anyone she fucked.

Greer rolled to the side of the bed just as her cell phone rang. "Hello."

"Fluharty here. Get your ass in my office, and I mean *now.*"

CHAPTER SEVEN

Fred Fluharty strummed his fingers on the old metal desk in his office and glared at her. The sound bounced off nearby file cabinets with an annoyingly tinny resonance. He looked tired and his clothes were wrinkled like he might've slept in them, again. She knew about his divorce but chose not to cross the line into his personal business unless he invited her.

"Don't you want to know why I called you in?" he asked.

"I've got a pretty good idea." Sweating, she tried not to blush. She hated having the sergeant call her into his office, especially when it involved personal matters. She was guilty, with no defense.

"Why did I tell you I couldn't assign JJ to review the Saldana case? Do you even remember that conversation?"

Greer nodded without looking at him. He had done so much for her, and she repaid him by acting like a horny schoolgirl.

"I want to hear you say it." Fluharty's expression soured. He propped his arms on the desktop and his pudgy fingers fanned out from his hands like he was trying to resist the urge to strangle her.

"He'd try to get in Eva's pants."

"Right, so imagine my surprise when he woke my ass up at two in the morning, drunk, to tell me you'd taken on that task. His language was more colorful. You *fucked* this woman?"

She flinched at his use of the word but wasn't sure why. That's exactly what she'd done, but to hear the sergeant or JJ refer to it in such terms bothered her. She nodded again.

"Have you suddenly gone mute? That would definitely be a first."

"I messed up." She'd disappointed him, and though it probably shouldn't have happened, she couldn't bring herself to apologize for having sex with Eva.

"You know what I need to do."

Taking her off the case was the right thing. She'd violated a basic rule of police work: don't get personally involved with victims, witnesses, or family members. But she also wanted to get to the bottom of Paul Saldana's death—for her own peace of mind, to vindicate JJ, and for Eva. Still, she struggled for a logical reason to stay on the case. Fluharty stared at her as if waiting for a rebuttal. "I got nothing, Sarge."

"Damn it, Greer. I counted on you. I *need* you on this."

"I'm sorry. If it wasn't for you, I don't know how I would've survived the last two years. After Clare—" She fought back a choking feeling in her throat. "I owe you a lot."

"It's not about owing. It's about doing a job. Can you promise this won't happen again?"

Greer finally met Fluharty's stare. "No."

Her answer obviously surprised him. "She means something to you?"

"I wouldn't say that exactly. She's different. But I won't lie to you if I'm not sure."

"I appreciate that. You're a hell of a detective, and I want you to finish this, fast. Eva's not directly involved with the case, though that's splitting hairs. I'll have to do some damage control with JJ— once he gets over the shock of losing a piece of ass like that to you. Sorry."

"Why doesn't he want me to do this review, Sarge?"

"Maybe he thinks he missed something and will be embarrassed. Maybe he's hiding something. Maybe something in his past. Damn if I know. You two need to talk. So, you'll try to keep it in your pants and clear this ASAP?"

"Absolutely."

"Got anything so far?"

"I didn't find anything in the crime-scene photos and we don't have any forensic evidence. But Eva found an address in Paul's BlackBerry of the warehouse he was scouting."

Fluharty shuffled some papers on his desk but his gaze held Greer's. "And?"

"I checked it but didn't see anything out of the ordinary. But I might go back. I didn't get through the whole thing."

"Don't waste your time. He didn't die there, and the fact he'd been there probably won't help us. Anything else?"

"Not so far, but I'll keep you posted."

Fluharty rose from his desk, signaling the end of their meeting.

Greer moved toward the door. "And thanks again, Sarge, for giving me this chance. I'll try not to screw it up—literally."

Eva sat in her car in front of the *New Hope Tribune* building convinced that after today she would understand the police department and maybe Greer Ellis better. Thirty minutes early for a meeting with Tom Merritt to review the information he'd compiled for her, she entertained herself with the navigation system by plotting escape routes from this town. But just like last night, her mind wandered to Greer.

Though the mixture of grief and hard, hot sex puzzled her, it diverted her from the other frustrations in New Hope. Greer had obviously enjoyed herself. The memory released another flood of desire. Eva had recalled Greer's essence on her body this morning as she showered. She'd tucked her hand between her legs and relived Greer's forceful penetration and the strength with which she possessed her. When Eva's body had burst into orgasm with Greer's fingers still inside her, it was perfect. And as she recalled the moment now, heat poured from her again and dampened her clothing.

Greer's restrained whimper as she came had infused Eva with the need to hear that passion totally unleashed. Unless her radar was way off, Greer would agree to another round sometime. At least it had seemed that way until JJ showed up and acted like a complete moron. When he mentioned Clare, everything changed. Had Clare prompted that faraway look in Greer's eyes after sex? Maybe Eva would solve that mystery also today.

Even though Greer still wasn't firmly on her side, she'd practically hit JJ defending her honor. Surely that meant something. Eva's father would've been proud. She'd masterfully used all available resources, especially Greer Ellis and Tom Merritt, to accomplish her goal. She rubbed between her thighs one final time to calm the ache that seemed a constant companion and got out of the car.

"You're just in time." Tom walked up from behind and linked his arm through hers. His red hair was neatly combed and he smelled of too much cologne. "Shall we get to work?"

"Definitely." She played along, snuggling a bit closer than necessary.

Tom commandeered a small room that looked more like a hallway. The absence of windows made it a bit claustrophobic, and the old wooden walls still reeked of cigarette smoke, scorched coffee, and the mustiness of long-stored paper. File folders covered a round table in the center, where Tom motioned for her to sit.

"You want some coffee or something?"

"No, I'm already buzzing, but thanks."

He joined her at the table and pointed to the stacks of files. "I searched our databases back ten years. That's how long Fred Fluharty has supervised the homicide squad. None of the detectives in the unit has been there that long. Jake's got the most seniority with eight years. I didn't find much of interest. We don't have many high-profile cases. They're mostly open-and-shut drug killings."

Eva looked at the files on the table, confused. "Then what are these thirty or more folders?"

"Most of them pertain to one case, but I'll get to that in a minute. The small stuff first." He reached for the file closest to him. "Someone killed the son of the chancellor of our most prestigious college four years ago in a home invasion. Jake Johnston handled the investigation. It turned out the boy was dealing drugs and wanted a bigger cut, but his supplier took offense. Case closed. No problems with the investigation other than the parents' denial. Jake eventually found the boy's notebook where he'd logged every transaction over a two-year period. The parents quieted down after that."

"What's next?"

Tom threw that file on the floor and picked up several at once. He fanned through them as he called out their contents. "Three prostitutes knifed by pimps; four ex-lovers, various modes of death;

six drug shootouts over product; numerous suicides, mostly pills; and a few accidental overdoses."

Eva flinched at the last one. She'd read the *Tribune* article on Paul's death—a small blurb on the last page. The account was condensed to fit neatly in the Law Enforcement section. The caption read, OUT-OF-TOWN MAN FOUND DEAD. Her insides recoiled at the unspectacular announcement.

"Was anything unusual about these cases or how they were handled?" She needed to concentrate on work before her emotions took over.

"Nope." Tom paused and looked at her with sympathetic eyes, like he was unsure if he should proceed.

"What? Go on."

"I'm sorry about your brother. I meant to say that the other day, but I was a little surprised to see you in person. From what I could tell, his cause of death looked pretty definitive."

"Appearances can be deceiving, Tom. You should know better than to take anything at face value. People who didn't know Paul could easily categorize him as another accidental overdose and move on. I can assure you he didn't die that way. I don't have proof yet, but I won't stop until I do."

Tom straightened in his chair and returned his attention to the single file still in his hand. "And then we come to this one."

Eva's heartbeat increased as she sensed something important, finally. "Tell me."

"Not a homicide, but an ongoing drug investigation in this area for over three years. I wouldn't have pulled the file, but Greer and Derrick Bastille's names flagged it. He worked undercover with DEA for a while and she helped track down the main supplier. They eventually got enough information to secure a warrant on the guy, Johnny Young."

"What's significant besides Greer and Bastille?" Sometimes reporters were awful drama queens. Their livelihood depended on hooking readers quickly and keeping them interested.

"Wait for it." He grinned and his fair-skinned face turned a light shade of pink. "The investigation is ongoing because every time the police get close to the head man, he gets killed and another one takes his place. The last one was Mr. Young, two years ago, which leads us to this case." He placed his hand on the bulky file on the table. "It's the town's only double homicide."

"Double homicide. Who else died?" Tom kept his hand on top of the folder and his green eyes shone with the excitement of a big scoop. He was obviously thrilled with whatever he was about to say. "Tom?"

"A nurse named Clare Lansing."

Eva heard the gasp and initially thought it came from Tom. *"Oh, Deus."* She had to be Greer's Clare. The news hit her with an unwelcome wave of emotion, as if she'd known the woman personally. She bit back another gasp for air.

Tom looked disappointed. "I take it you've heard about Clare?"

Eva shook her head. "Only the name. I don't know anything about her death."

Tom's disappointment vanished and he once again looked like a man ready to spill the day's big story.

"You knew her, this Clare?" Eva asked.

"She came to town about twelve years ago to work at the hospital. She was a great trauma nurse and was pretty soon running the ER."

"How did she get involved in a shooting?"

"She went to the police station that afternoon. Johnny Young did too. No one's sure why, since the police had a warrant for his arrest. Sergeant Fluharty came out of the building as the two of them were walking up that long set of steps at the entrance. He recognized Young and pulled his weapon. But Young had already started firing. He shot Clare in the back before Fluharty killed him. She didn't have a chance. The bullet pierced her heart."

Eva grabbed her chest. She couldn't imagine something so horrible happening to someone she loved. No wonder Greer was distant and wore her loss like an extra layer of skin. "How long had she and Greer been together?"

"So you know about their relationship?"

"Greer mentioned her the other night, but no details. She obviously loved Clare very much." Everything Eva said was true. Maybe a bit misleading out of context, but she wanted more information.

"Their love was obvious to everyone and the whole town accepted it. I guess Bessie and Ruth cleared the way for that. They were open about who they were and very involved in the community. Bessie actually introduced Greer and Clare. They were inseparable from day one, dated a few months, and then Clare moved in. They were together for ten years."

Eva tried to imagine a love that strong, that unifying. "Greer must've been devastated when she died."

"You have no idea. She blamed herself, still does, I think."

"Why? She wasn't there when it happened."

"Exactly. But she was part of the team searching for Young. Every time they got close, he was a step ahead. Greer believes if she'd caught him, Clare would still be alive."

Eva's eyes stung with tears, and she blinked to hold them back. "What an awful burden."

"She was wild when she arrived at the police station and realized what had happened. The chief marshaled the entire force to secure the scene until they processed it. Greer still tried to break through the line. She fought to go to Clare until Chief Bryant finally knocked her out cold. She's got a scar over her left eye as a souvenir, as if seeing her lover dead on the steps wasn't reminder enough."

The truth about the scar disturbed Eva more than anything she'd imagined. No one should have to endure a mental image of her lover's dead body combined with a physical reminder of her own perceived failure to protect her. Eva ached for Greer. She couldn't fathom losing a lover to senseless violence. Losing her brother was proving difficult enough.

"People around here don't talk much about that day, but we'll never forget. After it happened, the whole town adopted Greer."

"That must've comforted her on some level."

"I'm not even sure she noticed. She withdrew completely, didn't even talk to Bessie for weeks. The only thing she did on a consistent basis was go to work, always through the back door, never up those front steps. Sergeant Fluharty and Jake carried her workload. She wasn't capable of much for a while."

Eva had a hard time picturing Greer Ellis the cop as anything but confident and cocky. But her eyes told the story of a soul tormented by deep loss—conflicting personas struggling for dominance. After two years she appeared to live a normal life, but her spirit was still burdened. How *did* one recover from such profound sadness?

Tom cleared his throat. "Well, that's all I have."

"Thank you for putting this together, Tom. Do you mind if I read through some of these files and take a few notes?"

"No problem. Take all the time you need. I'll be at my desk. Don't forget our deal. Anything else?"

Sometimes nothing worked as well as a direct inquiry. "You never questioned the homicide detectives' methods or their integrity?"

"Nope, and I look for crap like that in a small town. The only unusual thing is this three-year drug investigation, and that was a DEA case. And I know Jake was in Boston before he came here but that's it. As far as I can tell, everybody's on the up-and-up."

Eva felt disappointed and relieved. She wanted to believe somebody had overlooked something in Paul's case, but she also wanted to trust Greer and the institution to which she was so loyal. "Do you have a contact at the Boston PD?"

"Yep." He whipped a small notepad from his back pocket, wrote the number down, and handed it to her. "Let me know what you find out, for curiosity."

"Will do, and thanks again for everything."

When the door closed behind Tom, Eva wondered about small-town mentality. New Hope reminded her of Lagos, with its community atmosphere and cohesiveness. That type of neighborly concern had comforted her when she was a child, everybody helping each other. But could she live in such a place as an adult, where folks knew your business whether you wanted to share it or not? The townspeople certainly protected Greer. Maybe that wouldn't be a bad thing. Eva hadn't allowed anyone to look out for her in a long time. She thought about her sexual encounter with Greer and quickly dismissed the accompanying pang of guilt.

Maybe the end didn't always justify the means. Was she exploiting Greer's loss by using sex to secure her assistance? Eva cringed at the possibility. She could be ruthless in her work, but not intentionally cruel. Maybe she'd talk with Greer, to clear the air…and her conscience. If they agreed on a temporary liaison, they could both benefit.

But right now she had work to do. She dialed the Boston PD number, identified herself and her connection to Tom, and stated what she needed. The detective promised to get back to her as soon as possible. She read through the entire file on Clare Lansing and Johnny Young. How horrible for Clare's friends and family to have her name forever linked to a dealer of drugs, addiction, and death. The basic details of the incident were as Tom explained, and Eva found nothing else significant.

When she slid the large folder away, several hours had passed. She now understood more clearly Greer's loyalty to JJ and Sergeant Fluharty. JJ had helped Greer through the most difficult time of her life. How could she not be grateful and devoted to him? And Fluharty had killed Clare's murderer. Greer probably would've preferred to handle that task, but the next best thing was another cop. Instant justice satisfied on many levels: the killer dead; Greer not having to see him again; the criminal-justice system spared a lengthy trial, possible appeals, and housing him for life. Some smarmy lawyer, representing a client who was obviously guilty and had no other defense, wouldn't have a chance to attack the evidence or the police department. Eva had covered too many high-profile cases to be naïve about the criminal-justice system.

She stretched and had started to gather her belongings when her cell phone rang. The Boston detective hadn't taken long to get back to her, she thought as she answered. "Hello."

"I told you to leave town, Eva. This is your last warning."

CHAPTER EIGHT

"Eva? Are you all right?" Tom stood in the doorway of the conference room with a concerned look in his eyes.

Eva held the cell phone away from her body like it might attack her. "Yeah, sure."

"You're as white as new snow." Tom crossed to her and placed his hand on her shoulder. "What's happened?"

The call had stunned Eva and she was a little embarrassed that it bothered her. The caller's tone, which sent chills down her spine, worried her more than his words. "I got another threatening phone call."

"What do you mean another one?"

"Somebody told me to get out of town a few days ago. I thought he had the wrong number. This time he knew my name and was more specific."

"Jesus, who have you pissed off? I mean besides the entire police department and half the town. The suspect pool is pretty large." Tom joked to ease her tension, but only increased it.

"His voice was deep and penetrating, kind of creepy. But it didn't sound familiar."

"We need to call the police and check this out."

Eva stared at him. Did he realize how he'd contradicted himself? "And what if he *is* the police? Would a cop go this far to avoid a simple case review?"

"Anything's possible. At least let me drive you back to the motel. I'm not sure it's a good idea for you to be way out there by yourself. Hurley isn't the best area of the county."

"Tom, you're very kind, but I'll be fine. If somebody wants me out of town, they'll have to do better than a couple of threatening phone calls."

Eva grabbed her purse and walked toward the door with Tom close behind. "Promise you'll call if anything else strange happens."

"Promise." On the way back to Hurley, the Boston detective called with information on Jake Johnston. He'd left the Boston PD for no specific reason after handling a highly publicized case. His clearance record was impressive, his investigations top-notch, and his professional reputation beyond reproach. There had been speculation about an affair, but she didn't see JJ leaving anywhere because of that. Extramarital affairs seemed standard issue in police work. Maybe he'd out-fished his social watering holes or simply needed a change of pace. Policing stressed the body and the psyche, especially in large cities.

When Eva arrived at her motel room, Greer sat out front straddling her huge Harley with a sour look on her face. How could a woman look so edible without even smiling? Warmth coursed through Eva's body and she steadied her breathing.

"To what do I owe the pleasure, Detective?"

Greer swung her leg over the motorcycle seat and hooked her thumbs in the back pockets of her ragged jeans. Her black leather jacket gapped open, revealing a rib-hugging T-shirt and no bra. Eva licked her lips in anticipation, praying the visit was a social one.

As if reading her thoughts, Greer answered, "This is business."

Eva unlocked the door and stepped aside for Greer to enter. As she passed, Eva inhaled the fragrance of pine and damp night air that clung to Greer from her ride through the woodsy back roads between New Hope and Hurley. Outdoor smells had never struck Eva as particularly appealing, but adhering to this woman they were not only appealing but also compelling.

"I understand you've been getting threatening phone calls."

"Damn it, Tom," Eva mumbled under her breath. "It's nothing."

"It might be nothing if we weren't reopening your brother's

case. It might be nothing if you weren't asking questions all over town. And it might be nothing if you were just another citizen passing through. But none of those things are true, so it definitely feels like *something* to me."

Eva wasn't sure if the feeling that trickled down her spine was a result of the low, resonating rumble of Greer's voice, the fact that she actually seemed concerned for her, or irritation at Tom for involving Greer. "Tom shouldn't have told you. I'd prefer you spend your time on Paul's case."

"When did they start?" Greer wasn't giving up.

"The day I arrived. It came to my room. The guy said to get out of town. I thought it was a wrong number. Today he called me by name and said it was my last warning."

"So, he's known who you were since you got here. He had to ask for you by name when he rang the motel desk. I'll check with the manager. Maybe they keep a log or have a computer system that tracks incoming calls. What number did he call from tonight?"

Eva pulled out her phone and checked, hoping what she'd seen earlier had miraculously changed. "Blocked caller, private number."

"Was anything distinctive about the voice? Had you heard it before? Any background noises, anything?"

"The voice was deep and sort of intense. He didn't have an accent and I couldn't make out any background sounds. The call was short and took me by surprise. But you're making too much of this. If it goes beyond calls, I'll be concerned."

"Somebody is threatening you and we need to know why." Greer started toward the door but Eva placed a hand on her forearm. That single, light touch made Eva want more.

"Since this isn't exactly an emergency, could we talk a minute—about the other night?" Greer's blue eyes locked on hers and sparked with uncertainty. "I don't want any discomfort between us, since we have to work together." Not entirely true. She also wanted a replay. She'd been too needy the first time and hadn't properly explored Greer's abilities. Eva was hopeful to experience her full repertoire.

"I'm not uncomfortable." But Greer's subtle twirling of her wedding ring said otherwise.

"I wanted say thanks and assure you I have no expectations. I was in a bad place and being *close* helped." She swept her hand down Greer's chest, heard the sharp intake of breath, and paused at the waistband of Greer's jeans. "We both know when this review is over, I'm leaving."

"It shouldn't have happened the first time. I told the sergeant I'd keep it professional."

Eva momentarily struggled for words. "You talked to your sergeant about our—the fact that we—" She wasn't sure how she felt about that. To be taken seriously, she had to maintain her professionalism. But she wasn't interested in what the people of this small town thought. And she certainly had no rules against mixing business with pleasure. Eva nuzzled Greer's ear and licked her lobe, hoping Greer would accept her interest in a rematch sooner rather than later.

"I didn't exactly have a choice. JJ couldn't wait to spread the word, and I wouldn't lie. I'm lucky the sarge didn't yank me from the case. So why don't we just concentrate on work?"

Greer backed away and opened the door. "And stop snooping around in my personal life."

"I wondered when we'd get back to that. This is very personal to me. I need to know that the people entrusted with Paul's case are reliable. If that upsets you, so be it."

"Trust is a two-way street. If you want to know something about *me*, ask. Then I'll have the option of answering and your information will be dependable. But I'd prefer we stick to the case and leave my past out of it." Greer pulled the door closed as she said, "Lock this after me and don't open it unless you know who it is."

"Will I see you again tonight?" Eva heard the expectation in her voice and tried to recover. "I mean, you know, to fill me in on whatever you find."

"Probably not."

Eva locked the door behind Greer and fell across the bed. She wanted Greer so much the ache that pounded in her center was painful. What did she find so compelling about this blindly devoted Podunk cop, or did their cat-and-mouse game challenge her?

❖

As Greer walked to the motel office, an uncomfortable feeling crawled up her back. She had the sense of being watched. The area supported a plethora of peeping Toms and stalkers with its various nooks and alleyways. A hodgepodge of multi-use facilities surrounded the office that sat back off the main road. She darted between opened and closed establishments, pausing in the darkness to check her surroundings.

When she arrived at the office, she stood beside the double glass doors and looked in. A middle-aged attendant nodded behind the desk. The man started as a bell over the door announced her entrance.

"Help you?" The clerk stood and wiped a hand across his oily face.

She flashed her badge and ID. "The manager still around?"

"No such luck. He skips before dark. But I'll give it a shot. What'd you need?"

Greer looked over the tall desk and examined the phone system. Her hope vanished. "Any chance you keep a log or computer record of incoming calls to the rooms?"

"Snowball's chance. Haven't replaced our phone system yet, and we don't keep hard copies of anything except registration information."

"Any suspicious persons hanging around recently, say the last week?"

"Officer, half our clientele is suspicious, but we don't ask questions."

Greer was wasting her time and breath. "Got it. Thanks."

She stepped outside and started back by a different route. Greer didn't consider herself a skittish person, but the night sounds seemed too close and unfriendly as she made her way through the darkness. The sharp smell of urine reminded her that she wasn't on a main street. She tucked her right elbow, and the service weapon against her side comforted her. She surveyed the open patch of ground ahead and moved away from the building. Cold air trickled down her back like a draft. She froze.

The light breeze carried the stench of foul body odor. She sniffed the air for a directional clue, but too late. A twig snapped and she whirled just in time to see a large object coming toward her head. She ducked and heard what sounded like a rock hit the wall behind her. Greer looked at her assailant, nothing but dark arms, legs, face, and clothing. She considered her options. Without confirmation that he was armed she couldn't shoot him. She had to fight.

Greer swatted the shadows as the man anticipated her strikes and avoided them easily. The lack of contact threw her off balance. She dodged another round of blows but inadvertently backed into a building. He punched her, solid and powerful. A fist to the gut knocked the wind out of her. She doubled over gasping for breath. Then a boulder seemed to crash on top of her. Her attacker drove her into the ground with his locked hands. She hit the dirt, dazed but conscious, certain that at any moment he would finish her.

But the kill strike didn't come, only the sound of pounding footfalls. After a few seconds, she regained her senses enough to stand. The area was completely deserted. Her stomach and head ached, and a scratch on her cheek burned. What the hell was that all about? If it was meant as a message, it was vague. If it was a robbery, they forgot to take anything. The only scenario that made sense was a thrill-seeker mugging, but this guy seemed too skilled and quick to be a druggie or street thug. She walked slowly back to her bike.

Greer considered reporting the attack but decided against it. The guys would laugh at her inability to defend herself, then be pissed about another unsolvable assault. Greer's instincts about the incident, like so many other things lately, led back to the Saldana case.

The guys were upset. Someone was threatening Eva and had attacked her. Maybe it had nothing to do with the case, but she didn't believe in coincidences. Perhaps Eva was right and someone had killed her brother. That would account for the murderer trying to scare them off the case. But they'd messed with the wrong detective. If anything, she was more determined to find out what was going on.

She straddled Icarus and stared at Eva Saldana's motel-room door. The thought of leaving Eva alone after what happened didn't sit well. And if her attacker was in any way involved with Paul's death, Eva could also be in danger. She brushed at the stinging scrape on her cheek, dismounted, and tapped on Eva's door again.

"Yes, who is it?" Eva asked from the other side. At least she was being cautious.

"Greer." The door opened and Eva's gaze swept over her before settling on her injured cheek.

"What happened to you?"

"Never mind that. Pack a bag and come with me. You're going to my house for the night. It's not safe here."

Eva pulled her inside. "What do you mean, not safe?"

"Somebody jumped me over by the office. I don't know if it's connected to this case or you, but I don't want to take any unnecessary chances."

"I'm not going."

Greer shook her head. "Could you not argue with me? You might be in danger here. I don't want that on my conscience."

"I don't feel threatened and I'm not about to run from shadows. If somebody wants to get at me, they'll have to come straight on." Eva edged closer to Greer and her tone softened. "But you could stay here if you feel that strongly about it."

Maybe Eva was in danger, but if she didn't take the threats seriously, Greer couldn't force her to take precautions. Greer was tempted to stay and wasn't sure if her motivation was concern for Eva's safety or her own selfish desires. She looked at her wedding ring. Sometimes even satisfying an itch felt like she was betraying Clare's love. "I'd better go, but I'll call the Hurley police and have them check by during the night. If you hear anything, call them and then me."

"Whatever you say, Detective." Eva's tone held more than a hint of disappointment.

Greer closed the door without looking back, cranked her bike, and sped back to New Hope. But her day wasn't over. She had snitches from her narcotics days that survived on a few dollars for information. And news of overdoses spread quickly through the junkie population. Maybe someone had heard something and was willing to talk four months after the fact.

Greer cruised the drug-infested warehouse district and looked for her most trustworthy informant, Bo. She thought it unusual that a detective had to "prove an informant reliable" before he could use him. How reliable could a junkie or thief be, especially when he was being paid? But this one had proved himself in the past.

She spotted Bo dressed in his long army green trench coat, camouflage pants, and toboggan and pulled up beside him. "What's new, Bo?"

"I knew it was you. Ain't nobody else got a damn bike that freaking loud. Put some mufflers on that sucker. It gives me a headache."

Bo was a dark-skinned African American, maybe forty but looked sixty. He'd been on drugs most of his adult life, and his wrinkled face and bony frame showed it. "You heard anything about a hotel suicide or overdose about four months ago, out-of-town guy?"

Bo stopped walking and Greer killed the ignition. "A little late with the investigating, ain't you, Detective?"

"Give me a break, Bo. Have you heard anything or not?"

He pulled the stocking cap off and scratched his bald head. "Nope, and that's a shame too, 'cause I could use some cash. Times is hard on the street right now."

"I'm open for anything else you got." Greer wanted to help the man even though any money she gave him would probably go into drugs or alcohol.

Bo stepped a little closer and lowered his voice. "I don't like stuff like this, but I heard we got a bad cop. He rips dealers off and takes their drugs to resell. That's why you keep chasing your tails."

After twelve years on the force Greer couldn't recall a time when that rumor wasn't rampant. "Yeah, well, I need more than that if you want to get paid."

"Word is the new drug boss, Baron Wallace, is nobody to play with. He's psycho, but you don't pay for rumors." He pulled his cap back down and walked off. "When I have something, you'll be the first to know."

Greer rolled Icarus along side Bo. "Here." She dug into her jeans pocket and pulled out two twenties. "Get yourself a room and a hot meal." At least maybe he'd have one night's sleep in a room instead of a cardboard box under the overpass. If Bo got anything more concrete, she'd pass it along to DEA. For now, she filed it for future reference.

As she cruised along the backstreets the local street urchins slid into the shadows, taking any chance of further intel with them, so she went home.

❖

Greer rubbed the small goose egg on the back of her head and her headache worsened. She took a couple of aspirins, threw herself on the bed, and pulled Clare's throw across her while she finished reading the autopsy report on Paul Saldana.

The medical examiner noted no external injuries to Paul's body, no obvious signs of forced drug usage, and no defensive wounds. Either Paul took the drugs willingly or someone forced him with a weapon. The lack of damage to internal organs supported the theory that he wasn't a consistent or extensive drug user. But the coroner couldn't determine if this had been his first time using, only his last. Greer needed more than an inconclusive autopsy report and a threatening phone call.

Next, she turned her attention to the witnesses JJ had interviewed, if they could even be called true witnesses. The hotel manager stated he'd checked Paul in earlier the same day and had no other contact with him. A housekeeper found the body the next morning and notified her boss, who called the police. Occupants of the rooms around Paul's had been out for the evening and offered nothing of substance. Greer flipped through the file for the hotel register of occupants to make sure the investigators had contacted everyone.

But she didn't find a guest register. JJ wouldn't make a mistake like that. He would have obtained a register of possible witnesses or contacts immediately. She double-checked but still didn't find a guest list. Maybe some of the paperwork had fallen out of the file accidentally. Greer checked the time. She dreaded going back out, but she wanted answers. No one would be in the office at this hour, and she could check without the guys giving her grief.

In fifteen minutes she walked into the darkened homicide office and left the lights off until she reached the sergeant's office. When she closed the door behind her, she flipped the switch and moved toward the cabinet where Sergeant Fluharty kept the closed cases. The space where Paul's folder should be was empty. She looked in front and behind to make sure nothing had been misfiled and even checked the gap between the cabinets. If she believed in coincidences, they were beginning to pile up. Greer was disappointed that JJ had probably missed something. She turned off the light and stepped outside Fluharty's office.

As she started toward the exit, somebody grabbed her from behind and stuck a gun in her ribs. "Freeze."

Chapter Nine

M ove and I'll blow your fucking brains out." Her captor shuffled them toward the office door and flipped on the light. "Greer?" He pushed her away.

"Breeze, what the hell are you doing pulling a gun on me, man?"

"Why are *you* sneaking around in the dark like a burglar?"

"I wasn't sneaking."

"Could've fooled me. What were you doing in the sergeant's office?"

Anybody in Breeze's place would think the same thing. She understood his position and decided on the truth. "The guest register from the hotel is missing from the Saldana file. I didn't want to upset JJ by asking him about it. I thought it might've fallen out so I came to look."

"In the middle of the night?"

"Less questions and snippy comments from the rest of you. Breeze, I didn't ask for the job. I want to prove JJ right as much as anything."

Breeze propped against the door jamb, his gaze never leaving her. "I believe that, but it feels too Internal Affairs–ish. We expect them, but not one of our own, to second-guess us."

Dressed in black jeans and pullover, Breeze looked like a special-ops soldier. A fanatic about anything sports related, he prided himself on his body and physical abilities. Then she noticed an abrasion on his knuckles. "What happened to your hand?"

He laughed. "A little roughhousing with the kids earlier got too rough. They're getting big enough to whup my ass." He shoved his hands in his pockets. "Sorry about the gun. You and JJ need to talk about this shit before it gets entirely out of control. You're friends."

"I know." As Breeze opened the door to leave Greer said, "Could I ask you something?"

"Sure."

"When you worked on the drug task force with DEA, did you hear anything about a dirty cop working with Johnny Young's outfit?"

"A few rumors, but we didn't find anything substantial. Why?"

"Something an informant said tonight. By the way, what are you doing here so late?"

"Killing time. Couldn't sleep and thought I'd check the court docket for tomorrow. They hadn't put it out when I left earlier."

"Yeah, they're pretty slow with that. See you later." When Breeze left, Greer turned her attention back to the case. Something wasn't right and she was missing it. Even though it was late, she decided to take another ride out to Hurley. If Eva wasn't asleep, she'd let her in on the investigation. Perhaps another set of eyes would help.

Greer's ride back to the motel went even faster than the one two hours earlier. Was she kidding herself that this was about the case? Normally an outing this time of night featured a quick romp with the evening waitress at the diner. Maybe she needed an excuse to see Eva without feeling guilty. As she pulled to a stop in front of the room, she'd convinced herself this was only about work.

The light was still on in Eva's room, so Greer unstrapped the small leather case from the seat and tapped lightly on the door.

Eva answered immediately. She swung the door open and stepped aside. "Please come in."

"I told you not to open the door unless you knew who it was." Greer tried to sound stern and businesslike, but when she saw Eva, she softened her tone. She was stunning in a nightgown that clung to her breasts, dove into ample cleavage, and stopped just above her knees. Eva's olive-skinned body was silhouetted through the sheer garment, highlighting every curve and dip. She looked like a confectionery delight, sweet and addictive. But like those delicacies, Eva's substance would soon vanish and she'd be left with only essence. To calm her butterflies and uncertainty, Greer reminded herself of her purpose.

"I don't know anyone else who drives a machine that sounds like a jet and would be knocking on my door this late."

Greer suddenly felt self-conscious and unsure of herself. "Yeah, I guess I shouldn't be here. It is late."

Eva looped her arm through Greer's and led her to the edge of the bed. "Please don't start with the *shoulds* again. I thought we were past that. You're welcome here anytime for *any* reason, but I assume this is work since you have file in hand."

She smiled and Greer lost focus as lovely dimples formed on her cheeks. The deep crimson of her lips churned up desire, and Greer's throat parched. For the first time since Clare died, Greer wanted to kiss someone but knew she wouldn't. It was too soon and to her a kiss wasn't just a kiss. It was an invitation—one she wasn't ready to extend.

"Would you like to sit or shall we talk standing?"

Eva's question broke the wayward drift of her thoughts and she settled on the edge of the bed. Eva plopped beside her in a meditation pose, flimsy fabric barely covering the dark patch of hair between her legs. Greer forced herself to concentrate on the folder she held.

"Would you look at the scene photos—not the pictures of Paul, just the setting? If it won't disturb you too much."

Eva's smile vanished and the cute dimples disappeared. "Okay. What am I looking for?"

"You know your brother and his habits. See if anything looks out of place or unusual. It might not seem significant to me." She handed the pictures to Eva and hoped this wasn't a mistake. It was difficult to predict relatives' reactions to such things, and she didn't want to cause Eva any more pain.

Eva held the photos and took a deep breath, as if steeling herself for the task. "Thank you for trusting me with this. I know it wasn't easy." She slowly flipped through the pictures, examining them carefully, saying nothing. Greer watched the array of emotions flash across her face as she viewed each photo. When she'd made her way through once, she repeated the process and eliminated all but three. "Here." She handed them to Greer. "This isn't right."

Greer looked at the photos. "I don't see anything unusual."

"His shoes and socks are scattered around the room."

"And?"

"Remember I told you that Vincent, Lucio, and I tormented Paul with worms and bugs?"

"Yeah."

"He was afraid of creepy things and didn't take off his shoes until he got into bed—I mean *immediately* before bed. And his shoes were *always* right beside the bed with the socks tucked neatly inside in case he had to get up. He started the habit as a child and it carried over to adulthood. We teased him about it when we went on family vacations." She pointed to the strewn shoes and socks. "Either someone took them off or he was under tremendous pressure."

Only someone familiar with Paul's routine would notice something so seemingly trivial. Had he been too strung out to follow his normal rituals, or did someone force him to inhale the cocaine? Was this Paul Saldana's last message? Anything was possible. Why would anyone want him dead? He was a stranger in town. Had someone followed him here to kill him? Or had he stumbled into something dangerous in New Hope? If someone had killed him, what was the motive?

"Anything else?"

"He kept his camera with him all the time, but it's not in the photos and it wasn't in his personal effects. Do you believe me now that he didn't overdose?" Eva stared at Greer with eyes full of hope.

Greer reviewed only the undisputed facts: cocaine beyond street-level purity, a victim with no history of drug use, Eva's threatening phone calls, and her own assault. The shoes seemed a small thing but, based on Paul's history, at least noteworthy. And now a missing camera. Maybe Paul's death *was* more than an overdose. She didn't want to give Eva false hope, but she wanted to be fair. "I've always been willing to *consider* it."

Eva's smile returned and her face seemed to glow. She moved the pictures from between them on the bed and scooted closer. Tears formed in the corners of her eyes as she took Greer's hands in hers. "Thank you, Greer."

Her name rolled off Eva's lips with a combination of gratitude and promise. The gentle *r*'s of her accent sent a thrill through Greer's system. "Please don't get your hopes up. I can only go where the evidence leads, and we don't have much right now."

"I understand. I'm so happy you're willing to look deeper." Eva wiped at her tears and, without thinking, Greer placed her hand on Eva's shoulder to comfort her.

"It'll be all right," Greer said as Eva rested against her. Her body was hot and soft. The hunger that gnawed in Greer earlier returned, ravenous. Her arms tightened into the soft curves of flesh covered by only a thin layer of fabric. She buried her face in the chestnut waves of Eva's hair and inhaled the fresh scent of orange and ginger.

"I know this isn't fair." Eva's tone was apologetic, her words soft and pleading. "But I need you."

The desire in Eva's voice persuaded Greer. She momentarily thought about her conversation with Sergeant Fluharty, then dismissed it. Her resistance slipped. She stretched out on the bed and pulled Eva with her.

"Thank you." Eva pressed her body against Greer, surged against her breasts and pelvis, and whispered in her ear. "I want you so much. Make me feel alive."

The cravings Eva elicited were too strong. Greer shucked off her T-shirt, then peeled her jeans and boots off. "Get undressed."

Eva sat up, grabbed the hem of her nightgown, and teased it slowly up her body. Greer savored each inch of olive skin. Eva's legs were firm and taut, though not muscled like her own. Her skin was smooth, like a silky coat of caramel. When Greer saw the glistening hair at the apex of Eva's thighs, her abdomen tightened. She stared as Eva inched the negligee higher.

Eva paused before pulling the gown over her breasts and Greer breathed, "Yes." The fabric clung beneath Eva's firm breasts, and when she tugged, it came loose and they bounced free. Greer stared in appreciation at the treasures she'd only been able to touch the first time. "God, you're beautiful."

Eva cupped Greer's face and brought their lips closer together. Greer could feel the proximity of her mouth and nearly succumbed. "No kissing. I remember," Eva said, and lightly blew her breath across Greer's lips.

Greer opened her mouth as though receiving a probing tongue, and the peppermint-scented air burned a path down her throat. She licked her lips, wanting more but forcing herself away from Eva's seductive mouth.

Eva pulled Greer down on top of her and buried her face in Greer's neck. "It's sex, nothing personal."

Greer wondered if Eva knew how bizarre that statement sounded. If sex was nothing else, it was personal, the most personal thing you could do with another human being. But personal didn't necessarily equate with intimate. Maybe that was the distinction she was missing. Sex for her recently had lacked intimacy, but she wasn't capable of any other kind.

She shifted down Eva's body enough to capture her breasts and bury her face between them. Desire swelled inside as she savored the soft fullness. She licked a dark nipple and watched it pucker as Eva shivered beneath her. Greer sucked and kneaded the tender flesh in her mouth and hands until her thighs were slick with arousal.

Fire raged where their skin touched as Eva wrapped her legs around Greer's thighs and ground against her pelvis. The contact was urgent and purposeful. Greer felt Eva's need building, her thrusts already a steady rhythm. Then, with their legs still entwined, Eva rolled them over and topped Greer.

"I want to make you come," Eva said as she stared into Greer's eyes. "Will you let me?"

"You can do whatever you like except—"

"Kiss you." Eva lowered her body on top of Greer and shifted until their breasts and crotches were in maximum contact. She slid up and down, back and forth, her full breasts coming within inches of Greer's mouth. Each time Greer tried to capture one, Eva purposely moved. Greer wanted more direct stimulation but Eva seemed determined to tease her. Greer reached to caress Eva's body, but Eva pinned her arms to the bed. The pressure increased.

"Why are you tormenting me?"

Eva's chuckle was seductive as she licked the edge of Greer's ear and dipped her tongue inside. "I want to make sure you're ready for me to touch you."

Greer rocked her pelvis against Eva's with the rhythmic probing in her ear. "I'm ready."

"Do you like penetration?"

Greer wasn't used to women who asked questions or gave instructions about sex during sex. And she certainly wasn't used to answering such questions. That Eva wanted to know what pleased her was a turn-on she hadn't anticipated. She usually did the pleasuring and was in control. She decided to be honest. "At the end. I like a lot of clit play."

Eva tucked her hand between their bodies and lightly rubbed Greer's engorged flesh. Greer's hips jerked and eagerly met each stroke. "Like this?"

"Oh, yeah, harder."

Eva increased the pressure, and the delicious tightening started in Greer's lower abdomen. Eva cupped a breast in one hand while continuing her cadence with the other. The regular rub-and-release pattern above and below met like a fireball in Greer's center. Her mouth dried and she suddenly craved a wet, probing kiss.

Greer grabbed the sheets on either side as Eva licked a path from her breasts to the top of her pubic mound. Her timing was exceptional as she shifted from finger strokes to tongue licks without missing a beat. When Eva's moist tongue made contact with her clit, Greer arched her hips off the bed. "Oh, yeah, more."

"You like that?" Eva asked.

"Yes," Greer answered as she threaded her fingers in Eva's hair and held her in place. "Faster."

Eva increased her tempo and the tingling release began in Greer. "Yeah, that's it." Her hips responded to every lick of Eva's tongue as the pressure crested. Eva shifted onto Greer's leg and rode the flexed muscle with each stroke. Eva's guttural moan shot through Greer like an accelerant and she exploded. "Yes, yes…" Her orgasm tore loose and ravaged her body like a marathon workout. She hugged Eva and held on as Eva's cries of pleasure mingled with her own until they were indistinguishable.

Greer collapsed into a satisfied stupor as her breathing returned to normal. She enjoyed Eva's embrace after being so completely satisfied. Unlike recent encounters, she didn't feel like the sexual repairwoman who'd done her duty and was now expected to leave. The woman in her arms stirred. "God, that was fantastic. You're amazing."

Eva nestled against her side, a hand resting between Greer's breasts. "Thank you. You're the only enjoyable thing about this trip—sexual relief from all the stress. I'll miss you."

With one statement Eva put Greer back in her place—a temporary balm to an itch. But what had she expected? Eva's stay in New Hope was temporary and their connection couldn't be anything else. The momentary feeling of disappointment surprised her. Obviously a great orgasm clouded her mind. Greer didn't want anything permanent either. Clare was her true love. She was certain she'd never love like that again.

Greer gave Eva a perfunctory hug and rolled away from her. "Guess I should be going." She turned her back and quickly dressed. When she looked at Eva again she was sitting in the middle of the bed still nude. God, she was splendid, even with her wavy hair going in every direction. Eva's skin had that fresh-fucked glow and her lips were plump from sucking her clit. Desire pounded anew in Greer's sex and she had to leave.

"Sure you can't stay? I know you're good for more than one." Before Greer could answer, Eva's cell phone rang. She motioned for Greer to wait while she answered. "This is Eva Saldana."

While Eva listened to the caller, her expression changed from playful to serious. "Yes, I'm interested. I understand. Of course I'll meet you. That's fine. Good-bye." She dropped the cell and stood next to Greer.

"Anything I need to know?" Greer asked.

"Some guy says he has information about Paul's death and wants to meet me. He won't go to the police because he doesn't trust them. I agreed to meet him at the warehouse on Lewis Street tomorrow."

"It doesn't feel right. It's too convenient. Did the voice sound familiar? Was it the guy who threatened you? Was it another blocked caller?"

"It wasn't the same guy, but it sounded like he was purposely disguising his voice. And, yes, the number was blocked."

"Even more reason not to do this, Eva. Let us handle it."

"He'll expect me. I can't risk scaring him off if he could be helpful."

"Then I'm going with you."

"What part of 'no police' don't you understand, Greer? I can't risk it."

"Well, at least let us cover you. And take someone else with you, anybody."

"No police, obvious or otherwise. This is too important. I'll ask Tom Merritt to come along. He's keen for a story."

"Does everything with you have to be a challenge? Why can't you accept that I know how to do my job?"

"Because you seem wed to some set of rules and restrictions that I don't find necessary or helpful. I like to look for other options. Sorry if that doesn't work for you, Detective."

Greer considered Eva's scenario: two reporters meeting an unknown subject, possibly dangerous, in an abandoned warehouse with no obvious police presence. This wasn't a promising setup. She'd talk with Sergeant Fluharty about providing discreet cover. "I guess Tom would be okay. What time did he say?"

"Two o'clock tomorrow afternoon."

That would be long enough to arrange protection and get in place before the meeting. "Okay. Call me the minute it's over. I mean the *exact* minute. If I'm sidelined, at least let me know what you find out. I'll be waiting to hear from you."

Eva walked her to the door. "Of course, I'll call you…and thank you for letting me do this." She gave Greer a warm hug. "Be careful driving home."

❖

When Greer turned in the driveway of the main house, the kitchen light was still on. Bessie was definitely waiting up. She didn't want to chat but couldn't risk that something might be wrong. After parking her bike in the garage, she walked to the house and knocked to announce herself.

"Well, this is new." Bessie gave her an appraising stare and sat down at the kitchen counter with her coffee.

"What?"

"Your trysts don't usually take this long on school nights. Anybody I know…like maybe that gorgeous Portuguese reporter?"

Greer turned quickly away from Bessie to hide any facial tells. But her aunt would've made a great cop. She didn't miss anything.

"It *was* her. Great."

"Bessie, I said no such thing. Don't jump to conclusions."

"Darling, you don't have to say anything. I've got eyes."

"Don't start planning the wedding. She'll move to her next assignment when this investigation is over." Stating the obvious out loud for the first time seemed surreal. Though she'd told herself the same thing many times, the words sounded both wistful and final.

"You're right. A fling is all it can ever be."

Of all the things her aunt could've said, that was the last Greer expected. From her not-too-subtle nudging in Eva's direction, Greer thought Bessie liked Eva and hoped something might develop between them. Had her matchmaking gene taken a nap? "What did you say?"

"I said enjoy it while it lasts."

"Am I missing something here? I thought you liked Eva."

"She's wonderful and probably perfect for you, but you can't care about her."

Now Bessie had her complete attention. "That's right." But were they on the same page? "Why do you say that?"

"Because she's a wanderer. She's never in one place long, either because of her job or by choice. That's an unforgivable sin to you. You see anyone who can't stay put as flawed."

Greer started to object but considered Bessie's statement. Was that possible? Loyalty was important to her, and while permanence of place contributed to that sense of dedication, it wasn't mandatory. She thought about her parents and Clare. They'd all left her, not by their own choice, but her feelings of loss couldn't differentiate. Could she truly care about someone who intentionally chose to leave again and again, someone who favored an itinerant lifestyle to a stable home? How could she speculate about some hypothetical emotional nuance? But she couldn't dispute Bessie's assessment either, which bothered her. "Maybe you're right."

"And maybe it's time to look at your priorities. Staying in one place has nothing to do with loyalty." Bessie stood and gave her a hug. "I can go to sleep a happy woman now. I've had my say. Good night, honey."

❖

Eva listened at the door until the reverberations of Greer's motorcycle faded. The farther away the sound, the more alone she felt. Lying in Greer's arms earlier had comforted her and she'd been reluctant to let go. At the same time, she hadn't relaxed enough to relinquish control during sex. That was more power than she'd ever given anyone. Her remark about leaving reminded her of her boundaries. The moment she'd said it, the distance between her and Greer grew like a living entity. But honesty was best in her affairs. She couldn't justify hurting anyone the way her father had repeatedly hurt her. She wouldn't offer hope that things could be different then leave anyway. Her lovers had to know that their liaisons were short-lived.

But sex with Greer had been different this time. Though Eva controlled their interaction on both occasions, tonight Greer was more engaged, more present. She hadn't seen the distance in Greer's eyes that had been so apparent before. They'd reached mutually agreeable work-and-play limits. Greer was an active and fully informed participant. If any using was going on, it was reciprocated. Eva released the guilt that nibbled at the edge of her consciousness. She considered taking a shower but decided she'd prefer to smell Greer's scent on her body as she snuggled beneath the covers.

Pulling the blanket around her, she concentrated on tomorrow's meeting. Who was this man who claimed to have information about Paul's death? And would his news support her belief that her brother had been murdered? The meeting could be a setup, as Greer suggested, a ruse to kill her as well, but if someone meant her harm, he wouldn't have to work so hard. She wasn't difficult to find and she was usually alone. She remembered her promise to have Tom accompany her and reached for the phone.

Eva sent him a quick text and his enthusiastic reply boosted her confidence. They arranged to meet at his office and walk to the warehouse together.

As she drifted into a restless sleep, she thought how nice to finally have Greer on her side. Paul's investigation would now benefit from the duty and deep loyalty Greer wore like a garment.

She wished Greer could be at the meeting tomorrow for backup. But she'd insisted on handling it alone. *Idiot*, she thought. *Stubborn, arrogant idiot.*

CHAPTER TEN

G reer was sitting in Sergeant Fluharty's office when he came in the next morning.

"Let me fix my coffee first. It can't be good if you're here early." He took the lid off his cup and scooped in four large spoonfuls of sugar, tasted, added more sugar, and settled at his desk. "Let's hear it."

"You look like hell, Sarge. You okay?"

"Says the woman with road rash on her face. Thanks for the commentary, but I'm fine. So, what's up?"

"Eva, Ms. Saldana, is meeting an informant about her brother's case at two this afternoon. We need to cover her."

"Where did this mysterious informant come from?"

"I have no idea, Sarge. He called her directly, refusing to go through the department. Said he didn't trust us."

"When did he contact her?"

"Late last night."

"And you know this how?"

Greer hesitated. Total honesty wouldn't help her cause or her credibility at this point. "She told me about it." That wasn't completely true but wasn't an outright lie.

"Jesus, it sounds like an epidemic. Who the hell doesn't trust the police? Don't answer that." Fluharty took another sip of coffee. "Did *Eva* ask for our help or is this your idea?"

"She's too proud to ask for anything now. She wants to handle it herself. But this may be a setup. Somebody jumped me last night after I left the motel office, and Eva's gotten two threatening phone calls."

"He did that?" He pointed to her cheek and she nodded. "Did you report the assault?"

"Nah, nothing to report. I didn't get a good look at him, and what cop wants to admit they got ambushed? It would end up another unsolved case in our unit that adds to the crime stats. I'm not even sure it's connected to what I'm working on."

"Still, you better be more careful. Anything new on the case?"

"That's why this doesn't feel right. We're getting nowhere and this guy comes out of the blue with information. It sounds like an intentional attempt to lead us in another direction."

"I'm not sure this makes sense, Greer. But if you feel strongly about it, we'll cover her. I'll tell the rest of the squad at lineup in a few minutes."

Greer's initial enthusiasm plummeted. How receptive would the guys be? She walked through the squad room trying to make eye contact with each detective as she passed. Breeze gave her a quizzical look. Craig spoke in his usual monotone from behind his computer screen. JJ grunted but didn't look up as she stopped in front of his desk. This wouldn't be easy.

"Can we talk?"

JJ propped his size-thirteen boots on the desk. "Sure. Go ahead."

Greer nodded toward the interrogation area at the back of the office, hoping for a more private chat. She didn't want to discuss the case, his bratty behavior, the intrusion into Eva's motel room, and his ratting her out to the sergeant in front of the other detectives.

"It's time for lineup. Say whatever you have to say."

She sat on the side of his desk with her back to Craig and Breeze and lowered her voice. "Why are you so upset with me for doing my job? You taught me everything I know about being a detective, and you've never turned down an assignment."

"You wouldn't understand."

"Try me, JJ. We're friends. At least I thought we were." The words were harder to say than she'd anticipated. JJ's expression softened with a flicker of emotion and his boyish grin reappeared. This was the face of her friend and mentor. Maybe she was finally getting through.

"It's just that when I—"

"So you've told him about last night?" Breeze asked from behind her.

Greer stiffened as a chill returned to the air around them.

JJ's eyes filled with suspicion and his expression hardened again. "What about last night?"

Breeze looked from one to the other and shrugged. "My bad. Thought you'd already had *that* conversation." He sauntered back to his desk like he didn't have a care in the world.

"Something you need to tell me, Greer?" JJ nailed her with his bad-cop stare.

"I thought something was missing from the Saldana file, so I went in the sergeant's office after hours last night to look for it. Breeze came in and got the wrong idea."

JJ rolled his chair directly in front of her. "What the hell do you mean, something was missing?"

"Okay, guys, huddle up." Fluharty called the group to order before Greer could answer. JJ was fuming. She added this to the growing list of things unresolved between them. The more time that passed without resolution, the more distanced they'd become.

Fluharty addressed the squad in his usual matter-of-fact tone. "Greer needs our help this afternoon. Ms. Saldana is meeting an informant about her brother's case. The guy refuses to contact us directly, so she's securing the info."

Breeze and Craig started mumbling to each other. JJ was surprisingly quiet.

"The meet is at the warehouse at 247 Lewis Street and I want everybody available. I'll have an op plan worked up by thirteen hundred hours. Be back here by then for assignments."

"Bullshit." JJ stared directly at Greer.

"Don't start, Jake," Fluharty warned him.

That was absolutely the wrong approach. Greer cringed as JJ stood and addressed the group. "*Bullshit.* Just because Greer's tapping that reporter's ass doesn't mean we should drop everything to help her." The room went deathly quiet as this new information registered. Everyone turned their attention toward her.

Breeze started. "You're screwing Saldana? Jesus, she's hot."

Craig whistled. "Damn, girl, you're fast." It was the first

time Greer had heard the young computer guru say anything even remotely suggestive.

JJ was not deterred. "What's the matter, Greer, need help proving I'm a lousy detective? And after the stunt she pulled last night, you're still backing her, Sarge?" Greer wondered if JJ hated her. His recent behavior certainly wasn't that of a friend. It had to go deeper than this case.

Now JJ had Fluharty's attention. "What stunt?"

"Tell him, Breeze." JJ obviously wanted everybody involved in her humiliation.

"Somebody better damn well tell me, and now," Fluharty bellowed.

Greer decided it would sound better coming from her. "I was in your office last night looking for a document from the Saldana file. Breeze came in, thought I was a burglar, and nearly shot my ass."

Breeze defended himself. "Well, you *were* sneaking around in the dark."

"Did you find it?" Fluharty asked. "I gave you everything in the file."

"No, I didn't find anything else."

"That's beside the damn point," JJ said. "I don't think we should let a reporter do our job for us. If this informant has anything to contribute to the case, we should get it directly from him, not through a third party. How reliable is that?"

Sergeant Fluharty motioned for everybody to calm down. "Look, the guy isn't comfortable with us. He'll talk to her. If he provides something new, we'll do what we usually do—verify. I want this thing settled ASAP. I'm tired as hell of all this bickering on the squad. We're covering her meeting today and that's that. Be back here at thirteen hundred for assignments—and bring a better attitude—all of you. And, Greer, my office before you leave."

Greer swore under her breath on the way to the sergeant's office. She wanted to catch JJ before he slid out and resolve their inventory of differences. This impasse couldn't continue. Sooner or later he'd have to face her and all the questions piling up between them. She tried to call his cell but he didn't pick up.

Fluharty didn't offer her a seat. "What were you looking for in my office last night?"

"I thought there should be a guest register from the hotel, but I guess JJ didn't get one. I couldn't find it."

"Ask next time. It looks damn suspicious having you poking around my office after hours. Ever think of asking JJ directly?"

"He isn't exactly open to chatting with me about this case or anything else right now."

"Straighten this shit out. It's getting on my nerves." He waved her toward the door.

Greer gathered her briefcase and walked to the parking lot. She spent the morning conducting follow-up interviews and making courtesy calls on victims who were still hospitalized. Even though she wasn't getting any new cases at the moment, she still had a pending caseload. The routine tasks occupied her mind and kept her from doing the one thing she deeply wanted to do—call Eva. After a quick sandwich at the diner and another attempt to contact JJ, Greer finally dialed Eva's cell number.

"Eva Saldana."

"It's Greer. Have you come to your senses yet and decided to let the police handle this?"

"Well, hello to you too, Detective. I'm meeting the informant, but Tom's coming along, so relax. It'll be fine. Besides, I promised to call you afterward."

But Greer detected a note of uncertainty in Eva's tone. She wasn't quite as confident as she'd been the night before. Greer's guilt about going behind her back to provide cover disappeared. If anything happened to Eva, she wouldn't be able to forgive herself— from a purely professional standpoint. And the political fallout would be disastrous. She envisioned the headline: CNN REPORTER INJURED WHILE INVESTIGATING BROTHER'S DEATH. The thought made Greer's stomach churn.

"Greer, is there anything else?" Eva asked.

"No, just making sure you hadn't changed your mind. Please be careful."

"I will."

"Okay, then, good-bye."

"Greer, thank you for last night. It was…" Eva seemed to be trying to choose the right word. In the silence Greer imagined the slightest hint of affection and the need to express exactly the right sentiment. "Nice."

Nice? Nice was the kiss of death. Nice was what you said to someone you didn't want to encourage. Nice was just shy of boring. Her disappointment surprised her. "Yeah, right. Talk later." She hung up and headed back toward the office for the briefing.

An hour later the squad was strategically positioned inside the warehouse on Lewis Street waiting for the meeting between Eva and the informant. Dark clouds intermittently shaded the afternoon sun and made the ramshackle building seem even more ominous. Sergeant Fluharty covered the back exit, JJ was a quarter way around the interior behind some boxes, and Craig was diagonally across from JJ under a loading platform. They could've used Breeze, but he'd been called into court at the last minute.

The warehouse was a large area for only four officers to cover, but they'd make the most of it. Greer was stationed across from the sergeant, lying in a shallow vehicle service bay. The musty smell of the warehouse mingled with the faint remnants of oil and lubricant that discolored the concrete surrounding her. Everybody was in place and well hidden when Eva and Tom arrived at exactly 1400 hours.

They moved toward the center of the space and Greer heard the low hum of their chatter. The sun penetrated the clouds and blackened windows barely enough to distinguish color and features. Even in this dusty, unkempt setting Eva looked gorgeous. Her casual clothes were immaculately tailored, and the bright shades complemented her olive complexion. An emerald green turtleneck and a multicolored blazer topped a pair of rust corduroy slacks. She seriously outclassed the dilapidated surroundings and her jeans-and-T-shirt-clad companion. Greer's discomfort grew as she watched Eva and the time slowly ticked by. Something was off. She could feel it but couldn't put her finger on what it was.

Thirty minutes passed and the guy still hadn't shown. Confidential informants were notoriously late, and her squad mates would have even less patience for this one. Since this was her operation, sort of, she could probably call it, but she wanted to give the man and Eva the benefit of the doubt.

"Okay, guys." Sergeant Fluharty's voice sounded in her earpiece. "I've got movement from the rear but can't see anybody yet. Be sharp."

Greer poked her head over the rim of the service bay and looked in Fluharty's direction. She couldn't see anything in the shadows that covered the back of the building. As she strained to detect any shape or movement in the darkness, adrenaline surged through her. She wanted to alert Eva, but that would defeat the purpose of being there.

Another shaft of afternoon sun suddenly broke through a crack in the crumbling building and illuminated Eva and Tom like a spotlight. A gunshot exploded like a bomb in the quiet, then another, and a few seconds later a third. The sunlight disappeared as quickly as a flashbulb and Greer couldn't see anything. She didn't move initially, waiting for the next volley. When her vision adjusted, she looked toward the center of the room and saw Tom and Eva hit the floor like marionettes cut loose from their strings.

Greer vaulted out of the service bay, weapon drawn, and sprinted toward the fallen pair. She scanned her surroundings looking for a target, but couldn't acquire one. She reholstered and dropped to the floor, skidding to a stop on top of Eva and Tom, shielding them with her body. "Stay down," she ordered. "Don't move."

Greer's heartbeat drowned out any other sound, and her nose burned from the sulfuric odor of gunpowder. She looked around and saw the other officers peering from their hiding places. The effects of her adrenaline surge would wear off soon and she'd be able to hear. Unsure if the threat had been neutralized, she remained in position and prayed the people beneath her were unharmed. The anxiety she'd experienced about Eva changed to fear. If she was hurt—

"Greer?" The voice was muffled. "Greer, is that you?"

"Eva, stay down." Greer looked toward JJ as he emerged from his place of cover. He gave the thumbs-up indication that all was clear. She rolled off Eva and grabbed her in a hug. "Are you all right? Are you hurt?"

"No, I'm fine but…"

Greer followed the direction of Eva's gaze. Tom Merritt was lying on his back and a patch of blood stained his white T-shirt. "I need an ambulance," she yelled to JJ.

"On the way," he answered. "I've got patrol setting up a perimeter to look for this guy."

"Craig, take care of Eva," she called. Then she turned to Eva. "Please stay with Craig until the ambulance arrives. You don't need to see this." She directed Eva away from Tom's body and knelt beside him.

Greer pulled up Tom's shirt and saw the bullet hole in his chest. She bent over and listened for breathing but heard none. She checked for a pulse, nothing. Greer went through the motions of CPR until the ambulance arrived and took over. The look they exchanged confirmed that Tom was already dead.

She sat back on her feet exhausted from her efforts. Her hands were coated with thick, sticky blood, and the sickly sweet smell assaulted her senses. Thank God it wasn't Eva's, but what the hell happened?

She cleaned her hands on a wipe the paramedics provided and walked toward where JJ, Craig, and Eva were standing inside the doorway. JJ issued orders to arriving patrol units and directed the crime-scene techs. She looked around for the sergeant, thinking he was probably coordinating the units outside. But he usually checked on his guys first thing.

As if she and JJ had the same thought, they stared at each other. At that moment her earpiece clicked open and she heard a faint voice. "Officer down. Officer down."

"Jesus, he's hit!" Greer ran toward the rear exit where Sergeant Fluharty had been positioned. The sergeant lay behind a stack of shipping crates, a pool of blood spreading out from his body. "Medic, over here." She knelt beside him and visually searched for injuries. Blood oozed from a wound above the vest line. Fortunately, his chest rose and fell with each breath. He was still alive.

The paramedics arrived and took over, nudging her aside. JJ placed a hand on her shoulder. "He'll be all right. Why don't you go to the hospital with him? We'll need updates on his condition. Craig and I'll stay here and start the investigation."

She wanted to stay and help, but she also wanted to be with Fluharty, and Eva looked like she was in shock. Maybe she needed to be checked over as well. "Okay. I'll wait for you there." She took Eva's arm and steered her toward her vehicle. Greer doubted that Eva had ever seen someone she knew gunned down, much less been standing beside them when it happened. Her brown eyes were wide with fear and she was uncharacteristically quiet.

On the drive to the hospital, Greer thought about the meeting gone wrong and the case. Somebody definitely wanted Eva Saldana dead. What did she know? Was she withholding information about her brother or the investigation? The "informant" had no way of knowing that Tom would be accompanying her, so Eva had to be the intended target.

The thought of Eva being on a killer's hit list unleashed rage inside Greer. Eva hadn't been in town long enough to make any real enemies. And for someone to want her dead because she raised questions about her brother's death disturbed Greer. Someone had a great deal at risk—enough to kill for. She tightened her grip on the steering wheel as she pulled up to the hospital.

When they stopped at the emergency-room entrance, Greer placed her hand over Eva's where it rested on the seat between them. She hadn't spoken the entire trip. "How are you doing? That was pretty rough back there."

Eva looked at her with eyes drowning in tears. "He's dead, isn't he?"

Greer wanted to reassure her, to say something to ease her pain, but she couldn't sugarcoat the truth. "Yes."

Eva's tears fell freely. She turned away from Greer as sobs shook her body. "I don't know how you do this job. And your sergeant—what if he—" She wiped her cheeks. "I've seen people shot before, not quite so close and not anyone I knew. I'm sorry. I know this isn't easy for you either. Let's go check on him."

"Would you mind if I hugged you first?" Greer wasn't sure where the request came from, only that it was heartfelt. She wanted confirmation that Eva was okay and that she'd be with her as she faced Fluharty's condition.

Eva scooted across the seat and into Greer's arms. Her hug warmed and comforted her, like Clare's old blanket did. Greer relaxed into the embrace and absorbed the consolation that Eva offered. It had been too long since she accepted solace from another person. She held tight for several minutes then eased away. "I guess we should go in."

When they entered the ER doors, Bessie was waiting inside and embraced them both. "Are you all right?" Her concern was obvious as her cool blue eyes made a quick examination of Greer for injuries. "Do either of you need to be checked out?"

"Eva may be in shock."

"I'm fine," Eva said. "See to the others."

"If you're sure, honey." Bessie turned back to Greer. "Take her to my office. There's fresh coffee. I'll come get you when I know something about Fluharty."

"Thanks, Bessie." Greer led Eva to the office around the corner from the emergency room. She poured them each a cup of coffee and sat in a chair by the window while Eva paced.

"What happened out there, Greer? What were you doing at the warehouse? Had you heard something about the meeting?"

"No, I decided I couldn't let you go alone. I asked the sergeant if we could cover the meeting." Greer paused, considering whether to censor her next comment. But having faced death, Eva had earned her honesty. "I'm so glad you're okay, and I'm sorry about Tom."

"It's my fault he's dead. I shouldn't have involved him in this." Eva gestured around the room like her situation was obvious, then dropped her hands in resignation.

"You couldn't stop Tom when he smelled a story. That's one of the things I admired and disliked about him. He was excellent at his job and he wouldn't want you to feel guilty. It's not your fault. But I promise we'll find out who's behind his death. The meeting was obviously a setup, but why and by whom?"

"We're missing something, Greer. Someone must have killed my brother because of something he inadvertently discovered. Whoever did it thinks I have access to that information."

Greer crossed the room and hugged Eva against her. Eva's return embrace was as natural as if they'd done it hundreds of times—close but not demanding, stimulating but not sexual. A hunger flared in Greer deeper than the flesh, but she refused to acknowledge its source. "Don't think about that right now. Let me find out about the sergeant and I'll get back to work. I *will* get to the bottom of this."

The afternoon sunlight that flooded the small office had melted into twilight before Bessie finally came back with news about Fluharty. "He's okay, honey. The shot was a clean through and through below the shoulder. If it had been a few inches lower, he'd be a goner. He's sedated, but you can see him for a few minutes. The chief and the rest of your squad just arrived and wanted to go in together."

Eva followed Greer and Bessie down the narrow hall but stopped at the exam-room door. Her reserve slipped as the emotions of the day overwhelmed her. She couldn't look at Fluharty without seeing Tom and wondering why he died instead of the sergeant. "I can't do this."

Greer looked surprised. "You don't have to go in. But don't leave, okay?"

"Go check on your friend. I'll wait here." Eva gave Greer a forced smile and turned toward a small seating arrangement near the exam area. When she saw Greer and Bessie go into the room, she collapsed on a small settee.

The energy suddenly drained from her. She'd managed since the shooting, but now her defenses refused to hold together. As she recalled the scene, her hands shook. Bullets whizzed through the air. One ricocheted off a piece of metal somewhere in the cavernous space. The second ended in a dull thud next to where she stood. That was the shot that struck Tom in the chest. The third and final shot was more muffled and indistinct. How did she so clearly remember three gunshots and the unique sound of each?

Eva wiped at the perspiration that formed on her forehead. She'd interviewed soldiers and police offices after shooting situations, and they often couldn't remember how many times they fired. But she was certain of her recollection. Her auditory senses had captured the incident in slow motion and replayed it precisely. None of the memories she carried from her assignments in war-torn areas were as vivid or frightening.

But while bullets were flying around her in the center of that chilly, abandoned warehouse, Eva wasn't panicked or even noticeably afraid. Her past didn't flash before her eyes. She thought about all the things she'd die without doing—the future she wouldn't have. At that moment she regretted most not having a stable life with a loving partner.

Eva remembered the feeling of safety when Greer shielded her with her body. She was certain that Greer would protect her no matter the cost to her personal well-being. How did a person learn to be so selfless, to face death for someone she barely knew? If Greer would sacrifice herself for a virtual stranger, what would she do to protect someone she loved? Eva buried her face in her hands and cried. She'd never know that kind of love and devotion.

❖

When Greer stepped into Sergeant Fluharty's room, the smell of disinfectants and alcohol overwhelmed her—the supposedly sterile odor of a hospital that she'd come to despise after twelve years on the job. JJ, Breeze, Craig, Chief Bryant, and a man she didn't know stood around the sergeant's bed. Fluharty was pale, his eyes closed, and a bandage covered his left shoulder. An IV bag hung from a pole and a line of clear fluid trickled into his veins. A heart monitor beeped rhythmically in the morbid silence.

"Any update, Bessie?" the chief asked.

"He's been patched up and given some pain medication, but he needs to rest. He might not wake up for a while."

"Thanks." Chief Bryant motioned for the officers to move to the side of the room out of Bessie's hearing. He nodded toward the slender middle-aged man beside him. "This is Special Agent Rick Long with the SBI. He'll be handling the case." The chief introduced the detectives and indicated who had been present during the shootings. "You'll have our full cooperation, Rick." He pointed toward JJ. "Detective Johnston will be your liaison."

"Thank you, Chief. I'll try to make this as quick and painless as I can." Agent Long placed his briefcase on a side table, opened it, and pulled out a handful of evidence bags. "First, I'll need your service weapons. Place them in these bags just as they are." He handed each officer an evidence container and retrieved the sergeant's weapon from underneath the gurney. "Fill out a receipt including the make, model, and serial number of your gun. Keep a copy and place the other in the evidence bag."

The officers all looked at the chief and he nodded his consent. "Has to be done, guys. You were the only people that we know were in that warehouse. We have to eliminate you first. Go to the supply room when you leave here and have a temporary weapon issued. You'll get yours back as soon as possible."

Agent Long secured their duty weapons in his briefcase and said, "Don't talk to each other or anyone else about what happened this afternoon until I've conducted my interviews. Is that clear?" Everybody nodded. "I'm sure your Internal Affairs guys will be following up as well."

The next few days would be hectic, and Greer needed to connect this incident to Paul's overdose. Most sobering of all, the gunman had targeted Eva today. "I'd like to get back to work, if that's okay, Chief."

Bryant and Agent Long exchanged a glance before the chief responded. "You're free to work on anything as long as it isn't *this* case—and that includes the Saldana investigation. The SBI will be taking over since it probably led to what happened today." Greer started to object but the chief stopped her. "And that goes for the rest of you.

"JJ, until Fred gets back on his feet you're in charge of the squad and liaising with Agent Long. Contact your informants and follow up leads at the direction of the SBI, but no cowboy antics. We have to let them handle suspects or we'll taint our case. Understood?"

He waited for each officer to acknowledge his instructions. "Now, everybody go home and get some rest. The scene has been cleared and there's nothing that can't wait until morning."

Greer wasn't sure she could abide by the chief's order. Too much had happened during this investigation and now it had gotten personal—someone had killed a friend of hers, shot another, and targeted a third. She could be discreet but she couldn't be idle. Greer stepped to the side of the bed and took Fluharty's hand. "Sarge, you'll be fine. The squad's all here."

The sergeant's eyelids fluttered as he struggled to open his eyes. He rolled his head from side to side looking at each officer as if trying to recall him. His lids drooped, his gaze faltered until he found Greer. He pointed at her and moved his lips but made no sound.

"What, Sarge, do you remember something?" JJ asked.

He licked his lips and stared directly at Greer. "Why did you shoot me?"

CHAPTER ELEVEN

Everyone in the small exam room stared at Greer like she was public-enemy number one. Her stomach flip-flopped into a nauseous roil and her mouth dried. It took every ounce of her restraint not to deny Fluharty's ludicrous accusation. The expressions on the faces of her coworkers varied from disbelief to outright hostility, but no one spoke. They would voice their suspicions in private, not in front of a stranger or civilian personnel.

JJ's face wrinkled in distaste, his eyes full of questions, the most concern she'd seen from him since she started to review the Saldana case. She wanted to talk to him and straighten out all their differences, to have him on her side again. The look they exchanged told her that wouldn't be happening any time soon.

The only person not regarding her like a suspect was Bessie. She stared at Fluharty as if he'd gone into cardiac arrest, then moved to his side and adjusted the IV drip. "He's obviously too heavily sedated to know what he's saying."

Sergeant Fluharty's arm dropped like a dead weight beside him on the bed and his eyes closed again. The room was eerily quiet. Greer resisted the urge to defend herself though everything inside her screamed to declare her innocence. Everyone would view an adamant denial in response to an incoherent question as an overreaction. Right now she needed to assume that the pain medication had affected the sergeant's memory and not say anything.

Finally Chief Bryant spoke. "Don't jump to conclusions. I want clear heads to prevail. The loss of a good man and the injury of one of our own has upset us all. Agent Long will talk to Fred when he's feeling better."

The squad members filed out of the room without speaking to Greer. She met Agent Long's appraising stare as he closed his cell phone. If the sergeant's outburst had affected him at all, he didn't show it. From the few minutes she'd been in Rick Long's presence, Greer already knew that he was professional, efficient, and direct. She hoped these admirable qualities would serve her well if the facts pointed toward her as a suspect.

"I'd like to talk to you," Agent Long said to her. "If that's okay." He looked at the chief, who gave him a resigned nod.

"Now wait a minute." Bessie crossed to Greer's side. "If you're planning to interrogate my niece based on the ranting of a drugged man, you might want to think again. That doesn't sound very reliable to me."

Greer's shoulders tensed. This wasn't headed in a good direction. "Bessie, it's all right. Let me handle it." She nodded toward the door but Bessie wasn't going quietly.

"I won't have anybody railroad her. Do you understand me, Sam? Tell this SBI man that Greer isn't capable of something like this."

Chief Bryant had seen Bessie riled before and tried to calm her. "He's doing his job, Bessie. Greer will be fine. Let's go wait outside." He nudged her toward the exit.

"Stop pushing me, Sam. If he's doing his job, why isn't he questioning the rest of the guys too?"

Agent Long, to his credit, tried to reassure Bessie. "I won't allow any railroading on this investigation. Detective Ellis needs to address a few things tonight." His voice was calm, his words sincere.

Bessie looked at Greer, and she visually pleaded with her to leave. "I'll see you outside in a few minutes. Check on Eva."

"All right, but I'm holding you," she jabbed her finger at Rick Long and then Chief Bryant, "and you accountable."

Long waited for the chief and Bessie to leave the room before he turned back to Greer. "She's quite a champion to have in your corner."

"She certainly is. Now what can I help you with, Agent Long?"

He moved two chairs together next to a small side table and motioned for her to sit. "Look, Detective, I know Sergeant Fluharty's medicated, but if what he said is possibly true, I have to ask you a few simple questions right now. You do understand that."

"Of course. Do what you have to."

Agent Long recited Greer's Miranda warnings, even though it was unnecessary since she wasn't in custody. He was probably being overly cautious, just in case. "Do you understand your rights as I've explained them to you?"

"I do." Unlike the administrative investigation that Internal Affairs would conduct, Greer had the option of not answering Long's questions. But she would only look more like a suspect. The sooner she got her side on record the better.

"Tell me about the shooting. I'll be taping your statement." He placed the small recorder on the table between them, dictated the time, date, location, and those present, and motioned for her to begin.

She started with Eva's anonymous call and her decision to cover the meeting, based on a hunch it might be connected to the Saldana case. She covered the briefing in which each officer received his assignment. As she laid out the plan, she could see it in her head as clearly as if she was looking at the sergeant's drawing on the old chalkboard. Her position was directly across from Sergeant Fluharty's, with JJ and Craig opposite each other. She recounted the incident from the time they assumed their posts, being certain to cover every detail she could recall.

Long let her continue uninterrupted. When she finished, he remained silent for several minutes, reviewing notes he'd scribbled on his pad. "Who made the actual position assignments at the briefing?"

"Sergeant Fluharty."

"Even though it was essentially your operation?"

"Yes."

"Isn't it usually standard operating procedure for the officer in charge to make the assignments and brief the squad?"

"Usually." Fluharty had assumed the lead role because the squad was already upset about the review of the Saldana case. He thought they'd follow his lead more easily. She wasn't about to tell Rick Long the internal issues of her squad. But if somebody else did, it could look bad for her. She could only hope that her fellow detectives would hold to the thin blue line of confidentiality on that particular issue.

"Why did he deviate on this occasion?"

"You need to ask the sergeant that question. I was reviewing the original file."

Agent Long seemed to consider her answer, then jotted more notes on his legal pad. "So you were positioned directly across from the sergeant?"

"Yes." Greer had already been down this road in her head. Neither JJ nor Craig would've had a line of sight in the sergeant's direction. She was the only one, aside from the real shooter, who could've made the shot that injured him. But the one that killed Tom appeared to have come from the opposite direction. Something wasn't adding up.

"You came out of the service bay with your weapon drawn?"

"Yes."

"Any chance you fired unintentionally as you ran toward Ms. Saldana and Mr. Merritt?"

"None."

"How can you be so sure?"

"I'm not a rookie, Agent Long. I don't run with my finger on the trigger. I scanned the room for the shooter, but couldn't find him. I wouldn't have fired indiscriminately without acquiring a target. You'll be able to verify that my weapon wasn't fired."

The SBI agent visually scanned her body and his gaze lingered near her feet. "Do you carry a throw-down?"

"No."

"Do you mind if I check?"

The question rankled but she would've asked it if she'd been investigating this case. "Help yourself." If she had used a throw-down, she would've gotten rid of it ASAP. That was crooked cop 101.

Agent Long patted Greer's body in the usual places a gun might be concealed and concluded at her ankles. "Thanks. I realize this is unpleasant for you."

"I want to know who killed my friend and shot the sergeant. If that means inconveniencing me a little, so be it. Anything else?"

"Actually—" A light tap sounded at the door and an SBI criminalist entered the room. "I'd like to swab your hands for a GSR test."

"I'm not comfortable with that. Those tests aren't dependable. I'm sure you've read the studies. I handle my weapon every day and fire it at least once a month." The FBI had discontinued gunshot-residue tests several years ago because of unreliability. Handling a weapon, even a clean one, could result in trace amounts of GSR transfer.

"I'll take that into consideration. It's just for a preliminary finding."

"Then why didn't you test everybody else before they left?"

"Sergeant Fluharty didn't accuse one of them of shooting him. He accused *you*."

Long was right and she hated it. If she refused, she'd look guilty and he could probably convince a judge to give him a warrant to compel her cooperation. On the other hand, if the test was positive, it could be damning. Sometimes she hated the nuances of the law, but they kept cops and lawyers in business. She reluctantly extended her arms and the lab tech swabbed the thumb and forefinger area of both hands.

"One last question, Detective Ellis. *Did* you shoot Tom Merritt or Sergeant Fluharty?"

Greer met his stare. "No, sir, I did not."

"Very well, that's all I have for now. I'll follow up later if necessary."

Greer checked on Sergeant Fluharty and exited the room. When she stepped outside, Eva and Bessie were still in the waiting area. Eva was resting her head on Bessie's shoulder and looked as though she'd been crying.

"Are you okay?" she asked Eva. They both stood as she approached and put on what Greer considered their strong faces.

Eva wiped her eyes. "Fine, and you? What was all that about?"

Bessie didn't waste any time getting her two cents in. "It's about blaming somebody for this mess. But it won't be my girl. Not if I have anything to say about it."

"Jeez, Bessie, defensive much? The man is just doing his job. I'd do the same thing if I was in his shoes." Her aunt's protectiveness warmed Greer, and for the first time since Clare's death, she missed the closeness they used to share. "But I do love how you look after me."

Eva stared at her in disbelief. "They actually think you might have something to do with Tom's death and Fluharty's shooting? You risked your life to save me and Tom."

"Exactly," Bessie said.

"Look, we're all exhausted. Let's get out of here." She placed a hand on the small of Eva's back, looped her arm though Bessie's, and guided them toward the door. "Walk us out?"

Bessie accompanied Eva and Greer to the exit and turned to her. "Don't worry about what Fluharty said in there. He's out of it. Go home and get some rest."

"I'll try. I'd like to invite Eva to stay at the house for a few days, until things settle down, if it's okay with you."

"Of course it is, honey. She's always welcome. Besides, we have to take care of each other." Bessie gave them both a parting hug. "I'll be late tonight. I'm meeting with the evening shift before I come home. There should be enough leftover lasagna for dinner."

"Thanks." The drive back to the motel and the few minutes it took Eva to throw some clothes into an overnight bag were too quiet—none of her usual questions or speculation about the case. Maybe Bessie should've checked her out for a delayed reaction to the violence before they left the hospital.

As they got back in the car, Greer asked, "Are you sure you're all right?"

"Fine." But the silence continued until they arrived at the house.

When Straw Dog and Frisky jumped enthusiastically for their homecoming greetings, Greer seized the opportunity to divert Eva's attention from the day's events. "Would you feed these guys while I scrounge through the fridge for that lasagna Bessie mentioned?"

"Sure." Eva followed Greer's instructions and busied herself preparing the dogs' food. The more she interacted with the two bundles of energy, the more animated she became. "They're amazing creatures, aren't they?"

"They're little food and emotion absorbers. It's uncanny the way they pick up on feelings and do their best to comfort. Do you have pets?"

Eva shook her head. "I travel too much. I couldn't put them through the trauma of having the one they love leave constantly for long periods of time. I know how that feels."

Eva looked sad and far away. Were they still talking about pets? Maybe the past had desensitized her to the effects her life of constant rambling had on those around her. "How do you know about being left?"

Eva drew a couple of deep breaths as if she might not answer. "My father was a journalist. He volunteered for any assignment that took him somewhere new. I was too young to understand that his leaving had nothing to do with me, so it felt very personal. Mother tried to compensate for his absence, but I could tell it affected her."

"I'm sorry." Why would Eva follow in a profession that had obviously caused her so much pain? "My wise and nosy aunt would say that staying put doesn't ensure loyalty or love. So I guess the opposite is also true."

"Maybe, but I worry that I'm like him, constantly on the move, not committing to anything but my job. The personal life I want doesn't seem possible."

"You can always change your mind. Just because you've done things one way doesn't mean you have to continue if it doesn't work for you." She stroked Frisky and Straw Dog lovingly on the head. "These guys will be the ones leaving me pretty soon. Bessie takes them in, nurses them back to health, and finds them a good home. It's hard to see them go."

"Bessie's very sweet—what she said about taking care of each other."

"My aunt is a caretaker, in case you hadn't noticed. She

believes we were put on this earth to help one another. If she finds an opportunity to do that, she makes it her mission. She'd probably adopt the needy population of New Hope and move them onto this land if she could—make them her extended family."

"That kind of caring must make you feel very loved."

Bessie had probably sacrificed a lot early in life to nurture her after her parents died. But Bessie didn't dwell on the past. She and Ruth had given her every advantage they could. "Yes, I always knew they loved me."

The kitchen grew quiet again as Greer placed the warm lasagna on the table, along with toasted garlic bread and a salad. As the tangy fragrances of tomato sauce and garlic filled the air, she poured them each a glass of wine and invited Eva to sit. "I know it'll be hard, but you should try to eat, at least a little."

Eva took a couple of gulps of wine and returned the glass to the table with a shaking hand. She pushed the lasagna and salad around on the plate with her fork but didn't taste either. "Have you ever killed anybody?"

"Not directly." Greer regretted her answer immediately. "If you mean in the line of duty, the answer is no. I've been lucky."

"I was trying to imagine what it would feel like to hold another person's life in your hands and know you were about to end it. What would flash through your mind? Would you consciously choose or would you decide without thinking in the immediacy of the moment?" Eva's voice sounded strained, as if she was on the verge of tears.

"Don't think about those things tonight, Eva. You've been through a lot."

"That's what I did today, you know. I ended another person's life." She pushed her plate away and rose from the table. "I have to talk to his family."

"Eva, don't do this to yourself. Go upstairs and take a long bath while I clean up down here. Then we'll discuss this more. Will you do that for me?"

"Did he have a family?"

Greer considered which would be worse, to have no one from whom to seek absolution or to face the loved ones left behind. Each was its own special hell. Her answer wouldn't comfort Eva. "No, Tom had no family and he wasn't married."

Eva's eyes filled with tears as she looked toward the stairs and back at Greer. Her expression was like a lost child, unsure what to do next. "Where should I go?"

"The second floor's all yours. Pick any room you like. They both have en suite bathrooms. I'll be up in a few minutes to check on you."

Eva retrieved her overnight bag from the entry and started toward the stairs. Her guilt hung like a yoke around her neck. She didn't know how to handle her culpability in Tom's death or how to seek forgiveness—if such a thing was even possible.

As she slowly ascended the stairs, Greer asked, "Are you sure you're okay?"

"I'll be fine. Don't worry." But her answer sounded hollow.

Eva reached the second-floor landing and looked at the similar bedroom suites on either side. One contained pictures and personal items and had a more lived-in look. She chose the one with a simple cream-colored duvet, white sheer curtains, and no sign of personal touches. After she pulled a robe from her bag, she headed for the bathroom and thought about her earlier conversation with Greer as hot water filled the tub and steam coated the large mirror.

What would she have done if she'd known Tom would die this afternoon? She certainly wouldn't have asked him to go with her to meet the informant. But what if she'd known only seconds before the shooting? Could she have done anything to prevent it? Would she have risked her own life to save his? She wondered how law enforcement or military personnel made such a decision in a fraction of a second, then lived with it forever.

It had only been four months since Paul's death, Tom had died at her side today, and someone was probably targeting her. One of those things was enough to put her on edge, but she'd hit an ill-fated trifecta. Talking with Greer about her father and love had made her more anxious. She usually gathered information through personal chats, not disseminated it. But something about this one nibbled at her beliefs about her life and choices.

Eva stripped and settled into the hot water, enduring the prickly sting as partial justice for her failings. She couldn't name anyone, aside from her brothers, that she was certain she'd risk her life for. She felt a responsibility, but not a real connection, to every person she'd interviewed in the course of her work. If she was honest, she'd never had the sort of connection she'd witnessed between Greer and Bessie or her friends with their partners. She couldn't even maintain a relationship with a pet because she wasn't home long enough.

She remembered the hundreds of times her father had left the family in search of the next big story, promising the current trip would be his last. As a child she blamed herself for not being enough to hold him. In adulthood, she realized his dreams and his demons had driven him from place to place. Some people just weren't suited to domestic life. Eva couldn't imagine doing to a partner what her father constantly did to her mother. As a compromise, she didn't get involved.

But maybe Greer was right. Her father's departures didn't mean he loved his wife or children any less. He came back for a reason; maybe that was his definition of love. She'd assumed her lifestyle prohibited a fully committed and loving relationship. That premise was based on a model that appeared to have flaws. Perhaps she abandoned her sexual liaisons so she wouldn't become too invested. What if her job was only an excuse to keep from getting hurt?

Eva splashed water on her face and relaxed into the huge soaker tub. It couldn't be that simple. She kept her trysts short and uncomplicated to protect lovers from the uncertainties and disappointments of her life—at least that's what she told herself. She closed her eyes and prayed the warm water would dissolve the emotional distress of today. Her guilt over Tom's death and her unflattering personal history weighted her down like an anchor.

❖

As Eva sluggishly climbed the stairs, Greer tried to reconcile the emotionally burdened woman with the confident, fearless reporter she'd been dealing with. This story didn't feature some anonymous person gunned down in an old warehouse. Not only had Eva known and liked Tom Merritt, she'd been standing beside him when he was killed. Was Eva even more drained because she'd probably been the intended target?

Greer was angry at herself for not insisting that Eva take her to the meeting. If she'd been closer, she might've been able to prevent Tom's death. All the seemingly unrelated bits of the case that hadn't yet fallen into place confused her. She wanted to help Eva, but her own emotions were frayed, her control tentative. However, naked fear had settled closest to her heart—fear that someone would harm Eva and she wouldn't be able to stop him.

This woman, with the energy of an overcaffeinated teenager and the determination of a marine on a mission, was beginning to matter to her. Greer panicked again and her chest tightened. Eva, not Tom, could be dead. She didn't know Eva well enough to *care* about her. But beneath her finely honed defenses she experienced a flicker of hope when she saw Eva, desire when they were near, and arousal when they touched. God, how could this have happened?

Greer threw the dishcloth into the sink and paced. It was ludicrous to invest in any woman, especially one who would soon be leaving New Hope. Eva Saldana was simply a woman in pain and Greer wanted to help her, nothing more. She took another drink of wine and climbed the stairs to the second floor.

When she walked by her old room on the way to the guest bedroom, she slowed. Something was out of sync. She turned toward the space she hadn't entered in two years. Eva lay under the old cream duvet—in her bed—the bed she and Clare had shared for ten years.

CHAPTER TWELVE

G reer stood in the doorway of her old bedroom, unable to move because of the pain. A kaleidoscope of pictures flickered through her mind: Clare lying in that same position, her long strawberry blond hair fanned out across the pillow; Clare's hand outstretched, summoning Greer to join her; Clare nude, rolling playfully from her; the two of them making love in the same bed that another woman now occupied.

The scent of Clare's flowery perfume filled her nostrils and she inhaled it like a drug. The distinctive moans of pleasure Clare made as she climaxed filled her head. The taste of Clare in her mouth overpowered her and she licked her lips. As the memories washed through her, Greer swayed unsteadily and grabbed the door frame. Her pulse raced. Why hadn't she told Eva to take the other bedroom? "Oh, God."

Eva sat up and looked at her. "What's wrong? You're so pale." When Greer didn't answer, Eva's gaze swept around the room and settled on her again. "This was yours and Clare's room, wasn't it?"

Greer could only nod.

"I chose the one that looked unused. I'm so sorry. I'll go."

Greer stood still. Sooner or later *someone* would sleep in this room. Clare would've liked Eva, so why couldn't it be her? She needed a safe place and a friend to talk to. Greer steadied her breathing and her heartbeat leveled. "It's okay. I was surprised. It's been a long time since I've been in this room, much less seen anybody else in it." As she spoke, tears ran down her cheeks. She swiped at them and turned to leave.

"Please don't go. I know this isn't easy for you."

Greer couldn't remember the last time she'd cried. She hadn't been able to at Clare's funeral; her shock and guilt had coalesced into a rage so profound that it blocked all other emotions. And she hadn't allowed herself to engage the grief long enough since then to purge it. Right now all she wanted was to cry. She walked slowly to the edge of the bed and sat down. "I miss her so much."

Eva drew Greer down on top of the covers beside her and wrapped an arm around her. "Tell me about Clare."

A small sob escaped her lips. "I'm not sure how—" Eva's steady hand along her side and the soothing cadence of her voice calmed and soothed the turbulence inside.

"Take your time."

After a few minutes, Greer said, "She was magnificent. Reddish blond hair, blue eyes, and the heart of an angel." Emotion bubbled up and her voice cracked. "She loved me and—" Something ripped loose in her chest and she wailed. The sound was foreign and frightening as it came in waves accompanied by a continuous flood of tears.

"Let it go." Eva stroked her back and whispered through her own tears, "We honor them with our memories."

Greer nestled against the cover separating her from Eva and allowed herself to be comforted. She didn't try to stop the tears or temper the ache that flowed from her. She thought about the love she and Clare had, the time they shared, and the bottomless pit of emptiness that now served as her heart. With each memory of their life together, Greer savored the intimacy and ached for the bond now missing. She'd floundered since Clare died, touching but not feeling, joining but not engaging, going through the motions of living but not experiencing life. "How do you—let them go—when it hurts so much?"

Eva whispered, "We *never* let go. We carry them in our hearts. The pain doesn't end. It only becomes more bearable." Her voice was tight with emotion as she stroked Greer's back. "Eventually we're able to talk about them, to share our memories with others who loved them, and to move forward a little at a time. But first we grieve."

Greer heard the pain in Eva's voice, her sorrow fresh and raw, as her tears soaked through the fabric between them. The death of her new friend and peer so soon after the loss of her brother was taking its toll. Eva Saldana had never tried to mask or suppress her emotional vulnerability. Greer both admired and wondered about her capacity to feel so freely and emote so easily. Here in Eva's arms, for this moment, Greer wanted to release the restrictive bands around her heart and let the pain out.

"How do you grieve a loss so deep it threatens to break you?" Greer had asked herself and Bessie that question so many times it seemed a mantra. The essence of Clare was woven through her as intricately as the vital systems that supported her life. Was it possible to disengage without destroying?

"Cry. Let the feelings out. Don't think about it. Don't worry what happens next." Eva rocked her gently. "Just cry."

And she did. Eva held her, rocking and whispering reassurances, as they both wept. It seemed forever, yet no time at all until the tears slowed and eventually stopped. She felt relieved and instantly guilty. "I killed her, you know." The words rushed from her lips before she could stop them.

"What?" Eva rolled Greer toward her and searched her face. "Why do you blame yourself?"

The question shook Greer. She'd borne that burden for two years but no one had ever asked about it directly. Nausea settled in her gut as she recalled the hopelessness of that day. "I put her in harm's way—I can't talk about this."

"You don't have to. Maybe I'm trying to understand what I've done. I got Tom involved in this case. I put his life in danger. I killed him as surely as if I pulled the trigger."

Greer relented as the sadness and horror on Eva's face transformed her lovely features into a mask of despair. Today's events had obviously affected Eva more than she thought. Perhaps someone with fresh grief and guilt of her own could understand the depth of Greer's loss. She clamped her fists together until her fingers turned white. Could she utter the words she'd directed at herself every day since Clare's death?

"I—I put her in the line of fire." She swallowed the lump in her throat. "I asked her to meet me at the station because I was running late. If I'd picked her up at the hospital like we'd planned, she wouldn't have crossed Young's path. She'd still be alive." A bitter taste crawled up her throat and Greer thought she might vomit. "I killed her."

Eva slid her hand up Greer's chest. "Oh, darling, you didn't kill Clare any more than I killed Tom. But the difference between knowing and feeling is huge, isn't it? We both have to come to terms with that." Eva hugged her again and some of the tension disappeared. "I'm so sorry about Clare, so very sorry."

Greer had no idea how long they lay wrapped in each other's arms, giving and receiving comfort. As the ache in her chest slowly subsided, she realized she'd been holding another woman for hours with no sexual intent. Their intimacy intoxicated her. Her interactions the past two years had lacked this kind of familiarity, which didn't necessarily come from sex. It rose from a deeper place, from a union of more than the flesh—the joining of two souls at the point of greatest vulnerability. Suddenly she felt awkward and shifted toward the edge of the bed.

"Are you okay?" Eva asked.

"Yeah." But Greer wasn't sure. *Was* she all right with being used and discarded, as she and Eva had earlier agreed to do? Eva had opened a door that Greer planned to keep closed forever. Could she go back to one-night stands after this tiny taste of real intimacy?

Eva seemed to pick up on Greer's mood. "Why don't we change the subject?"

Greer relaxed as she pushed the disturbing thoughts aside. "Good idea. I'm sorry for this. I was supposed to be taking care of you tonight."

"We sort of took care of each other." Eva gave Greer more space on the bed, paused for several seconds, then asked, "Do you trust Jake Johnston?"

Greer resisted the intrusion and the return to reality. Before Eva came to town she would've answered that question with a quick, definitive yes. But she couldn't easily dismiss her emotional connection with Eva, and, lately, she had begun to doubt JJ, which she truly detested. She didn't want to believe that any cop, especially JJ, engaged in deceitful or unprofessional practices. Integrity and honor were basic to law enforcement. If you corrupted your values, you'd better find another profession. If she let these basic principles waver, she weakened her foundation.

"Yes, I trust JJ." Her answer lacked conviction. "I owe him a lot."

Eva paused, seeming to weigh her next comment. "I've heard how he helped you after Clare's death. That kind of support deserves loyalty."

"Without the sergeant and JJ, I probably wouldn't be a cop now. You can't get that close to someone and not trust him. JJ has faults, but he isn't professionally dishonest."

"Then I trust your instincts. I'm trying to figure out who's behind all this. And JJ hasn't supported you lately. He's the only person I've met who's been uncooperative, even openly hostile."

Greer agreed with everything Eva said but didn't want to take sides against her friend. "Something's going on with JJ, and I need to find out what it is. He hasn't been himself since the sergeant assigned me this review. I've been trying to talk to him, but he keeps avoiding me. After today, I'm afraid that just got worse."

"Would you let me talk to Agent Long?"

"I don't think that's a good idea. Besides, what could you say? You don't know who shot Tom or the sergeant."

"I know you didn't."

"Thanks, but it'll take more than a vote of confidence to clear this up."

"I'll do whatever I can to help, if you'll let me."

Eva shifted in bed and the sheet slipped below her breasts. Greer tried not to stare but was suddenly very aware that Eva was nude under the covers and she was still fully clothed on top of them. The intimate but platonic closeness they'd shared earlier now disappeared as Greer's body ached. She averted her gaze but not before Eva noticed her discomfort.

"I'm sorry." She pulled the covers over her exposed flesh. "So what happens now—with the case, I mean."

Disappointment washed over Greer when Eva's breasts disappeared from sight, followed by a twinge of guilt. She couldn't have sex with Eva in this room, in this bed. She would be betraying Clare. If she ever started a new life with someone, they would have to begin somewhere they could make new memories. Besides, tonight wasn't about sex. She and Eva had shared something deeper and more intimate. Uneasy, Greer turned and rose from the bed to put some distance between them.

"I'd like to go through Paul's personal things that you picked up at the station. We might've missed something, and a second look could be helpful. But we have to keep this on the QT because the SBI is officially in charge of the case."

"Oh, good, a secret operation. Let me know when. It's all at the motel."

"I better let you get some sleep." Greer walked toward the door. "And, again, I'm sorry about earlier."

Eva smiled and the tiny dimples formed on her cheeks. "No need to apologize. I'm glad you trusted me."

"Good night, Eva. I'll be downstairs until Bessie gets home if you need anything. And don't worry about intruders. We have an excellent four-legged alarm system." Eva's olive-skinned body looked gorgeous against the pale bedding. Now seeing Eva in Clare's bed didn't make her so anxious. Surreal but not unpleasant.

Greer was sitting at the kitchen table staring into a cup of cold coffee when Bessie got home from work. "Where's Eva?"

"Upstairs…in my room." She didn't need to look up to know Bessie was giving her an oh-really stare. "She needed to rest and I told her to go up. She chose that one."

"Are you okay?" Bessie rubbed Greer's shoulders with the loving strokes of a devoted parent. Her touch had always relaxed and calmed Greer even in the worst of times.

"It shocked me at first but I'm better." She poured Bessie a cup of coffee and waited for her to sit. It had been a while since they had a late-night chat after work. Greer was usually out back in the apartment, having a swim, or working when Bessie came home. But something about this day and her conversations with Eva made Greer crave the connection she and Bessie used to share.

When Bessie settled in the chair across from her, Greer said, "I've missed you. It's my fault we've grown apart."

"Honey, we haven't grown apart. You needed some space for a while." Greer finally met Bessie's gaze and tears burned her eyes. "Have you been crying?" The surprise in her voice mingled with concern.

"A little. Eva and I talked about what happened today…and about Clare. We were both emotionally exhausted."

"Thank God. I'm so glad you finally shared some of that. You've bottled it up too long."

"I'm sorry I couldn't talk to you, Bessie. You understood exactly what I was going through. I just couldn't, especially after seeing how you suffered when you lost Ruth."

"Don't ever apologize for that, honey. You did the best you could. I have to confess, though. It seemed like I lost you and Clare at the same time. I've missed our talks, even our arguments." Bessie's eyes reflected the same pain and sadness that Greer had lived with the past two years.

"I'm sorry I put you through that. I know you loved her too."

"Does this mean you're letting go of the guilt?"

"I'm trying." Greer smiled and playfully poked Bessie's arm. "But I'll remind you about that argument crack next time we have a knock-down-drag-out."

They sat in companionable silence for several minutes, sipped coffee, and alternated scratching the dogs' ears. "Sooo…"

"So what?"

Bessie feigned exasperation. "You're making me act like a nosy aunt. So, how are things with you and Eva?" At that moment Nina, Bessie's ball of black furry cat, pounced into her lap, as if she too wanted to hear the answer. Bessie stroked her and waited patiently.

"Nothing's changed."

"Doesn't sound like that to me. You both cheated death today and it sounds like you shared something pretty intense tonight. I'd say that's a change."

"Except that she's still leaving when this is over."

"Ever think she might need a reason to stay?" Bessie waggled her eyebrows. "Every woman wants to believe she's wanted, special. Haven't I taught you anything, girl?"

"I can't be that reason for her, Bessie. She has to *want* to stay for herself, not because of me. Besides, I'm not sure I have anything to offer her. It's too soon. So, I guess this means life is pretty much back to normal, huh?" When Bessie didn't have a snappy comeback, Greer looked up from her coffee. "What?"

"Normal might be relative for a while. I went up to check on Fred before I came home. I knew you'd want an update. JJ was skulking outside his room."

"Did you talk to him? He's been avoiding me lately."

"He wanted to know if Fred would recover. But he'd been drinking, heavily. When I told him to leave, he argued with me. That's not like Jake. He usually acts respectful to me and the staff."

Greer recalled her encounters with JJ since Eva Saldana came to town, and none of them had been pleasant. When the sarge assigned her the case, everything seemed to change. But maybe he was hiding or afraid of something else, something personal he couldn't tell anyone. That would account for his uncharacteristic drinking and aggressive behavior. Whatever was going on was affecting his work, his friendships, and probably his entire life. She made a mental note to track him down and get to the bottom of it sooner rather than later. She refused to let their precious personal and working relationships slip away without knowing the reason.

"So did you check on the sergeant?"

"He woke up before I left. He was still groggy, but he's asking anybody who'll listen why you shot him. That SBI agent was in with him when I clocked out. Honey, I don't like the way this thing is shaking out. If they're trying to pin this clusterfuck on you, I won't stand for it."

Having Sergeant Fluharty accuse her of shooting him once was one thing, but continuing the accusations was another. Maybe he hit his head in the fall and was suffering short-term memory loss. Maybe the events had become scrambled in his mind, and seeing her kneeling over him before he passed out made him think she was the shooter.

"Don't worry about it. I didn't do anything wrong. When the drugs are out of his system, the sergeant will set everybody straight. He may have even seen the gunman." But the stormy blue of Bessie's eyes said she was no more convinced than Greer that they would resolve the issue that easily.

CHAPTER THIRTEEN

The next morning Greer slipped a note under Eva's bedroom door asking her to call when she was ready to go through Paul's belongings. She sprinted to the garage and pushed Icarus to the end of the driveway so she wouldn't wake Eva. As she sped toward the hospital to check on the sergeant, she reluctantly thought about the other reason for her early departure. Facing Eva after their evening of emotional intimacy scared her more than being charged in the shootings. A sleepless night hadn't cleared her mind or erased her powerful connection to Eva. She needed more time.

When she parked her bike in the hospital parking lot, she saw the white SBI vehicle in one of the law-enforcement spaces. Her stomach tightened. What had Sergeant Fluharty already told the investigator about his shooting? As she turned down the hall to the sergeant's room, Agent Long emerged from it.

"Good morning, Detective." His smile was entirely too friendly for someone who suspected her of murder and assault.

"How's he doing today?" Greer asked.

"Better, I think. He's more lucid than yesterday. He recanted his statement that you shot him." Long watched for her reaction but Greer gave him nothing. "But I'll keep looking until I find out what really happened. Maybe we can talk later, after I've had a chance to interview your squad mates."

She should probably feel relieved, but Rick Long hadn't given up on her as a suspect yet. It would be unprofessional to do so. "Sure. I'll be around the station. We have Internal Affairs statements today."

Greer watched Long disappear at the end of the hall before

she entered Sergeant Fluharty's room. He appeared to be asleep, his breathing even, his face drawn and colorless.

"Have you come back to finish the job?" Fluharty opened his eyes and grinned, motioning for her to come closer. "Can you believe that pencil dick? He thinks you shot me and Tom Merritt."

"Well, you *did* ask me last night why I shot you."

"I was doped out of my gourd. I know it wasn't you."

"Did you see who it was?"

Fluharty shifted positions and winced in pain. "I didn't see a damn thing. How could I get shot from the front and not see who did it? I heard the first shots and ducked behind the crates for cover. The bullet must've come through them. But how did somebody get inside the warehouse, shoot me and Tom, and get back out without being seen?"

"That's the big mystery. I seem to be the only one who was in a position to shoot you, at least that's what Long believes."

"I think I set him straight, but don't let him bulldoze you."

"Thanks, Sarge." She looked at the single vase of flowers on his bedside table. "Did anyone call your wife?" She immediately regretted the question. Fluharty hadn't mentioned his wife in a very long time, and it was apparently still a sore subject.

"You mean my ex. She wouldn't come anyway. She only wants to see me if I have an alimony check in my hand or she thinks it's time to collect on the life insurance."

Greer shifted uncomfortably. When they first separated, he'd been devastated, but the acrimonious proceedings had made him bitter.

"Forget about her, tell me about your case."

"They've relieved me for now. The chief turned it over to the SBI because it's probably linked to yours and Tom's shooting. I think the perp was after Eva."

"Why? Have you uncovered something new on her brother's case?"

"No, but apparently somebody thinks she's found a lead. We're going back through Paul's belongings today to see if we come up with anything." She stopped, realizing that she'd admitted her intent to violate the chief's order to stay clear of the Saldana investigation. "Uh, I mean—"

"Don't worry, kiddo. I'd much rather you solve this case than let the Staties get their jollies making us look stupid. Keep it quiet and keep me posted."

"Will do, Sarge. Do you need anything before I go?"

"Nah, just be careful. It looks like your girl could be right about her brother's death. Don't take any chances."

This was the first time somebody else had acknowledged that Paul Saldana's case might be more than it seemed. Greer exited the hospital and walked toward her bike. She wanted to tell Eva, or maybe she was just missing her. Before she could crank the bike, JJ pulled his souped-up sixties pickup into the lot. She kicked the stand down and waited for him to park. She wasn't about to let him get away one more time without talking to her.

JJ didn't have a welcoming expression, but she didn't care. "Good morning, JJ."

"Whatever it is, I don't have time." He closed the truck door and started toward the hospital. "I want to check on the sergeant and, in case you forgot, we have IA interviews today."

She blocked his path and forced him to look at her. His eyes were bloodshot and his breath reeked of stale booze. "I haven't forgotten, but we need to talk. What's happened to us?"

"Nothing, so leave it alone." He sidestepped her and kept walking.

She caught up to him and grabbed his arm. "Come with me." She steered him toward the diner across the street from the hospital. "You need coffee if you're talking to IA today."

"Let go of me, Greer. I'd hate to deck you out here in public."

"Do it. Deck me if it'll make you feel better. Maybe then we can have a real conversation. I'm tired of tiptoeing around you like I have something to hide. *I* need to talk to my friend. I miss you."

Her last statement seemed to calm JJ's blustery attitude. His shoulders sagged and he looked like he might cry. She'd never seen him so emotionally vulnerable. "Jesus, I can't go in there." He pointed toward the diner. "Janice is working now. She's doing doubles since—"

"Since what?" Greer tried to remember the last time she'd seen Jake and Janice together. They'd been married for years, and when they moved to town from Boston, she'd gone to work in the diner and soon became the assistant manager. But JJ's work behavior had distracted Greer so much she hadn't looked beyond the job for the source of his problems. "What's happened, JJ?"

"Get us some coffee." He turned around and headed back to his vehicle.

Greer brought two large black coffees back to the truck and handed one to Jake as she settled into the passenger's seat. The interior smelled like new leather and Armor All. He treated his antique ride with the care due a mistress. Greer admired some of his detailed handiwork and gave him time to decide how to approach this conversation. Any question from her might sound like an indictment, which would only shut him down more. Jake was worse than her at emotional discussions. He took a few sips of the steaming coffee and finally turned toward her.

"Janice caught me screwing around. She left me."

It's about time, Greer thought, but she said, "I'm sorry to hear that. When?"

"That first night I saw you at the motel over in Hurley. I told her I was working late but she followed me from the station. At first I thought you told her."

"You could've asked. I didn't like your fooling around, but I couldn't tell your wife. It's not my place."

"I know that now."

"Do you want her back?"

Jake rubbed his hands over his face as huge tears welled in his eyes. "Yeah, I do. I love her, but it's too late. I admitted everything, every time I'd cheated on her—and it was a lot. I don't think she'll ever trust me again."

Greer tried to imagine cheating on someone she loved but couldn't conjure up an instance in which that might happen. When she was with Clare, no other woman even turned her head, much less her thoughts or desires. They trusted each other completely. "Trust has to work both ways, JJ. You've got to prove she can trust you again. That could take time. Are you willing to make the effort?"

"All I've been able to do so far is get drunk and beg her to take me back. It's not doing much good."

"Can you blame her? Who wants a cheating drunk? I don't

mean to be harsh, but put yourself in her place. What does *she* need and how can you give it to her?"

They were quiet for several minutes, as JJ seemed to consider her advice. "Yeah, I guess you're right. I've been feeling sorry for myself."

Greer waited, and when it appeared JJ didn't intend to say anything more, she asked the question that had been bothering her. "What else, JJ? More's going on between us than the breakup of your marriage."

"Jesus, and I thought you women were supposed to be sensitive. Isn't that enough?"

"Sure, it's enough to send you over the deep end, but I didn't have anything to do with that. So why are you treating me like I'm the enemy?"

JJ rolled his coffee cup between his hands and stared ahead at the hospital. "Did I ever tell you why I left the Boston PD?"

"When I brought up the subject, you said you got burned out and needed a break."

"That was part of it."

A warning tingle shot up the back of Greer's neck. "And the other part?"

"I investigated the overdose death of the mayor's son. It should have been an open-and-shut case, but the media tried to make it something else. They supported his opponent and would use anything for political leverage. The mayor asked for an outside review of my case, which I saw as a vote of no confidence." JJ paused and met Greer's gaze for the first time. "I may not be a loyal husband, Greer, but I'm an honest cop. I couldn't let that happen. It would've tainted my career, so I left a week before I was scheduled to render the final disposition on the case."

The cylinders clicked into place as the mystery surrounding JJ's behavior unfolded. "So, the case was still open and they handed it over to someone else. They didn't consider you the detective of record since you didn't clear the case, and your reputation was intact."

"Yeah."

"And when the chief ordered us to review the Saldana

investigation, also an overdose, you saw it happening again—questioning your integrity and investigative abilities."

"When you say it like that, it sounds pretty egotistical. But can you understand? As a cop, if you lose your integrity, you don't have anything."

It wasn't easy, but Greer restrained from pouncing on JJ for his narcissistic pride and unwillingness to come clean with her. "You could've told me. It would've been easier for everybody. Not to mention I could've used your help. It's not about proving you wrong."

"You got the case right after Janice left, and I wasn't thinking straight."

"Doesn't say much for your trust in me." Greer tried to understand how it would feel to have someone question her loyalty and integrity. Along with love, they were the touchstones of her life and career. As much as she disapproved of his behavior, Greer sympathized with JJ. "I understand how that messes with your head. But we need to clear up a few other things." How could she bring up his behavior in Eva's motel room?

"I know what you're about to say. I acted like a complete ass at the motel that night. I shouldn't have said the things I did about you and Eva, and I definitely shouldn't have brought up Clare. That was shitty even for me. I'm sorry, really."

Greer studied JJ for any hint of deception. But his words seemed sincere, his tone even and apologetic, and his eyes filled with remorse. "Okay, I forgive you. But don't *ever* talk about Eva like that again or bring Clare into a conversation that isn't about love. I mean it, JJ."

He nodded and hung his head. "It looks like I fucked up the case anyway. Somebody must have killed that guy. If not, why's a shooter after his sister, unless he was targeting Tom?"

"Well, since you're the liaison with the SBI, you'll be able to keep tabs on that. But I don't think they were after Tom. He wasn't even supposed to be there. Somebody thinks Eva has stumbled onto evidence that her brother had and wants to get rid of her before it comes out. We have to figure out who and why. Are you finally with me on this, JJ?"

"Partners again." He held out his hand and they sealed the deal with a handshake. "I'll keep you posted on the shootings and you stay with the Saldana case, on the QT, of course."

"So why didn't you get a register of guests at the hotel the night Paul was killed?"

"I did. You know that's one of the first things I do—list everybody present, verify, and interview them." He paused, as if putting some pieces together in his mind. "Is that what you were looking for in the sergeant's office the night Breeze caught you?"

"I knew you didn't forget, so I assumed somebody had misplaced or misfiled it. I guess that's still what could've happened." They looked at each other like neither believed that scenario. "Was anything unusual about the register?"

"Not that I remember. I conducted all the interviews myself."

"I need it. I'll go back to the hotel and see if they kept the records."

"Let me know what you find, and I'll do the same from my end."

As they settled into their old professional rhythm, the tremendous weight of misunderstanding lifted from Greer's shoulders. She had her friend and partner back. They could bounce ideas around, come up with possible scenarios, and discuss their findings. Jake was a top-notch investigator and she wanted to count on him again.

"One more thing. Stay out of the bottle. We need to focus on the case, and you have to get your wife back. Agreed?"

"Agreed. Now let's go give our statements to IA and get on with it."

When she and JJ walked into the IA office, Craig was coming out. The IA detective who escorted him looked at them and asked, "Who's next?"

"I'll go." Greer was anxious to get back on her case and JJ needed a couple more cups of coffee. Nodding toward the pot, she followed the investigator into his office and closed the door.

An hour later she emerged and smiled at JJ. "Piece of cake." She practically jogged to the police parking lot and drove to the Days Inn on the other side of town.

When Greer entered the standard-fare lobby it smelled like someone had hosed it down with pine air freshener. The scent was so strong her eyes watered. As she approached the desk, she recognized the attendant as someone she'd spent time with when loneliness rode her too hard. She was an attractive blonde, curvaceous and entertaining, as Greer recalled. But damn, she couldn't remember her name. As she got closer, the woman's brown eyes shimmered with enthusiasm and a radiant smile spread across her face.

"Greer! How wonderful to see you again."

"Good to see you too—" She glanced at the name tag drooping over the woman's left breast. "Debbie." Thank God for the protocols of the hospitality industry. "How've you been?"

"Not bad. Missing you." Debbie propped her elbows on the counter and offered Greer an unobstructed view of cleavage bubbling out of her lime green scoop-neck blouse. Overpoweringly sweet perfume wafted from her body and clashed with the heavy pine odor. She licked her lips and brushed at unruly hair with her hands. "Something I can do for you, I hope."

"I wish I could say this is a social call," she lied. "I need to look at your guest records for about four and a half months ago, June twenty-second. Any chance you keep them that far back?"

Debbie's smile lost some of its sparkle but her eagerness didn't wane. "We keep records for at least a year. I'll get you a printout." With her pink-tipped nails, she tapped a few keys on the computer and the old DeskJet printer on the counter whirred to life. "This could take a while. Want a cup of coffee while you wait?"

Greer's skin prickled with anticipation but it had nothing to do with Debbie's invitation. The least she could do was play nice while the real subject of her interest printed off one agonizingly slow page at a time. "Sure, coffee would be great."

Debbie opened the door leading from the common area to the office and motioned Greer inside. "Have a seat. I'll bring you a cup."

While Debbie was gone, Greer tried to come up with a subject for conversation that couldn't possibly lead back to sex. As she remembered, Debbie was good at turning a topic to her advantage.

"Here you go, lover." Debbie handed Greer the coffee and stepped back, her gaze creeping slowly up Greer's body like she was filming every inch.

"Thanks, Deb. How's work been lately?" The question sounded as lame as Greer felt for asking it.

"You know this town. Every horny businessman, cop, attorney, judge, and politician comes here for a quickie. It keeps me in business because this place isn't cheap and we don't rent by the hour. The next closest place is over in Hurley, and nobody wants to risk bedbugs for a fifteen-minute lay."

So much for steering clear of sex. "Guess I didn't think of your business quite like that, but I see the logic."

Debbie scooted up on the corner of the desk and her short skirt moved higher over her well-shaped thighs. She parted her legs enough for Greer to glimpse the signature black thong that bisected her patch of blond pubic hair. "I hear you've moved that reporter in with you out at Bessie's. Does that come with benefits?"

Greer was surprised that the news had spread so quickly. She hoped to keep Eva's whereabouts quiet until they figured out who was after her. "Who told you that?"

"Come on, lover, you know I can't reveal my sources. But if you aren't getting what you need, I'll be happy to fill the void. We were pretty hot together."

"I'm not having this conversation with you, Deb."

"That's one of the many things I like about you, Greer. You're discreet."

Greer swiveled sideways in her chair to check the printer and heard a low growl as the machine shot the last sheet of paper across the counter in their direction. She stood to leave. "You might want to have that thing checked. It sounds like it's on its way to the technology graveyard."

Debbie slid off the desk, gathered the printed pages from the countertop, and handed them to Greer. "Sure you can't stay a while? You haven't even finished your coffee."

"Wish I could, but this is important and I need to stick with it." She took the printout and winked before turning to leave. "Thanks, Deb. I'll catch you another time."

When Greer got back in her patrol car, she pulled JJ's witness list from the case file and compared it to the guest register. One by one she checked each name off as she found their interview in the documents. When she finished, everyone was accounted for. She dropped the papers on the seat in frustration. She'd hoped to find something of value on the missing register.

Greer watched the routine activities of New Hope for several minutes, feeling certain that she'd missed something in the case file. She picked up the register and read over it again, one entry at a time. Near the bottom of the page between two crossed-off names was an unchecked one, Carlton Williamson. She'd worked so fast that her marks overlapped that name as well. Mr. Williamson had been registered in the room beside Paul's the night of his death but left early the next morning—before housekeeping discovered Paul's body. No one had interviewed him because he wasn't there when the officers did the canvass or when JJ talked with everyone else.

She dialed JJ's number and hoped he was finished with IA. When he answered on the second ring, she asked, "Ever heard of Carlton Williamson?"

"Nope." She loved the way cops talked to each other, a sort of shorthand that didn't require etiquette or sensitivity. "Why? Who is he?"

"He was registered in the room beside Paul but checked out before the canvass. I wanted to make sure you hadn't left him out on purpose."

"Nope. Let me know what you find."

Adrenaline flooded Greer's body as the excitement of a new lead registered. She read the contact information and dialed the listed phone number. A secretary informed Greer that attorney Carlton Williamson was out of the country and would return in a couple of days. She left her name and number, requesting that he call as soon as possible. Could this attorney have witnessed Paul Saldana's murder? As she pulled away from the Days Inn, still psyched about this possible witness, her cell phone rang. She answered and the voice on the other end kicked her pulse up another notch.

"It's Eva."

Greer wanted to share the excitement about her latest discovery, but she had to be sure of actual progress before getting Eva's hopes up. She forced a calm response to cover her enthusiasm about both the case and hearing from her.

"Am I disturbing you?"

The only disturbing thing was the way her body reacted to the sound and thought of Eva. "Not at all. Did you get the note I left this morning?"

"Yes. I'm on my way back to the motel if you're ready to meet and go through Paul's belongings."

"Would you like to have lunch first? I'm starving."

The line was silent for a moment. "Greer, it's only ten thirty."

Greer was glad Eva couldn't see her blush as she fought to recover. "Well, I didn't have time for breakfast. If you've already eaten, you can have coffee and keep me company. Meet me at the diner in ten minutes? We'll need to drive separately anyway, because I have things to do later. Please, I need food to work."

"Of course." Eva's answer was as soft and reassuring as a caress.

Greer drove slowly, praying that by the time she reached the diner her emotions wouldn't be trapped in the continuous memory loop of intimacy she'd shared with Eva last evening. How could one brief encounter make such a profound impression on her? These new feelings rode her all morning like the nagging ache of a physical workout. She needed something to calm the persistent unrest inside—something from Eva. Maybe when the case was over they could spend some time together before Eva left town. But the possibility didn't comfort her. The next time they had sex, physical desire might be the initial impulse, but it wouldn't be the only one.

CHAPTER FOURTEEN

When Eva pulled up to the diner, Greer was getting out of her unmarked police vehicle. Tight blue jeans hugged her long legs and a faded T-shirt pressed tightly against her compact breasts. Eva gripped the door handle and tried to wipe her mind of the series of sexual fantasies Greer's body aroused. But today her attraction to Greer struck a deeper personal note. They'd shared something special last night, something more than sex, and that concerned Eva.

After Greer left, Eva had pulled the cover tightly around her as a chill settled on her skin, soaked through to her bones, and made her shiver. She was uncertain if the temperature actually changed or if she simply felt Greer's absence so acutely. This woman with her honor and loyalty and her raw sexuality burrowed into Eva's senses and refused to relent. Greer had risked both her professional standing and her life searching for the truth. Such devotion was hard to discount, but Eva wasn't accustomed to how it made her feel.

Keeping her liaisons as purely sexual encounters served her well. She was up front about her limitations and her intentions, which protected everyone. She always left before the connection grew too strong.

But she'd never had a secure, confident woman emotionally surrender to her so completely. Her heart had gone out to Greer as they grieved and comforted each other. That single interaction bonded her to Greer more fully than sex ever could. Maybe her lessons were wrong. Maybe extremes produced the same results: leaving too soon could hurt as deeply as staying too long.

Before she could examine the thought further, Greer tapped on her car window. "Are you planning to let me starve to death with food so near?"

Eva got out of the car and hugged Greer close, unconcerned with stares from passersby. "How are you?" She rested her head against Greer's chest, listened to the rapid beat of her heart, and inhaled the fresh fragrance of her skin. She sensed a connection here that had been missing in her life for too long. It invigorated and frightened her because she had no idea what to do about it.

"I'm starving." Greer's voice was tight with emotion and she stepped back, holding Eva at arm's length.

"I meant how are you *feeling*, after last night?"

"I'm good." She turned and walked toward the diner. "I appreciate what you did. It's the first time I've been able to cry in a while."

Eva didn't want to make Greer more uncomfortable but she had to know. "I hope your leaving so early this morning didn't have anything to do with me."

Greer wouldn't look at her, which told Eva quite a lot. She didn't address the issue and wasn't willing to lie. Eva's heart pounded as though she'd run a marathon. "Let's get you fed before you pass out," she said as they stepped inside the diner.

A busty brunette waitress took their order and returned shortly with Greer's stack of scrambled eggs, bacon, and hash browns. When the woman passed the fourth time and asked to reheat Greer's coffee without even a nod at her, Eva found her obvious interest in Greer amusing. But Greer seemed more concerned with her food than who was serving it.

Eva's stomach churned at the greasy offerings as Greer wolfed them down. She searched for a light topic for distraction. "Friend of yours?" This was a new experience for her, feeling the least bit interested in another woman's attention toward a bed buddy. But Greer was sexy in a quiet, unassuming way and attracted attention without trying.

Greer looked up from her breakfast for the first time. "Who?"

"Our waitress."

Greer's gaze followed the direction of Eva's nod. "Oh, that's Sandy."

"An ex?" She couldn't stop herself. Greer looked at her like she'd asked the most ridiculous question imaginable. And the look implied more—that she had no right to ask—and she was exactly right.

"Nope."

Eva was on emotionally unstable ground. Intellectually, she and Greer had an understanding about their relationship, but she'd stepped into a quagmire of emotions with this woman. The conversation made her uncomfortable, testy even, so she reverted to work mode. "Are we headed to the motel after breakfast?" An arousing picture of the two of them on her motel bed made Eva modify the question. "To go through Paul's things?"

"That's the plan."

"I was wondering about the camera again. Since it wasn't in his personal effects or in any of the pictures, shouldn't that tell us someone else was in the room?"

Greer rested her hand on Eva's. "I'll look into it. But we can't be certain he had it that night." Greer put money on top of the bill and stood. "Ready?"

Busty Sandy ran over and tried one final time to get Greer's attention. "Finished so soon? Sure I can't get you anything else?"

"No, thanks, Sandy. See you later." Greer turned to Eva. "Shall we?"

With a bit too much pleasure, Eva grinned and took Greer's arm. "Definitely."

As she followed Greer back to Hurley, Eva wondered why Sandy's amateurish attention to Greer bothered her. After a few unacceptable possibilities sprang to mind, she decided she didn't want to know the answer—at least not right now. She owed it to her family to clear Paul's name.

When she and Greer settled at the side table in the motel room, Eva pulled the evidence box from under the bed. She took a deep breath and opened the container slowly, as if afraid of what they might discover. Eva looked inside and her eyes filled with tears. She wanted to be strong, to hold her emotions in check at least until a degree of vindication tempered her grief. But these were the last items Paul touched.

Greer took her arms and guided her carefully into a chair. "Let me."

Eva watched as she reverently removed the contents from the box and laid them carefully on the table. Greer picked up the BlackBerry and scrolled through it. "I don't see anything unusual. Have you checked?"

She nodded. "The warehouse address and a map to the Days Inn were the only things that related to New Hope."

"The property receipt indicates a necklace. I don't see that."

Eva reached into the neck of her sweater and pulled the medal out. "St. Francis de Sales is considered the patron saint of journalists and writers. Paul wore it to honor my father and me. That's the kind of man my brother was."

Greer opened the Italian leather wallet, and Eva recited the contents without looking. When Greer held up two camera cards, she almost dismissed them out of hand. "Have you checked these?"

"Yes, but I didn't find anything significant—some pictures of the old warehouse."

"Let's do it again, to be sure. Get your laptop and we'll look together."

Eva powered up her MacBook Pro and slid the first camera card into the slot. Nothing; the card was obviously a spare. The second card produced a series of images. Most of the shots showed the exterior of the Lewis Street warehouse, with a few more of the inside. As she flipped through the last two pictures, a sick feeling settled in the pit of her stomach. The background was very dark and out of focus, as if Paul had been trying to take them without using a flash. She'd rushed past these before without much thought.

Greer moved closer and Eva heard her breathing quicken. "What's that? There, in the corner of that shot?" She pointed to the last photo. "Can you get it any clearer?"

Eva tried a few adjustments but the picture was no better. "Sorry. What do you think?"

"I can't be certain, but it could be two people in the shadows at the back. Maybe I can get Craig to work on it. He's good with anything concerning computers. Do you mind if I take it for a while?"

"Of course not. Let me know what you find." Eva thought about Tom Merritt. She would have gone to him with this, if he hadn't been killed. She prayed no one else would be hurt before they solved Paul's case. "Do you think your cohorts checked these camera cards before?"

"Maybe. If they were convinced the case was a suicide, they wouldn't have needed to. And even if they did, this isn't much of a lead."

When Greer stood and looked at her watch, Eva felt uneasy. "Leaving already?"

"I have to talk to Agent Long again, and I'd like to get this photo card to Craig. Will you be all right here?"

Eva started to speak and Greer stopped halfway to the door. "What?"

"Bessie asked, well, actually ordered, me to get the rest of my belongings and come back to your place. She said it's not safe way out here but—"

"And she's exactly right. Better do as you're told. It's much simpler that way." Greer's smile was both reassuring and welcoming. Eva wanted to hold her and feel her warmth soak into her bones.

"Are you sure it's okay with you?"

"Absolutely. I'll see you there later."

The certainty of Greer's response caught Eva off guard. She'd expected Greer to reluctantly acquiesce to Bessie's offer, but she actually sounded pleased. "Thank you, and before I forget, Bessie said dinner's at seven and you better not be late."

Greer laughed as she closed the door behind her. Eva gathered her clothes, packed her suitcase, and checked out of the Sunset Motel with more than a little relief. She was glad to be moving closer to town and, if she was honest, closer to Greer. She welcomed the unusual sense of security that being around Greer and Bessie provided. In her profession home was where she washed her clothes and packed a bag for the next trip. But right now this feeling of family was the only reassuring thing in her life.

❖

Greer couldn't stop the anticipation that had fluttered inside her since Eva had announced that she'd be staying at the house.

Her self-control had been tested all morning as she worked closely with Eva, breathing in her orange-ginger fragrance, watching her flip her long strands of wavy hair, hearing the hint of jealousy in her voice when Sandy touched her at the diner. And her expressive gestures as she talked made Greer want those hands all over her body. Everything about Eva Saldana was becoming more exciting, challenging, and sensuous. How would she manage with Eva living in the house just steps away from her?

As she pulled up to the police station, Greer told herself this wasn't the time to indulge her imagination or her hormones. She had to clear herself in the shootings of Tom Merritt and Sergeant Fluharty, then close Paul Saldana's case properly. Until she addressed those two major responsibilities, everything else would have to wait— including her growing attraction to Eva.

When Greer walked into the squad room, Craig Myrick was in his usual spot, at his desk on the computer. Greer handed him the camera card and explained what she needed and how quickly. "Any news on the sergeant today?" she asked.

"Getting better. Maybe going home tomorrow." He took the card, slid it into the computer slot, and pulled up the photos. "Check back in an hour." Sometimes his confidence annoyed Greer, but he always did a good job. When she asked if he'd seen Agent Long, Craig nodded toward the sergeant's office.

Rick Long had made himself comfortable in Sergeant Fluharty's office. His files and reports littered the desk, and empty coffee cups spilled out of the trash can. The smell of a sausage biscuit drifted from a crumpled container on the file cabinet. "I was getting ready to track you down, Detective Ellis."

"Here's the Saldana file, everything I was given." Greer conveniently left out the register of hotel guests that wasn't included with the original case. If he wanted that information, he'd have to work for it like she did.

"Thank you. Are you ready to get the rest of my questions out of the way?"

"Let's do it."

Agent Long shuffled papers, looked at his notes, and said nothing for a while. Greer let the time pass without filling the space.

She'd been to enough interview and interrogation classes to know what guilty people did at times like these. She wasn't one of them, so she patiently waited for Long to begin.

"The gunpowder residue test hasn't come back yet, so you're not entirely off the hook in spite of Fluharty's revised statement. I've been talking with the rest of your squad, other officers, and a few town folk. It's hard not to hear things in a place this small."

Greer's anxiety rose even though she had nothing to hide. She recognized Long's approach as a technique designed to throw her off-kilter. "Can we get on with the questions, please? I still have a job to do."

"Is it true you were denied access to the crime scene when your lover was shot?"

Greer dug her fingernails into her palms to control the anger and keep her voice even. She resented having Long drag Clare's name into another police investigation. "That has nothing to do with this case. But to be clear, Clare Lansing wasn't my lover. She was my partner for ten years, so when you talk about her, do so with respect." Her tone was flat and hard, and she realized that alone would reveal the significance of her statement.

"I understand and I certainly meant no disrespect. Did Sergeant Fluharty have anything to do with your exclusion from the scene? It goes to motive."

"Fluharty and about half the New Hope Police Department. They kept me from contaminating the scene. If that was motivation, I'd have gone after Chief Bryant. He's the one who knocked me out." Greer traced the scar through her left eyebrow.

Agent Long considered her comment as more time passed. He seemed in no particular hurry. "Your records indicate you were ordered to take a psych evaluation and leave of absence after the incident. Who made that decision?"

"You obviously already know the answer to that question."

"And?"

"It was Sergeant Fluharty, but you don't have all the facts, Agent Long."

"Then why don't you fill me in?"

"Sergeant Fluharty kept me out of Clare's crime scene. He

did his job and protected evidence. As soon as everything was processed, he took me to see her. And, yes, he ordered me to have a psychological evaluation and to take leave. He needed to be sure I was fit for duty. The safety of other officers was at risk, not just my own."

"I see."

"No, I don't believe you do." It pained Greer to talk about that time to a man who thought her capable of murder. But he needed to hear the truth and she needed to say things that she hadn't uttered for two years. "After the eval, Sergeant Fluharty also took me into the homicide squad, let me work at my own pace, and helped me through the most difficult time of my life. So, no, I didn't shoot him or Tom Merritt. Tom was a friend. We went to school together, worked as closely as cops and reporters can, and I had no reason to hurt him."

Agent Long looked at her for several minutes. If he was trying to make her nervous and contradict herself, he failed. She'd spoken the truth and didn't need to say anything else.

He finally stood and offered his hand. "Thank you, Detective. I'll be in touch." Before she got to the door, he asked. "Oh, by the way, why wasn't Detective Derrick Bastille on the stakeout at the warehouse?"

"I believe he had to go to court at the last minute."

"That's what he said. Thanks for your cooperation."

The squad room was empty when Greer left the sergeant's office. The other detectives had apparently gone for the day, and she cursed Long for making her miss Craig. Those camera cards might be her only lead. She stopped by her desk to check messages and saw a file folder with Craig's childlike scribble: *You owe me.*

She flipped the file open and examined the last two photographs. Craig had done an amazing job of enhancing the shady images enough to make out facial features of one of the individuals in the shadows. She recognized the man immediately—Baron Wallace, local drug lord. But how was he connected to Paul Saldana? Perhaps Paul *had* been a user and Wallace was his contact. Or maybe Paul stumbled on a meeting that he instinctively knew was important enough to photograph. But more likely the picture was a random shot. The answer was in the identity of the other person with Wallace.

Unfortunately, it wouldn't be as easy to identify that individual. The darkness veiled his features more completely. Whatever the connection, Greer had to find Baron Wallace to unravel it.

As she made a mental note of the locations Wallace frequented, she slid the pictures back into the folder and headed home. If she put Icarus in the wind, she'd make it just in time. The thought of Eva sharing a nice family meal with her and Bessie warmed Greer and made her twist the throttle a little harder. She decided to wait until after dinner to tell Eva about the pictures of Baron Wallace.

Eva wiped her hands on her apron and looked at the appetizing dishes with an odd sense of satisfaction. It had been years since she put a meal on the table that didn't come out of a takeout container. She'd insisted that Bessie let her help make a traditional Portuguese meal, in honor of her homeland and Bessie's affinity for the country. "This looks delicious. I hope Greer likes it."

"We're about to find out," Bessie said as the motorcycle rumbled past the main house toward the garage. "But, trust me, she'll eat anything that isn't nailed down." Bessie took Eva's hands and squeezed. "You have no idea how much I've enjoyed this. I miss some of the foods I used to get in my travels and the pleasure of someone else's company in the kitchen." Her eyes misted with tears as she ushered Eva toward the pantry. "Now get a bottle of white wine from the chiller before I start crying like a big baby."

Eva warmed at Bessie's obvious appreciation. Helping with dinner reminded Eva of many days with her mother doing the same thing. They'd worked effortlessly together, as she and Bessie had, anticipating the other and sliding into an easy rhythm of preparation and cooking. She hadn't imagined feeling that comfortable anywhere other than her childhood home.

Rummaging through Bessie's collection of wines, Eva thrilled at the variety. Her host was apparently a connoisseur of fine wine from many countries. She pulled a familiar bottle from the rack and read the label—Quinto do Vallado Douro 2007. "I can't believe you have my favorite wine. How wonderful."

"I thought you might like it. I made some of my fondest

memories of Portugal over a bottle of that very brand. Honey, would you mind giving Greer a shout to hurry along while I finish? We don't want this feast to get cold."

"Of course." As Eva crossed the backyard toward the garage apartment, Greer met her halfway. She held a file folder and her blond hair was wet and full of finger ridges where she'd combed it. Her T-shirt clung in damp splotches to her body, and the hiking shorts she wore stopped mid-thigh, revealing a long expanse of shapely legs. She'd changed from her earlier attire, and the skimpier version caused a sudden burst of arousal in Eva. Nobody should look this good. "I've been sent to summon you to dinner. We don't want our masterpiece to get cold."

"*Our* masterpiece?"

"Yes, Bessie let me help with dinner."

"But she hasn't allowed anyone in her kitchen since—"

"Since Clare, she told me. I'm honored. We worked together nicely. Your aunt is an amazing woman."

"She certainly is."

"What do you have there?" Eva indicated the folder.

"We'll talk about it after dinner." Greer pressed her palm against Eva's back and guided her toward the house. The small, possibly unconscious, gesture that initially annoyed Eva now felt protective and surprisingly enjoyable. Greer ushered her inside and held her chair, then Bessie's. "This smells great."

"Wait until you taste it. Eva and I created a touch of Portugal for your dining pleasure. Dig in, I've been looking forward to this all day."

Eva felt pride for having helped with the meal and grateful to share a cherished tradition with people who mattered to her. She hadn't felt this welcome at a family dinner table in a long time.

Bessie dug in first and rumbled appreciatively. "Mmm. This is some kind of good. It reminds me of a story."

"Oh, no." Greer groaned. "She *always* does this. Food *always* reminds Bessie of a story and it *never* has anything to do with the food. It's usually a made-up tale about my childhood."

Eva was immediately more attentive. "Do tell, Bessie."

"Well, as you can imagine, Greer has a bit of a God complex. When she was a child she convinced herself she could fly. Most kids go through that phase, but hers persisted and she tried numerous times to prove it."

"Oh, Bessie. You'll spoil my dinner."

"Shush," Eva said. "It's rude to interrupt."

"When Ruth and I were building the garage, Greer climbed to the roof and jumped. She was a horrifying and hilarious sight, after the fact. We were terrified. But this little tow-haired minx flapped her arms and yelled for us to watch her fly over the pond."

"Oh, my God. Was she hurt?" Eva stopped chewing, gazing at Greer.

"Not a scratch. She hit the ground, rolled a few times, and started back for another try."

"What?"

"She said she wasn't flapping her wings fast enough."

Eva and Bessie laughed while Greer stuffed more food in her mouth and shrugged. The dinner chat remained light and entertaining. Bessie told a few more stories about Greer's escapades, and Greer corrected and revamped the stories to suit her superhuman vision of herself as a child. Their laughter bounced off the high beams in the ceiling as they created memories of their own.

When the chatter quieted, Bessie pushed back from the table. "That's about the best meal I've had in years. You two run along while I clean up." Eva started to object but Bessie cut her off. "Nope, you helped cook and I wouldn't trust that one," she nodded toward Greer, "with my dishes after such a feast. She's already headed into a food-induced coma. Skedaddle. Washing up will give me a chance to savor it again…and lick the pots."

"It won't do you any good to argue with her." Greer hooked her arm through Eva's and led her toward the back deck. "Come on, we need to talk anyway."

"Thanks, Bessie. It was delicious," Eva said.

"The best." Greer retrieved the file folder from the counter and closed the kitchen door behind them. "I don't see how you kept your figure if you ate like that growing up."

"I've always been a runner. That helps, though I haven't had much time to indulge since I've been here. But you're stalling with the flattery, so let's have it."

"Jeez, I didn't use to be so transparent."

"Maybe I see the real you." She was simply stating her opinion, but it obviously made Greer uncomfortable.

She scuffed her sandals against the decking and hooked a thumb in the rear pocket of her shorts. "Yeah, maybe you do."

"What is it?"

Greer handed Eva the folder. "Craig made some headway with the photos on Paul's camera card. I recognize one of the people in the shadows." She waited while Eva looked at the enhanced images. "It's Baron Wallace, a.k.a. the Baron, top man in the local drug scene."

Tension grew between her and Greer as she stared at the man's face. "And you're thinking, what, that Paul bought drugs from this man? Are we back to that again?"

"Don't jump to conclusions, Eva. I'm not sure what to think. It's unlikely that Paul bought drugs, from everything you've told me about him, but I have to consider all the possibilities. When we clear his name, we don't want to have *any* unanswered questions."

When we *clear his name?* Eva was torn between the implications of the new photos and Greer's inclusion of her as a real part of the investigation. Greer didn't have to share this information with her. She could have withheld it until she found the connection. Perhaps Greer was starting to trust and believe in her. "You're right. I don't want questions. We have to find this Baron. I'll have the New Hope paper run a picture of him. I'll offer a reward. Somebody will come forward."

"You can't do that."

"Of course I can. It's the fastest way to locate him."

"And blow our chances of finding out what happened."

Eva didn't understand Greer. One minute she included her in the details of the case and the next she blocked her efforts to help. "I don't follow."

"We need to ID the other person in the picture. If there's a conspiracy, a media blitz will send Baron into hiding, maybe get him killed, and his boss will cover his tracks. Please let me handle this, Eva. I need to know you can do that, without interference. Will you trust me?"

Greer's plea touched Eva, and her urgency lessened. She stepped closer and placed her hand against Greer's cheek. "I trust you with my life. Don't you know that?" The words were out before Eva could edit them, but she meant every one. Pure instinct told her she could and should trust Greer completely.

Greer turned her face into Eva's hand and kissed her palm. The tenderness shot up Eva's arm and straight to her heart. Greer's stormy blue gaze dug into her soul as she slid her hands up Eva's sides, pausing at her waist. She knew what would happen next before Greer asked.

"May I kiss you?"

"Pleas—" Greer's mouth was on hers before she finished the word. She was gentle and timid, as if asking further permission. "Yes." Greer outlined Eva's lips with the tip of her tongue, her breath hot and sporadic. Eva placed a hand behind Greer's head and brought them together. "More."

Greer eased her tongue into Eva's mouth tentatively, as if kissing for the first time. But her technique was exquisite, the slow, deliberate pace of an intended seduction. It was torment of the sweetest variety—every stroke delicious, every touch an explosion of arousal, every spark of desire spiraling straight to her core. Greer kissed her deeper, pulling their bodies so close Eva could barely breathe.

She'd never had a kiss that felt so much like a request. Now she understood why Greer hadn't done this before. A kiss wasn't just a kiss to her. It meant something more significant, more revealing. As Greer's mouth closed over hers, she surrendered to whatever that something might be.

"Take me to bed, Greer." But the cool night air against her lips swept away her hopes.

Greer stepped back, her gaze a blend of desire and confusion, her breath coming in short bursts. "Not yet." She handed Eva the photo folder. "Keep these, but promise you won't use them until I give the okay."

Eva reeled from their kiss, not ready to relinquish the moment but desperately wanting to give Greer whatever she needed. "You have my word." Eva watched Greer walk toward the garage and for the first time in her life knew the pure, deep ache of a lover's parting.

CHAPTER FIFTEEN

Greer thought morning would never come as she lay awake in her small apartment and mentally replayed dinner with Eva and Bessie. They'd been like a family—wonderful women sharing a delicious meal, stories, laughter, and closeness. When she and Eva were alone on the deck, the feelings only grew stronger. She temporarily contained the desire to touch her, but something more demanding took charge. Her subconscious betrayed her by unleashing long-suppressed, often-denied feelings. Suddenly her need was more about sustaining the emotional familiarity she'd experienced with Eva than the physical union they'd shared.

The secret compartment in which she carefully stored all things poignant had suddenly burst open and flooded her senses. She was trapped in the moment as deftly as a moth captured in burning torment, and just as powerless to do anything about it. Though she'd been with women since Clare, the emotional and the physical had never merged. The combination was powerful, the desire to touch overwhelming. Her insides quivered with restrained energy, and as she'd reached for Eva her hands trembled.

The intimate physicality she'd avoided for two years loomed— kissing another woman. Uncertainty had plagued her as she'd slid her hands up Eva's sides, afraid she would feel nothing but more afraid of feeling too much. She stepped closer to Eva, focused on her moist, full lips. She'd requested permission as much for herself as for Eva. But that permission didn't relieve her of responsibility.

Her choice spoke volumes about her mental and emotional state. Kissing implied a deeper level of caring and served as an invitation to fully engage. As their lips met, her entire body hummed with the energy that flowed between them. Eva's lips were warm and eager, her mouth welcoming, and hungry. Greer's reservations dissolved in the waves of sensation that coursed through her. She'd made the right decision.

While she enjoyed the physical aspects, the emotional aura made her almost dizzy. Eva's affection and responsiveness made her feel worthy. This connection was unique; Eva was special. As their kiss deepened, she wanted more but forced herself to step back and reality intruded. Too many obstacles existed between them, and she needed to stay on her reliable behavioral path.

What *had* she been thinking? Nothing could possibly come of their liaison. It was what it was and soon would be over. But the part of her that defied reason wanted to believe they could have more. That part led, actually drove, her to kiss Eva—a natural progression of their recent interactions, and it felt painfully yet wonderfully right.

Did Eva feel the pull between them? She seemed to enjoy herself at dinner and joined the easy banter between her and Bessie. Perhaps sharing in their lives had let her glimpse a possibility beyond globe-hopping. Eva was not only capable of commitment but seemed to long for it as well. After all, she'd vowed to clear her brother no matter how much time it took. That level of determination spoke to deep loyalty and character.

Greer stopped her ramblings, chastising herself for wishful thinking. She had no idea what Eva Saldana thought or wanted. She wasn't even clear what was going on in her own mind. Did these developing feelings for Eva mean she'd forgotten about Clare? She twirled the platinum wedding band on her left ring finger. Had the time come to take it off and move forward? A twinge of guilt, then hope, flowed through her. Maybe when this case was over she'd think about her future and the possibility of another woman sharing it.

Thirty minutes later Greer straddled her bike and drove slowly past the house. Bessie stood on the back deck drinking coffee and shaking her head. Was the scowl for her skipped breakfast or her cowardly escape without speaking to Eva, again? Bessie had probably seen them kissing on the deck last night as she washed the dinner dishes. But Greer didn't have time to examine her own behavior, much less Bessie's. She waved on her way out of the driveway and blew Bessie a kiss for good measure.

When she walked into the squad room, a round of applause met her. JJ rushed over and threw his arm around her shoulder. He'd obviously told the other guys that they'd patched up their misunderstanding because Breeze and Craig were smiling and cheering as well. But even that revelation wouldn't warrant such a reception. "What's up, guys?"

"We've all been cleared of the sergeant and Tom's shootings, criminally and administratively. They set some kind of investigative record on this one. Agent Long gave us the good word a few minutes ago. He wants to see you." JJ nodded toward the sergeant's office. "When you're finished, get in touch. We need to talk."

Rick Long waved her into the office and she closed the door behind her. "I hear we've all been cleared. Is that true?"

Long hesitated and ran his hand over close-cut hair. "Congratulations, your GSR came back clean. And the direction of the gunfire is inconsistent with your location in the warehouse. So, basically, you've been exonerated."

Greer exhaled but immediately her pulse accelerated as she sensed something unsaid. "But..."

"But nothing."

"I'm not an SBI agent, but I know when someone's withholding information. If you have something about the sergeant and Tom's shooter, don't you think you should share it?"

Agent Long looked up from his files and smiled. "If you ever get tired of New Hope PD, I'd love to sponsor you for the Bureau. You're right. There is something, but I'm not at liberty to discuss it yet. I'm waiting for one more test to come back from the lab."

"Suit yourself." Greer stood and moved toward the door.

"Any luck on the Saldana case? I know you're still working it." Greer started to explain but he interrupted. "And I don't have a problem with that. I've got my hands full."

Greer debated sharing information with Long. Her initial impression of his integrity remained intact. He had worked practically nonstop to process the crime scene and interview the squad. And he had apparently pressured the crime lab to get critical test results back in record time to clear them all. Her gut told her she could trust him.

"I found a witness that wasn't on the original list. I hope to talk with him in the next few days." Greer paused and Long waited. Apparently she wasn't the only one who knew when someone was withholding information. In for a penny, in for a pound, she decided. If she expected his cooperation, she had to do likewise. "And it's possible our top drug dealer is somehow involved. I'll keep you posted, if you'll do the same. I'm not sure how these two cases are linked yet, but I'd bet my career they are."

"I agree with you, Detective, and I'll let you know what I can."

Greer nodded and went to find JJ. He was standing beside the industrial-sized coffee urn pouring another cup and offered her one. "Yeah, I skipped breakfast." She moved closer and was relieved that he didn't smell of alcohol, as he had in recent days.

"So what do you think?"

"I'm glad my ass is off the block for this one." Greer stalled. She wanted to hear JJ's take on what was going on before she offered her opinion.

"Something's hinky about this shooting. If Long has cleared the squad, he has to be looking at another suspect. We were the only ones in that place, that we know about."

Greer had the same thought. She and JJ were finally back in sync. This was what she'd missed about their strained friendship— being able to brainstorm about work and reinforce each other's hunches. "So who could it be?"

"You better find that doper, Baron Wallace. He could be the shooter or know who is." At Greer's quizzical look, JJ added, "Craig told me about the pictures. It sounds like a good lead and so does the new witness you turned up. You're on the right track."

"Thanks." Greer appreciated JJ's open encouragement. But that was all he could do because of his initial involvement in the case. His endorsement would have to be enough. "Did the sergeant get out of the hospital yet?"

"Yep. He was asking about you when I went by earlier."

"Is he at home?"

"If you can call it that. He's still at the Grandview Hotel, their extended-stay facility. What is it, two years now? His ex-wife wouldn't even let him go home to recuperate. And I have to tell you, he doesn't look good."

From the sadness in his voice, Greer knew JJ was thinking about his own domestic situation. "I'll drop by and see him before I start looking for Baron. Put the word out with your snitches. I need some help locating this guy." She patted his shoulder. "And don't worry about Janice. You'll get her back."

Greer got the keys to her unmarked car and drove to the small hotel across town. Strange that Sergeant Fluharty hadn't bought another house, or at least rented an apartment, after his divorce. He'd probably moved on, though, in retrospect, he looked more disheveled. Maybe she'd been too busy with her own life and grief to notice anyone else's predicament. She'd reach out to him. After all he'd done for her, the least she could do was listen, if he wanted to talk.

As she pulled up to the office, Greer regarded the Grandview, once a stellar tourist destination in the area, now in disrepair. Since the less-expensive Days Inn had popped up near the interstate, the place had gone steadily downhill. Overgrown ivy obscured the building's intricate brickwork. Window shutters swung back and forth in the breeze like drunks staggering down the street. She got the sergeant's room number from the seedy clerk, made her way around the dense bushes, and knocked on his door.

After a long silence the sergeant asked from inside, "Yeah, who is it?"

"Sarge, it's Greer. Came by to check on you."

The door opened only a crack and Sergeant Fluharty peered out. "Come on in." When she crossed the threshold, Fluharty secured a weapon in the waistband of his pants. "I was making a cup of coffee. Want one?"

"No, thanks, I've had my quota for the day."

He shoveled sugar into his cup and added a liquid concoction that looked more like motor oil than coffee. He was pale and drawn, his short hair scraggly, and several days' growth of stubble covered his face. It looked like he'd aged years since she'd seen him in the hospital.

"Are you feeling all right?"

Fluharty picked up his coffee cup and shuffled to an overstuffed chair, leaving her standing by the bed. Someone had moved the chair from its original location in front of the window and pushed it against the wall. "I think I'm having a reaction to the pain meds. It feels like I'm tripping every time I take one, then I nod off. And the pills taste bitter as shit too."

"Call your doctor and get it straightened out or call Bessie." Greer wasn't sure how to approach a personal conversation with Fred Fluharty. "So, how are you?" They'd never ventured beyond the work realm. It seemed awkward. Not only was he fifteen years older, but he was also her boss. Cops didn't cross some lines.

"My shoulder feels better, if that's what you're asking. If it's not, we don't need to go there. I'm still in this stink hole, which about sums it up." He motioned around the room. "I can't even answer the door without my gun." He patted his waistband.

Greer noted the sparse surroundings: a full bed dominated the cramped space, with a single nightstand to the side. The upholstered chair Fluharty occupied was the only seat. An old coffeepot sat on a counter outside the bathroom, and rumpled clothes littered the floor. Two trash cans nearby overflowed with fast-food wrappers. The room smelled of leftovers and unwashed clothes.

She couldn't help but contrast this setting with the home Fluharty had shared with his wife. Greer had visited them for Christmas and Fourth of July parties with JJ and Janice. The Fluharty home had been welcoming and immaculately clean, unlike this motel room that probably wouldn't pass a health inspection. She was concerned for him and wondered how things had gotten so out of hand.

"Can I help with anything? You probably can't do much with your arm out of commission."

"No, thanks—and I don't need your pity, damn it." His tone was harsh and the look he gave her wasn't one she was used to seeing. Perhaps the medication *was* having an adverse effect. "Tell me about the case. How's it coming along?" His voice sounded normal again and his interest seemed genuine.

As Greer updated the sergeant she noticed his energy level start to climb. He was more attentive and animated, but kept looking toward the door and window as if expecting someone. He must have taken his pain meds and was feeling the effects. "So now I have to find this drug dealer. He could be the killer or he could be working for somebody else. Any suggestions?"

Fluharty rattled off a few locations to check for Baron Wallace, all places that were already on her list. Then they talked for thirty minutes longer about the investigation into his shooting, Tom's death, the Saldana case in more detail, and finally her reconciliation with JJ.

The sergeant finished his coffee and placed the cup on the bedside table. "I hate to be a spoilsport, but I'm a little tired."

Greer walked toward the door and turned to say good-bye, but Fluharty had already nodded off. She made a mental note to have Bessie prod Fluharty's doctor to make a follow-up call and check on his condition. Something more than just his injury was wrong. She locked the door behind her and headed toward the part of town that drug dealers and users considered heaven.

The warehouse district was still the best place in town to score. Though a small town, New Hope had the big-city drug feel. Even its nickname, No Hope, had roots in the drug trade. The redevelopment commission was making some progress in turning the vacant properties over to the growing film industry, but the transformation was working its way from the city center outward, so this particular stretch of buildings would be the last to change.

Greer cruised along the trash-lined back streets and stopped periodically to check the crack dens and shooting galleries for possible sources. But the revelers from last night were still sleeping it off and the day was too young for dealers. She searched for her informant, Bo, and found him restocking his shopping cart from the grocery-store Dumpster.

"Hey, what's up, Bo? Need to earn a little extra cash today?"

Bo shot her a toothless grin and continued to scavenge the trash. "Got nothing on that reporter's death you asked about."

"I need to find Baron Wallace. Know where he is?"

"Can't say that I do, but you need to catch him before he hurts somebody bad."

The remark immediately piqued Greer's interest. "Why, what's he done now?"

"You didn't hear this from me, but he's hiding out. Changes places every day. Pays big money to flop in people's apartments overnight. Something's up."

"I need this guy, Bo. Will you call me if you hear anything?" She handed him a business card with her cell number on the back, certain that he'd lost or used the others she'd given him as get-out-of-jail-free passes. Then she pulled out a twenty and slid it in his jacket.

"What's that for? I ain't done nothing yet." He took the card and stuffed it in the pocket of his worn jeans.

"I know you'll come through." As Bo continued to forage in the Dumpster, Greer cruised the strip once more and came up empty. Sometimes the worst part about being a cop was the legwork—hour after boring hour of looking, talking, and waiting for something to happen.

❖

Eva stood in front of Bessie's kitchen window, stared at the garage, and, for the third time, dried the coffee cup she held. She'd heard Greer leave early this morning and wondered why she hadn't stopped by for breakfast or to check in. They still hadn't heard from her and it was midafternoon. After all, they had finally kissed the night before. Her previous behavior indicated that kissing was a very big deal. It certainly put a different slant on Eva's world. She hadn't slept all night wondering what this new development meant in her life.

"Don't worry, honey. It wasn't personal." Bessie scrubbed the final dish and handed it to Eva.

"What?" Eva tried to look innocent, but hiding feelings from Bessie was as unlikely as being in southern humidity without sweating.

"She gets pretty single-minded when she's on a case. Leaving without saying good-bye this morning wasn't necessarily about you."

Bessie was as bad at hiding things as she was, so the statement relayed her own doubts. "But it *could* have been about me. I don't want to cause her any more trouble. She's put herself on the line at work and now—"

"And now you've given her something worthwhile to think about, and it's past time."

"I don't want her to be distracted or put herself in jeopardy. The people behind Paul's death have proved they'll go to any lengths to avoid being discovered." Eva considered her next question, but had to ask. "Has she always been such a risk taker?"

Bessie's gaze shifted to the ceiling and the worry lines across her forehead deepened. A verbal response wasn't necessary. "I understand. She changed after she lost Clare, didn't she?"

"It was painful to watch. She wouldn't let me help. For a while she didn't care if she lived or died." Bessie emptied the dishwater and wiped her hands on her apron. "But I can see a change ahead. I think you have something to do with that."

Eva dried the dish she was holding and placed it in the cabinet. "I don't know, Bessie. I don't want her hurt for any reason." The idea of Greer being in danger because of her or in pain as a result of their relationship sent a shiver down her spine. Finding her brother's killer was important, but was she willing to let Greer sacrifice herself to do so? She prayed she wouldn't have to make that choice.

"I've got an idea. Why don't we go turn in that rental car of yours? There's no sense wasting money when we have a vehicle sitting in the garage gathering dust."

"I don't know, Bessie."

"It's my old Honda, nothing special, no sentimental value, so if you run it in a ditch, I'll collect the insurance money. Come on."

"Okay, if you insist. I *could* put the money to better use." Bessie's smile encouraged and warmed her as it had from the day they met. If nothing else came of this trip, she and Bessie had become friends and would remain so long after she returned to her life.

She wasn't sure she could say the same for her and Greer. Was Greer capable of moving on after losing Clare? Sometimes a loss that deep never healed. And if Greer was ready to try again, could she? Would she be able to have a fully committed relationship, given her career and lifestyle? In some ways they already seemed more than friends, but could their closeness survive separation? She considered all these questions but found no answers as they pulled up to the rental-car office.

After they returned the rental, Bessie insisted that Eva drive while she regaled her with tales about some of New Hope's more infamous residents. Eva navigated the pickup along the back roads toward home, trying not to wreck it as she laughed at Bessie's stories. She took her time, enjoying the scenery and Bessie's company.

Though it was barely twilight when they turned off the main street from town onto the side road, the tall trees along the roadway made it seem later and much darker. As Eva maneuvered the turn, headlights from behind lit the interior of the truck. "Back off, buddy," she muttered. "Don't you hate tailgaters? That's how I met Greer, you know. I was—"

Eva wasn't able to finish her statement. The vehicle behind them rear-ended the truck and it lurched forward, swerving toward the ditch. "Jesus."

"What the hell?" Bessie said, looking around for the culprit.

Eva's pulse pounded in her ears as she fought to right the truck's direction. It crossed to the other side of the road, and she brought it back under control. Her hands slipped on the steering wheel. "Bessie, see if you can get a look at the driver or the vehicle." Eva doubted she'd have much success with the combination of bright headlights, dust, and blacked-out windows. "I'll try to lose him."

"I feel like I'm back in a war zone. Who the hell does crap like this?" Bessie grumbled.

Eva sped up and their tail kept pace. Bessie hung on to the seat back and tried to get a look at the driver. All Eva had been able to make out was that the vehicle was a black or dark blue jacked-up truck with a push bar on the front. It had no identifying marks or tags on the bumper. She could only hope Bessie would notice something more significant.

Eva pumped the accelerator again, but their pursuer got closer. Eva looked at Bessie and shook her head. Her heart pounded and she was almost hyperventilating. "Tighten your seat belt. I'm sorry. I can't lose him." A second jolt from behind sent the truck fishtailing. Eva jerked the wheel to correct, overcompensated, and the truck careened off the road.

The out-of-control activity around Eva suddenly slowed. The suspect vehicle veered around them, made a U-turn, and headed back toward town. Their truck slid closer to the ditch and a large oak tree. Eva wasn't prepared for the violent jostling when the seat belt in Bessie's old truck gave way. She pitched sideways against the door, across the seat into Bessie, and back into the steering column. Her head hit something solid, and before everything went black, she thought about Greer and wished she'd been more open about her feelings.

Chapter Sixteen

As Greer made one final pass through the warehouse district on her way back to the station, her cell phone rang. "Ellis."

"Greer?" JJ's tone told her immediately that something was wrong. "Where are you?"

"On my way back to the station to get my bike and head to the house. What is it?"

"Come to the hospital. Bessie and Eva had an accident on the way home. An ambulance brought them here. It isn't serious."

She didn't hear the last part. Her pulse raced as visions of another injured loved one flashed through her mind. She executed a U-turn in the middle of downtown and floored the gas pedal. *"Tell me!"* The words were barely audible as she clenched her teeth to remain controlled.

"It's not serious," JJ repeated.

The air rushed from Greer's lungs and she gasped for breath. God, no, not again. JJ's reassurances still didn't register. Bessie was her only family. She couldn't lose her. And Eva—she wasn't sure about her feelings for Eva, only that she wanted a chance to find out. "Are they—?"

"Don't panic, partner. When EMS arrived, they seemed shaken but okay. It's a precaution. We haven't been able to talk with them yet."

Her anxiety eased only a little. She wouldn't be satisfied until she saw for herself. "Are you sure? You aren't keeping anything from me, are you?"

"That's all I know. I'll see you at the ER entrance."

"Make sure patrol doesn't miss anything...in case it wasn't an accident."

"I'm already on it."

Greer slammed her cell phone shut as the car skidded to a stop at the hospital. Several patrol officers near the entrance surrounded JJ. When she approached, she heard him say, "Scour that area with a fine-tooth comb if you have to. And report to me, only me." JJ broke away from the group and guided her into the ER. "They're in here." He pointed to the small private exam room. "I'll wait for you."

She paused at the door and took a deep breath. Whatever awaited her on the other side, she had to be calm and supportive. This wasn't about her or her past. She needed to take care of the people close to her in the present. She stuffed her emotions down and opened the door.

Eva and Bessie lay on gurneys side by side with nurses administering to them both. They were chatting and laughing as if nothing had happened. Bessie's lower lip was cut and swollen, and her right eye was developing quite a shiner. The left side of Eva's forehead sported a goose egg that had already begun to bruise. She showed no other physical signs of injury.

"Have you two been playing bumper cars or what?" Greer tried to deflect some of her anger at seeing her aunt and Eva even slightly hurt.

"Hi, honey. We're fine. Aren't we?" Eva nodded in response. Bessie's concern was obvious. She understood the anguish Greer was experiencing and tried to reassure her. "You should've seen this girl handle my old truck. I thought I was on a racetrack. But we're okay."

"Yes," Eva added, "just a few bumps and bruises. No permanent damage, but it's good to see you." She extended her hand to Greer.

It had been a long time since a woman offered her hand in such a simple and unassuming manner. The look in Eva's eyes said she was volunteering more than a gesture of reassurance. At this moment she held the key to Greer's peace of mind, and one touch—confirmation of her body heat, the cadence of her heartbeat—would make everything right again. But if Greer allowed her feelings to surface now, she'd be useless professionally.

Greer stepped between the two beds, took Bessie's and Eva's hand in hers, and kissed each lightly. "I'm so glad neither of you was badly hurt. I'm not sure what I would've done." The thought was too horrifying to verbalize. "Has the doctor checked you already?"

"Yes, honey. Being head of nursing has its advantages. They put us on the fast track and we're being cleared to leave as we speak." Bessie eyed her suspiciously. "Go ahead and ask. The cop in you is about to bust out at the seams."

She overruled her emotions and switched into work mode. As much as she didn't want to ask the question, she had to know. With everything that had happened lately, anything was possible. "Was this an accident?"

Eva and Bessie exchanged a look before Eva answered. "It definitely was *not* an accident. He intentionally rammed us twice. The vehicle was a truck, jacked up all around, dark, with tinted windows. I couldn't see the driver at all."

Greer forced the fear that rose in her into a more productive direction. Someone was definitely after Eva and they'd involved Bessie in the attempt. Fear gave way to anger as she made mental notes of Eva's details, then turned to Bessie. "Anything to add?"

"A humongous push bar on the front of the truck and a couple of horizontal dents across it. I'd recognize the pattern if I saw it again. But like Eva said, nothing on the driver. Honey, we may never know who it was."

"Oh, I'll know, one way or the other. Good work, both of you. Chances are the truck was stolen. We'll probably find it abandoned somewhere." Who dared to attack the people she cared about again? She hadn't been able to save Clare, but she *would not* fail this time.

Eva's grip on Greer's hand tightened. "This is all connected to Paul's case."

She could see the worry that suddenly clouded Eva's deep brown eyes. "Yes—and this is the second time somebody has gone after you. I intend to see that it's the last. I'll brief JJ while we wait for your discharge. Neither of you move until I come back. Are we clear?" They nodded.

True to his word, JJ was waiting outside the door. "Did you get anything?"

She filled him in on the sketchy details, though they probably wouldn't help much. "Eva is the link to this whole thing—Paul's death, Tom and the sergeant's shooting. She's the only consistent element."

"I'm afraid you're right. What can I do?"

"Stay on the patrol guys about the hit-and-run and help me find Baron Wallace. I've put the word out on the street but come up empty so far."

"Will do. I'll call you later." He paused and Greer could tell he wanted to say more but wasn't sure how.

"What is it, JJ?"

"I was wondering. Do you think we need to put a guard on Eva twenty-four seven? If all this is connected to Wallace, these drug guys mean business."

JJ was right, but so far the cowards had come after Eva one at a time from the shadows. If they continued that mode of attack, she was in a better position to stop them than a cop who wasn't familiar with Eva or the situation. But she didn't want to jeopardize Eva's safety for the sake of her own ego. "It couldn't hurt. Have the county boys swing by the house a couple of times a night, if they have time. Otherwise, Bessie, the dogs, and I've probably got it covered. They won't be able to sneak up on us with that pack of yappers we've got."

When JJ left, Greer took a seat in the waiting area outside the exam room. She needed a few minutes to gather her thoughts. This suspect had made the fatal error of involving people she cared about in his crimes. The outrage that rose in her again filled her with heat. Cops weren't supposed to investigate incidents involving friends or relatives because their objectivity went out the window. But more than most, cops understood the need to protect and avenge loved ones. They would back her all the way.

She thought about Eva and the recent shift in their relationship. What began as a contentious professional situation had become more. Though they'd known each other only a short time, they were connected. Greer had learned that time didn't necessarily diminish or intensify affairs of the heart.

Against the odds, Greer cared for Eva, and the thought unleashed conflicting emotions. She'd risked her career and several friendships to side with Eva against the department—but it was the right thing to do and it was her professional obligation. The rule-bound part of her wanted to dismiss these feelings as simple lust and return to life as before. She *shouldn't* encourage or engage in her physical attraction to this woman who was part of an ongoing investigation. Eva *shouldn't* be living in her home. Greer *shouldn't* have kissed her, no matter how strong the desire.

However, feelings this powerful didn't come along every day. Since Clare's death, Greer had been totally devastated, denied and absolutely refused to acknowledge Clare's absence, angrily stayed drunk all weekend and had the occasional sexual tryst, languished in deep bouts of depression, and finally, reluctantly accepted Clare's death. But it had taken that recovery time and more for her to feel this strongly attracted to another woman. To dismiss their connection out of hand was like laughing at fate. She didn't want to go through the rest of her life alone. Clare wouldn't have wanted that for her. But *could* she let go of the past with Clare for a future with Eva?

The panic she'd experienced when she thought Eva was injured at the warehouse and again tonight flashed through her mind. This wasn't merely a brief affair. If she didn't get the chance to explore what they had, she'd regret it. She wasn't sure how such a profound change had occurred, but it was a gift she didn't intend to take lightly.

Being with Eva reminded Greer what she'd been missing, and she wanted it back. She wanted to live again, not merely survive. Bessie's affection, her fulfilling work, and her loyal friends and colleagues made her life full. But she longed to plunge headlong into the fire of love again. Was it even possible? She had to know.

Eva settled into one of Bessie's cushy lounge chairs and sipped wine to settle her nerves. The disinfectant hospital smell still burned her nostrils and made her second near-death experience too real. She inhaled the wine's flowery bouquet and waited patiently as Greer questioned Bessie again about the accident. It would be her turn soon enough, and she refused to reveal the depth of her fear. Greer didn't need to hear how terrified she'd been or that she thought of her just before she blacked out. That had surprised Eva as much as the attempt on her life. That the two had occurred simultaneously concerned her. How could she separate them and figure out what she was actually feeling?

She hadn't thought about her job or the great satisfaction or acclaim it had brought her through the years. Or about her travels around the world and the amazing things she'd seen. Her colorful past full of women from many cultural and ethnic backgrounds didn't even appear. Surprisingly, she hadn't even thought about her family. She remembered Greer.

Maybe she'd flashed to Greer before the crash because Greer was in law enforcement and made her feel safe. Perhaps she regretted using Greer initially and wanted to apologize before her imminent death. But she'd wished that she'd been more open about her feelings. No matter how she tried to justify or explain it, she cared for Greer Ellis.

In that split second before unconsciousness, she'd wanted to share her feelings with Greer, though she wasn't sure why. Doing so couldn't change their interaction so far and wasn't likely to impact their separate lives in the future. They were worlds apart, independent women in accomplished careers, experienced in and injured by love. Nothing she could say would alter that. Strange how the mind functioned when death loomed.

If she hadn't come to New Hope, she wouldn't have found Greer. But now that she had, she wasn't prepared to walk away and pretend she felt nothing. Her life of casual liaisons in exotic locales hadn't stirred the exhilaration that Greer did. Those experiences had fulfilled her in some aspects, but not like her contact with Greer. She would always remember their interactions—both the good and the bad. Was she prepared to give that up?

When her domestic genes kicked in, Eva usually left town. It would be easy to secure another assignment and make some hasty departure excuses. But this wasn't a typical situation. She couldn't leave until they'd cleared Paul's name. And even if she could, she'd be deciding to continue living as she had been—alone and anchorless—just the way she'd sworn she wouldn't live. The thought of leaving Greer hurt more than the fear of Greer eventually rejecting her. Maybe it *was* possible to have the life she wanted. And when she and Bessie were run off the road, maybe her subconscious was telling her the time had come to decide what she wanted and to talk with Greer about her feelings. That would be a first for her, and the idea frightened her as much as being the target of a killer.

"Eva, did you hear me?" Greer asked.

"Sorry, I was daydreaming." More like a sappy romantic interlude.

"I asked if anything else surfaced about the truck or driver who ran you off the road."

"I'm afraid not. I wish I could be more helpful."

Greer started to say something else but her cell phone rang. "Greer Ellis." She listened for a few seconds and answered. "Yes, Mr. Williamson, I'll be happy to meet you at your convenience. Name the time and place." More silence. "That's perfect. See you then."

When she hung up, Bessie said, "Don't tell me you have to go back out tonight."

"No way am I leaving the two you of you alone after what happened. I can talk to this guy tomorrow."

Bessie waved her off as if to say she could handle any problems. "I dare the bastards to trespass on my property. I'll handle them myself and call for cleanup when I'm done."

"I know, Bessie, but I'm not taking any chances." She looked at Eva. "Will you try to be the voice of reason here?"

"I'm with you on this one, Detective. The more protection we have right now, the better." Eva wanted to be brave and fierce like Bessie. But tonight she needed to be with Greer, to feel comfortable in the confidence and security that seemed to surround her. She wanted Greer to hold her through the night. And as she and Greer climbed the stairs to the second floor, a sense of peace came over her.

❖

Greer rested fitfully as she kept watch over Eva. The room that once served as her safe haven now seemed like a staging area for the next assault. Every outside noise or creak of the house ramped up her adrenaline and kept her hypervigilant. Each time one of the dogs growled, she conducted another safety sweep through the house. Her mind whirred as she tried to assemble recent events into a recognizable pattern. The only comfort she allowed herself was listening to Eva's steady breathing until the black night turned gray.

At first light Greer eased out of the house and drove into town for her meeting with Carlton Williamson. Despite the early hour, several downtown shop owners had already put out their colorful umbrellas along Elm Street. The aroma of fresh bread drifted from the bakery and blended with the smell of brewing coffee from the diner. The sights and scents seemed more encouraging today and made her optimistic about her meeting.

As soon as she entered the diner, Greer spotted Mr. Williamson seated in a booth in the back. He was the only stranger and stood out in his striped button-collar shirt and loosely knotted tie. His salt-and-pepper hair was neatly trimmed and combed to one side. She offered her hand as she approached and introduced herself. Greer noted Williamson's empty coffee cup and motioned to Janice for another round.

"How can I help you, Detective?"

The man returned her handshake with a firm grasp and met her gaze with clear, light blue eyes. Greer hoped Carlton Williamson had something substantial to contribute to this case because he would make an excellent witness. Not only would his standing as an attorney impress others, but he appeared to be sincere and trustworthy.

"I'm following up on a death investigation that occurred a little over four months ago at the Days Inn where you stayed on your visit to New Hope. The incident would've occurred the night before you left. Did you see or hear anything unusual that night?"

Mr. Williamson lifted his suit jacket off the bench seat and retrieved a small calendar from the inside pocket. "Just a second." He flipped a few pages and ran a finger down the sheet. "Ah, here we go. Yes, there was something."

Greer controlled a twinge of excitement. "Yes?"

"You'll think me odd, but I document almost everything. It's a compulsion—drives my wife nuts, but it does come in handy. That night, I was prepping for a trial, probably two in the morning. It was very quiet for a hotel. Then I heard a muffled thumping noise and thrashing about, like wrestling on the carpet."

"And?" Greer didn't want to rush Williamson, but she sensed more to his story.

"I thought I heard somebody say 'please,' like they were asking for help." For the first time, Carlton Williamson's gaze shifted away from her. "And I'm ashamed to say, I did nothing. I didn't check to see if anything was wrong. I didn't call the desk to have them follow up. I didn't call the police. I became what I most despise about our society—an apathetic citizen."

Greer's hope vanished and she struggled to find something reassuring to say to this man who was obviously embarrassed by his behavior. "You had no way of knowing." It sounded patronizing but was the best she could do. Her disappointment was as palpable as his discomfort.

"But I did look out my peephole about half an hour later when I heard the door open. Guess I wanted to see for myself that this person was okay. I assumed the person I saw leaving was the occupant." Williamson paused as if considering another possibility for the first time. "You don't suppose it was—"

"Do you think you could identify this person if you saw them again, Mr. Williamson?" Greer was determined to keep him on track. Witnesses often became preoccupied with the process and modified their stories to avoid a lengthy involvement in the criminal-justice system. She needed him to commit to the details before that scenario took hold. But if Carlton Williamson was half as sharp as he seemed, he'd already played that situation out completely.

"I'm certain I could."

Hope returned as Greer took out her notepad. "Would you describe this person as fully as possible?"

"Caucasian male, probably about six feet—hard to say through a peephole—not very muscular, shaved head, and an earring of some sort in his left ear. He was wearing a tight red tank top that I found unusual for the fall weather. I couldn't see below the waist. I was looking through one of those magnifying peepholes, not the full-body variety."

As Greer noted the details, her enthusiasm rose with each new entry. The description sounded exactly like Baron Wallace, but she couldn't jump to conclusions. It was possible to challenge an identification made through a peephole into a dimly lit hallway. "Is there anything else, no matter how insignificant it may seem?"

Mr. Williamson thought for a few minutes and rechecked his calendar. "No, that's it."

"Would you mind if I looked at your notes?" When he handed over the small calendar, Greer wondered how he could possibly have reconstructed his story from the squiggles she saw on the page. "What is this?"

"My own personal shorthand. I started using it when I was in law school. I wasn't particularly attentive, so I trained myself to observe and make notes. It helped with studies and later in interviews with witnesses. It's become a habit, but I'm afraid it won't make sense to anyone else."

Greer envisioned a defense attorney asking to see Mr. Williamson's notes and receiving the calendar with his doodles all over it. The visual made her smile. "Would you be willing to look at a picture lineup?"

"Sure, anything I can do to help."

Pushing the coffee cups to the side, Greer removed the picture file and placed it on the table unopened. "Look at all the pictures before you make any comment. Study each one carefully, then I'll ask if you recognize anyone."

Williamson smiled at her. "I understand the procedure. I'm a criminal-defense attorney."

"Making sure to cross all the t's and dot all the i's, in case our suspect gets someone as sharp as you to represent him." Greer opened the file and pushed it toward Carlton Williamson. "Take your time."

As soon as he looked at the photos, Greer was certain he recognized the suspect. His eyebrows arched almost imperceptibly, a quirk that she imagined preceded the delivery of his most salient points in court. The wait was excruciating as she sipped her cold coffee and allowed him time to be certain of his decision.

"Okay." His gaze met hers and he waited for the question.

"Do you recognize anyone, Mr. Williamson, and if so, how?"

"This man." He pointed to suspect number four, Baron Wallace. "This is the man I saw in the hallway of the Days Inn hotel that night. I'm certain of it."

Greer retrieved the file, closed her notepad, and placed them both back in her leather folder. "Thank you. You've been very helpful."

He collected his coat and stood to leave. "You're very welcome. I'd hate to play poker with you, Detective. I have no clue if the one I chose is your suspect."

It wasn't exactly a violation of protocol to verify this information for a witness, but she'd made it a practice not to do so. But in this case, Carlton Williamson had come a long way and would be an excellent witness. She wanted to extend a little professional courtesy and respect for his efforts and keep him in a cooperating mood. "You've done very well." When he looked at her she nodded. "I'll be in touch if we go to trial."

After Williamson left, Greer remained in the booth reviewing their conversation. She now had a witness who had seen Baron Wallace in the hallway outside Paul Saldana's room the night he died. That same witness could testify to hearing a noise that was beyond those usually associated with early morning hours or sleeping. And, finally, Carlton Williamson heard someone, probably Paul Saldana, pleading for help. For the first time since she started this case, Greer was certain Paul had been murdered. But she still had no idea why.

"More coffee, Detective?" Janice Johnston stood behind Greer with a steaming pot at the ready. Greer wondered if she wanted to fill her cup or pour the scalding coffee in her lap. Janice wouldn't be happy with her for keeping the secret about JJ's infidelity.

"Yes, please." Greer tried not to flinch as Janice filled her cup with the steaming liquid. "How are things?"

The look Janice gave her wasn't the daggers-and-death stare she'd expected. Janice plopped into the booth across from her and rested the pot on the edge of the table. "They suck, if you want to know." Her highlighted medium brown hair was pulled back into a tight ponytail, making her face seem more aged and severe. The smile Greer had associated with this woman for years was sadly absent. "I miss the lying, cheating bastard."

Greer traced the mouth of her cup with her finger, unable to find a suitable response to the uncomplimentary but accurate description of JJ. "I'm sorry," she finally said.

"It's not your fault, so don't feel bad about not telling me. I know how you cops are with your damn code-of-silence bullshit. This one's on him."

"He misses you, Jan. Is there a chance you could—"

"Well, if it isn't my two favorite women." JJ's voice behind her accounted for Janice's pained expression. "Mind if I have a seat?" He indicated the empty space next to Janice.

"Sit all you want. I have to get back to work." Janice grabbed the coffeepot, swung it dangerously close to JJ's crotch, and headed for the next table.

"Guess you don't have to ask how that's going." JJ sat down but his stare followed Janice. "What are you doing here so early?"

Greer debated keeping her conversation with Carlton Williamson quiet. She wasn't sure how JJ would take the fact that he'd missed something during his investigation. "I interviewed a witness in the Saldana case. He heard what sounded like a scuffle in the early morning hours. *And* he saw Baron Wallace outside Paul's room shortly after that."

"Damn." For a second she thought that was all he had to say. But she could see the wheels turning. "I've learned a lot lately, Greer, mostly to be grateful for what you've got." His gaze returned to Janice as she worked the room. "Another is to give one hundred percent, especially in a job like ours. Because the minute you take a shortcut or think you've got it nailed, something jumps up and bites you on the ass."

The sadness in his voice told Greer these lessons hadn't been easy. Losing someone you loved was one of the most difficult things in life. And loss of respect or integrity in a job as honorable and public as law enforcement was its own kind of hell. Her heart went out to him, but nothing she could say would mitigate his situation.

"I let the pressure of a caseload and clearance-rate stats push me into making a quick, and wrong, call. That guy deserved better than he got, and I'm glad you're finally giving it to him."

"I'm sorry, JJ. I wanted you to be right on this."

"You did your job. I'm the one who fucked up, but I'll help you fix it. I've got my informants looking for Baron. I'll let you know the minute I get anything." JJ scooted forward in his seat toward her. "But right now, we might have a bigger situation than finding a drug dealer."

Greer experienced that tingling sense of foreboding that usually accompanied bad news or an operation gone wrong. "What?"

"Agent Long got the rest of the forensics results back from the state lab today. He left them on the desk in the sergeant's office. One of the perks of being the second is that I have a key." He lowered his voice as if everyone in the room had suddenly tuned into their conversation. "They found muzzle-blast residue on the sergeant's shirt."

His statement registered with a jolt. "*What?* Somebody in the lab screwed up. Because if that's true, it means—" What it meant and she couldn't bring herself to say was that whoever shot the sergeant was standing within three feet of him. *And* if the residue pattern was roughly circular around the entrance, that person was also about his size and the weapon was pretty near perpendicular when fired.

They sat in silence for a few minutes and Greer let the information ferment in her mind until it formed an ugly ball of disbelief and confusion. If the shooter had been within three feet of Sergeant Fluharty, he had to have seen him. But if he saw the suspect, why wouldn't he identify him? An equally far-fetched possibility came to mind. The sergeant *could* have shot himself. Greer dismissed the idea as totally ridiculous and surmised that the test results were simply wrong. "They need to retest."

"You know the other possibility as well as I do, Greer."

"What reason would the sergeant have for shooting Tom Merritt and himself? You know him better than I do. That doesn't make any sense."

"But that's the fly in the ointment, isn't it? We don't have a motive for any of this—Paul Saldana's murder, Tom's death, or the attempts on Eva's life, none of it. That's the missing piece we have to find. And—"

"Jeez, there can't be more to this nightmare."

"Long asked the clerk of court for the officers' sign-in sheet on the day of the shooting. Breeze told us he'd been called on a case and that's why he couldn't be on the stakeout. But he didn't have a case on the docket."

"This just gets worse. Let's keep this information between ourselves for now."

"Yeah, one more thing. We found the truck that ran Bessie and Eva off the road, reported stolen—no surprise there. But it had Baron Wallace's fingerprints all over the inside. He's not even trying to cover his tracks."

"That means he's more dangerous than ever," Greer said.

"That's what I was thinking. Want to split up and look for him?" She nodded. "I'll take the east side. Check back with you in a couple of hours…and be careful."

"Will do."

"And don't forget about Tom's funeral tomorrow."

As she picked up her folder and exited the diner, it was evident that JJ was as conflicted about this situation as she was. They'd both work night and day until they got to the bottom of it. Her head ached from considering all the unpleasant possibilities. She refused to believe that Fred Fluharty—the man she knew and trusted, the man who had mentored and supported her, the man who avenged her lover's murder—had any nefarious connection to this convoluted case. And she'd never known Breeze to lie about anything. If she couldn't trust these guys, what did that say about her instincts?

CHAPTER SEVENTEEN

Greer searched drug flophouses in the warehouse district for Baron Wallace until after midnight. JJ had given up hours ago and tried to convince her to go home and get some rest. But she kept looking, certain she'd find another clue. With each hour that passed without a credible lead, her compulsion deepened. She rubbed the tense muscles in her shoulders and focused on the faded numbers on the side of the wood-frame house she faced.

Her eyes burned from lack of sleep and her stomach growled for nourishment. Black coffee had been her constant companion and the caffeine had become ineffective. No one she'd spoken with admitted any knowledge of Wallace's whereabouts. Her frustration level made her grumpy and less than cordial with sources. She promised herself this would be the last stop.

She approached the dilapidated residence—an address where Wallace had lived ten years earlier with his mother. The chances of him being here were slim, but with no clues, she had to explore every possibility. She stepped to the side of the door and knocked. No answer. She tried again. After several minutes, something shuffled inside. Several more minutes passed before someone approached the door. Greer turned sideways and cocked her right hand on the grip of her weapon.

The door swung open and a very thin, balding woman who smelled of liniment appeared clutching a worn housecoat to her chest. "What in the name of sweet Jesus are you doing knocking on my door this hour of the night? *Excuse me*, I meant to say *morning*. Somebody better be dead."

Greer produced her credentials. "I apologize for the hour, but I need to locate Baron Wallace. Does he still live here?"

The woman wiped her eyes and squinted at Greer's badge. "Detective, huh? Well, if you *were* any kind of detective you'd know that boy hasn't even been to visit me in over four months, much less lived here."

"Then you're his mother, Brenda Wallace?"

"I try not to spread that around since he's turned out to be such an upstanding citizen and all, but I did give birth to him."

Greer's hope was fading as quickly as her patience. "Do you know where he's living now, a girlfriend's address, anything?"

"Nope, and I don't want to. Sorry, lady."

As Mrs. Wallace turned to go back into the house, Greer tried one last appeal. The timing was right and it certainly couldn't hurt. "You said he came by about four months ago. Did he spend the night?"

"Yeah, said he was on his way out of town *on business*. I know about his business and I'm not mixed up in that. But he looked pretty tired and wrung out. So I guess my mothering instinct got the best of me. I let him stay the night in his old bedroom."

"Would you mind if I took a look in his room? He might've left something behind."

"What's this all about? I don't think you said." She blocked the doorway and waited for Greer to answer.

"It's a homicide investigation."

Brenda Wallace grabbed the fabric at her throat and twisted. "Oh, sweet Jesus. You think Baron killed somebody?"

The woman looked truly shocked. It seemed easy enough to accept that her son dealt drugs to schoolkids. Was it such a stretch to imagine it ending in someone's death? But Greer had sympathy for the woman's dilemma. How difficult it must be to raise children in today's society with all the temptations and peer pressure. "I'm not sure, Mrs. Wallace, but I have to eliminate him as a suspect. May I look in the room?"

She stepped back and allowed Greer to enter. "I want no part of this. If he's done something like that, he's got to answer for it. It's in the back, on the right."

"Thank you, ma'am." Greer opened the door of the musty-smelling room and did a visual examination. The space was empty except for a single bed and a dresser that desperately needed repair. Starting at the entry, Greer worked methodically in a clockwise manner checking for possible evidence. She cleared the entire room before she approached the closet.

She opened the door and looked in. The only piece of clothing hanging on the rod was a blue windbreaker. A crumpled grocery bag lay on the floor, but nothing else. Greer carefully unfolded the top of the bag and shined her flashlight inside. Then she knelt for a closer look to confirm what she saw—a Nikon Coolpix camera.

Mrs. Wallace denied it was hers or that she'd ever seen it before. Greer left the bag in place and called for a lab tech. It had to be Paul's missing camera. If so, she'd added one more piece of circumstantial evidence in the case against Baron Wallace.

Greer waited hours for a crime-scene tech to respond to her location. The only two in the department were tied up on an early-morning fatality. But Mrs. Wallace seemed grateful for the company and made a pot of coffee. Greer shared it with her while listening to the challenges of parenting an ungrateful child. By the time the lab folks arrived and she got a couple of identifying digital photos of Paul's initials on the battery door of the camera, it was mid-afternoon. She barely had time to go home, change clothes, and make it to Tom's service. But she still had one more thing to do.

Forty-five minutes later Greer parked at the back of the New Hope cemetery, hoping to avoid the people gathering for Tom's burial. She removed the carefully wrapped bundle of lilies from the seat beside her and took the long way around to Clare's grave. It had been only a week since her last visit, but the cooler temperatures had already destroyed the petals of the flowers she'd left. Clare deserved fresh, live flowers, so the town florist kept a stock of lilies on hand year-round. Clare loved lilies.

Greer knelt, removed the wilted flowers, and put the fresh ones in their place on top of the headstone. She ran her hand along Clare's name engraved in the granite and shivered at the cold that penetrated her fingertips. It was impossible to equate a barren plot of land or a frigid block of rock to her once loving and vibrant partner.

She'd experienced only warmth and vitality from Clare from the moment they met. But this was the final resting place for her body and sometimes the only place Greer felt close to her. She came here frequently after Clare died, slept on top of the grave, and prayed to join her.

But today she had another purpose. Today she sought permission to live again. She needed to say aloud some of the things she'd been thinking and feeling lately. If they sounded right, they had to be true. Tears blurred her vision. Emotion gathered in her chest as the words came together in her mind and she began to speak.

"Hi, honey, it's me. I—I miss you and I love you so much it hurts." Greer stared at Clare's name as if she'd find the guidance Clare could no longer provide etched in the letters. "I have something to tell you." She took a deep breath and forced the next sentence out. "I've met someone who matters to me."

The sentiment wasn't exactly right and the words didn't ring true. She wondered if the sky would open up and rain down Clare's disapproval. Instead she experienced a sense of peace, as if Clare was challenging Greer in that calm, patient manner of hers to dig deeper. "You're right. She doesn't just *matter* to me. I think I'm falling in love with her." Greer buried her face in her hands and sobbed. "And I don't know what to do. I'm afraid that if I love her, I'll lose you."

But their love would never fade, *could* never fade. It was as firmly entrenched in her as the intricate system of nerves that permeated her body. Any attempt to sever their connection would destroy her. Clare lived in her heart, in her memories, and through their stories. Part of their happiness with each other had been their commitment to a full and satisfying life, in every possible respect. The best way to honor Clare now was by celebrating and living to her greatest potential—which included love.

As Greer cried, she remembered the last time she'd been able to grieve for Clare—in Eva's arms, on the bed she and Clare had shared. But that moment had been about more than grief. It had been about release of another kind—emotional liberation and a willingness to engage again. The intimacy of that moment returned and Greer surrendered to it and found both forgiveness and hope.

Clare would not have held her accountable for her death, nor would she have approved of the unfulfilling life Greer was living. If she held on to the guilt and denied the possibility of love, she was betraying their relationship.

When Greer's tears subsided, she stood and pressed her hand against the cold granite again. This time the chill was energizing, the stone anchoring, its strength enduring. "I will always love you, my darling. Thank you." She removed the wedding ring from her finger, placed it in her pocket, and walked toward the crowd gathered to say good-bye to a beloved friend.

❖

Eva closed her cell phone and reached for the last skirt in the pile she'd been trying on. Gray with a small pinstripe, appropriate for a funeral, she thought. As she pulled it on and tucked her white fitted blouse into the waistband, she wished she'd never met Tom Merritt. If she hadn't asked for his help, he'd still be alive. Had she put others at risk in the course of her job? Had any of them died because they helped her? She prayed not. She pushed the troubling thought from her mind, finished dressing, and went downstairs to join Bessie.

She'd passed the morning and early afternoon doing mindless tasks: showering, cleaning the bathroom twice, making the bed three times, and changing clothes over and over. Then she'd talked with Vincent and Lucio for the past hour to update them on the case.

Now she had to know if Greer was okay. She'd been out since the previous day. Eva had listened to the nocturnal sounds that turned into waking noises of the day then back to night and hadn't heard Greer come home. If this was life with a cop, she wasn't sure she could handle it. She laughed at her assumption. Maybe she was just on edge because Tom's service was today and her guilt and sadness had resurfaced. She put on a brave face for Bessie as she walked into the kitchen and inhaled the scent of freshly baked sweets.

"Wow, something smells great. What are you cooking?"

"I made a batch of chocolate pecan brownies and oatmeal raisin cookies. My staff is coming over for our monthly meeting and I'm in charge of dessert. Want some with a cup of coffee? I didn't want to disturb you earlier." The dark circles under Bessie's eyes told Eva that she hadn't rested well either.

Normally, Eva would've gratefully eaten a brownie, but today she didn't think her stomach could handle anything. "No, thanks." She tried not to ask about Greer, but the turmoil inside grew worse the longer she tried to contain it. "Where is she? Do you think she's all right?"

"Yeah, don't worry." Bessie placed her arm around Eva's waist and hugged her. "If anything happens, someone will contact us. I go through these sleepless nights when she's working an involved case."

"You aren't used to it—the hours, the not knowing, the danger?"

"I don't think it's possible to get used to those things. You learn to live with it and hope for the best. Greer's a good cop. She knows how to take care of herself. Besides, she knows that if she gets hurt, I'll kill her."

They laughed and Eva hugged Bessie tighter. Some of the tension in her body eased and she got another glimpse of the affection these two women shared. It had to be comforting for Greer to know that someone loved her so unconditionally.

"How are you holding up?" Bessie asked. "Are you ready for this service?"

"I'll be okay. I feel so helpless, though. I wish I could do something."

"Be yourself, honey, and if anything needs to be done, you'll know when the time is right. I'm a big believer in instincts and intuition, and you've got both in spades."

"You're good for a girl's confidence. Shall we go?"

Bessie pulled off her apron and tossed it on a chair. "Ready as I'll ever be."

"And what about Greer?"

"She'll be there. It won't be easy, but she'll be there."

"I know she and Tom were friends since school." Bessie went silent and the reason suddenly occurred to Eva. They were heading to a cemetery. "Are we going to where Clare is buried?"

Bessie nodded.

Their ride to the county cemetery was short and silent, like an unspoken agreement between friends of long standing. They respected each other's time for reflection without the need for meaningless prattle. Eva squeezed Bessie's hand as they approached the entrance.

A huge leafless oak tree stood on either side of the entry like barrel-chested sentinels at the desolate garden of souls. Eva thought it strange that a black wrought-iron fence surrounded the small memorial park. The residents had already transcended the constraints of the physical realm, and visitors were more eager to get out than in. The property was well maintained, but the cool temperatures of fall had turned the grass and flowers a dismal shade of brown. Somehow it seemed more fitting to the occasion than the lush spring foliage in Lagos when they buried Paul.

When Bessie parked near the burial site, Eva was surprised to see so many people. Greer had said Tom didn't have any family and wasn't married, so she hadn't expected many people. Patrol officers, plainclothes detectives, hospital workers still in uniform, EMS personnel, firefighters, and other folks who were probably Tom's coworkers from the newspaper huddled around the funeral-home tent for the graveside service as the minister began to speak.

Eva half listened to the scripture passages and obligatory prayers as she looked around for Greer. JJ and the other homicide detectives stood apart from the crowd behind Sergeant Fluharty, whose left arm was still in a sling. It appeared as though the assault had drained him of more than a little blood. He looked pale and gaunt, and when his eyes met Eva's, he quickly looked away. Greer wasn't with her squad, which Eva found odd. Greer valued only her personal commitments more than her professional ones.

She scoured the neatly maintained grounds and finally saw Greer walking toward her squad mates. In the distance behind her a fresh arrangement of purple lilies lay in stark contrast on top of a gray granite headstone. The poignant scene touched Eva. She couldn't fathom the devastation of burying the woman she loved, the inconsolable loneliness of visiting a patch of earth and slab of granite instead of a living person. What peace of mind or solace of heart did such rituals provide? Losing her parents and Paul had been traumatic enough, but she couldn't imagine losing a life partner. Eva tore her gaze from Greer, the pain on her face too explicit and too intimate for outsiders to intrude upon.

When Eva returned her attention to the service, the minister asked if anyone wanted to share a memory or story about Tom. Several of his coworkers told anecdotes about working with him that elicited rounds of laughter. When the last person finished, Eva stepped forward. She wanted to pay tribute to Tom for his sacrifice to the profession he loved. She owed him that and so much more.

"I'd like to say something, please." The minister nodded. "My name is Eva Saldana. I knew Tom only for a short time, but he seemed like a wonderful man. He offered to help me with a story when he could have easily refused..." *And still be alive.* Her throat tightened. "He was very direct and respectful. I admired his ability to be honest without being judgmental. Few people have it. I'm sure it made him an excellent reporter. I wish I could've known him longer. I think we would've been very good friends."

She moved back beside Bessie and grabbed her hand for support. Bessie's steady grip calmed Eva as tears streamed down her face. "That was beautiful, honey, exactly the right thing to do."

The minister said a final prayer and the crowd dispersed. Eva and Bessie were walking arm in arm toward Bessie's pickup when Greer caught up. She looped her arm through Eva's and walked alongside.

"That was nice of you. Are you all right?"

Eva nodded, so touched by Greer's concern that she didn't trust herself to speak. Greer's eyes were bloodshot and slightly swollen, like she hadn't slept all night and had been crying. Eva ached, realizing what being here must have cost her.

"Worked all night again, didn't you." Bessie's tone was more statement than question. "You won't be much good if you keep this up. Can you come home for a while?"

"Yeah, I need to talk with Eva anyway."

Greer's gaze locked on her and Eva's skin tingled and glowed with heat.

"You sure you're okay?" Bessie asked.

"I'm fine, Bessie. Stop worrying so much. I'll see you at the house."

"Something's up with her," Bessie said as she drove the short distance home. "And I think you're about to find out what."

"Should I be concerned?" Eva's pulse fluttered in anticipation. Part of her wanted definitive proof and closure in Paul's case; the other part wanted something she'd only imagined she could have—a life with Greer.

"Be ready for anything. You never know with that one." Her smile conveyed both mischief and concern.

When they reached the house, Greer was standing in the driveway. She asked Bessie, "You need any help? I know the ladies are coming for your meeting."

"Nope, got it covered, unless you ate all the brownies and cookies."

"Only a couple." She took Eva's hand and led her toward the garage. "Eva and I'll be in the apartment."

CHAPTER EIGHTEEN

This would be Eva's first time in Greer's private space, and the prospect excited yet intimidated her. Their joined hands felt intimate and right, the nearness of their bodies perfect, each broadcasting desire—or was she projecting? Her legs trembled as she climbed the staircase into Greer's personal domain.

The loft apartment was light and airy, with huge windows all around and an open barn-style door at the opposite end. It smelled of the outdoors and the clean freshness she associated with Greer. A king-sized bed dominated the room and a couple of barrel chairs faced the lake and woods. A small kitchenette and glass-block restroom occupied the space opposite the door. The fabrics, wall hangings, and artwork that decorated the room provided splashes of fall color and seemed appropriate for Greer's more reserved, traditional style.

"This is beautiful," Eva said. "It feels like you."

"Thank you, I think. Would you like something to drink?"

"Water would be fine."

"Have a seat." Greer motioned to the chairs overlooking the lake. After she retrieved two bottles of water from the fridge and handed one to Eva, Greer opened hers and drained it. She fidgeted with the bottle cap and finally tossed the empty into the trash can. "I need to tell you some things."

Eva grew more anxious at seeing Greer without her cocky assurance and professional cool. Emotions seemed to be the only thing that made her the least bit uncomfortable. Could *she* handle a personal conversation with Greer, if they both put their cards on the table? An overpowering need to find out replaced her uncertainty. "Okay. Whatever it is, it'll be fine."

Greer stopped in front of her. "I *kissed* you."

Eva's heart pounded rapidly. "You certainly did." Greer's acknowledgment excited her as much as the act itself.

"I haven't kissed anyone since Clare."

Would Greer apologize and say it couldn't happen again? Eva shuttered as if a cold breeze had blown through the room.

"I liked kissing you and I want to do it again, but—"

"You don't have to explain." As much as it pained Eva, she wanted to spare Greer any further discomfort. "I know you love Clare and always will. I admire that about you. I'll respect your boundaries from now on, promise."

Greer knelt in front of Eva and placed her hands on her knees. "I do love her, and you're right, that won't change. But I also have very strong feelings for you. You've touched a place in my heart that I thought died with Clare."

Greer's blue eyes pinned her and Eva drew a ragged breath that felt like it contained a narcotic. Her pulse hammered. Heat spread through her body. She was unprepared. She'd thought about a relationship with Greer, even fantasized about it, but didn't consider it a real option. She remembered wishing on the day of the accident that she'd been more open about her feelings. How could she be open when she was so conflicted?

"Wow. When you have something to say, you get right to the point, don't you?"

"It takes a while, but yeah. Sorry if it's too much."

"Greer, I don't know what to say." She looked down at the strong, lean hands on her knees. Greer wasn't wearing her wedding ring. She'd obviously made a decision about her life. The thought filled Eva with hope and trepidation.

"Don't say anything yet. Let me get this out and then you can think about it. I've been so screwed up for the past two years that I couldn't feel anything. You've changed that for me. The situation is complicated. You have a life that covers the globe. Mine is confined to this small town. All I'm asking is to be a part of yours in some way. Is that possible?"

Eva wanted to scream *yes* at the top of her lungs, but her past failures stopped her. "I'm not any good at this relationship stuff."

"I'm not sure anybody is. We do the best we can. Just think about what you've had and what you want. The answer should lie somewhere in between."

Eva placed her hands on either side of Greer's face and pulled her closer. "You're amazing, and I'd like for you to kiss me now."

Greer's lips were as soft and tender as Eva remembered, and the moment they met hers, all her doubts vanished. She wanted this. She wanted Greer, whatever that looked like, for as long as possible. Greer's mouth claimed hers in a flood of emotions: desire, respect, compassion, and love, all in one deeply arousing kiss. But most of all, Eva felt secure, like she belonged to this woman, in this place.

Eva scooted toward the edge of the chair, hiked her skirt up her thighs, and wrapped her legs around Greer's waist. She could hardly contain the urges that raged inside her. But this time the ferocity of those feelings went beyond the physical. This time she and Greer shared an intimate connection that hadn't existed before. Greer had been honest about her interest in Eva. And although Eva hadn't committed herself verbally, she felt the same way. Greer would know that when they made love. She'd hidden her feelings from lovers in the past, but she hadn't experienced this level of desire. Was it even possible to hide something so overwhelming?

Greer slid her hands around Eva's back, pulled her tight against her, and stood up. Eva was amazed and turned on at her strength as she rose from the floor, lifting Eva easily from the chair. "Now?" she asked.

"Yes, now I'm taking you to bed."

Greer eased Eva onto the side of the bed and again knelt in front of her. She flipped her shoes off and skimmed her hands up her legs and under her skirt. "You truly are gorgeous."

Greer's comment touched Eva. Women she'd bedded in the past hadn't bothered to compliment her beauty, usually too preoccupied with their own. "Thank you." She responded almost inaudibly, her breath coming in short bursts.

"May I undress you?" Greer asked.

"I wish you would, and quickly."

Caressing her way slowly up Eva's legs, Greer reached around and unzipped the skirt, then eased it down her body onto the floor. She kissed a delicate path from Eva's knee to the top of her thigh, switched to the other leg and did the same, avoiding the aching pulse point between her legs. Eva groaned and Greer smiled with understanding.

"Patience." Greer scooted Eva up on the bed, straddled her, and began to slowly, methodically unbutton her blouse. With each closure she released, Greer applied a kiss to the sensitive skin underneath. Her lips were hot and moist, like Eva's center, and she wanted the two joined soon. The pleasurable torture was pushing her too quickly toward climax.

"I can't take this much longer. I want you so badly." Eva dug her fingers into the top of Greer's shoulders and squeezed.

The last button on her blouse was just above her cleavage, and when Greer opened it, she let out a long, shaky breath. "Oh, my God—so gorgeous." She pushed the garment off Eva's arms and tossed it to the foot of the bed. For several seconds she stared at Eva's breasts, captured in a beige, lacy, front-clasp bra. "This is wrong." Greer unhooked the bra and cupped the malleable flesh in her hands. "That's more like it."

Greer palmed and rolled Eva's breasts back and forth, flicking her now-erect nipples with the tip of her tongue. Eva bucked as the pressure built, desperate for contact in the one place Greer circumvented.

As Eva pled for mercy once again, Greer stretched out on top of her and pressed her ear against Eva's chest. "Shh, I want to listen to your heart."

Eva ran her fingers through Greer's thick blond hair and pulled her closer. She'd never felt so appreciated as she did at this moment. Perhaps Greer's loss of a loved one helped her fully appreciate the mere heartbeat of another. The simplicity was poetic.

"You're amazing and so gentle."

Greer kissed her way up Eva's neck and nipped her ear. When Greer closed her mouth over Eva's, she responded eagerly. She sucked Greer's tongue in tempo to the thrusting of her hips against Greer's still-clothed leg. Her thong was soaked but too rough against her clit. "Get undressed. I need to feel you." Eva removed her remaining piece of clothing and waited impatiently for Greer to rejoin her.

Greer shucked her shirt off without unbuttoning it and wiggled out of her dress pants. She wore no bra or panties. Another wave of arousal engulfed Eva. She reached for Greer, who topped her again, rubbing her center against Eva's pubic mound and staring at her with a come-and-get-me look. Greer had been patient and controlled when Eva wasn't touching her, but that was about to end. Eva needed to reciprocate and she needed relief.

She cupped one of Greer's breasts and squeezed. With her other hand, she slid her middle finger between Greer's legs and stroked. "No more teasing."

"Ye-yes, okay." Greer stretched back on her feet, exposing her protruding clit. "Do that again. Please." Eva complied and Greer pumped her pelvis forward and back to meet her slow caresses. "Faster." Greer's head was thrown back and her small breasts rocked with their motion. Eva wanted to watch Greer's expression, to see her face, to stare into her eyes at the moment of climax, which wouldn't be long.

"Do you like that, Detective?"

"Oh, yeah."

The motion of Greer rubbing against her was testing Eva's limits as well. She didn't usually come without internal stimulation, but this would be one of many differences between Greer Ellis and every other lover she'd had. "Look at me, Greer."

When they made eye contact, Eva gasped. Greer's face was a canvas of transparent need. Her blue eyes were open wide, the irises pinpoints of focused desire. She looked so beautifully vulnerable as she captured her quivering bottom lip between her teeth.

"Sorry," she breathed. "Can't stop."

Greer cried out and thrust her hips forward one final time before her rigid clit trembled and eventually softened under Eva's touch. "Come with me," she pleaded. Before Eva could respond, Greer positioned Eva's leg between her own and entered Eva with her finger. The pace of her entry kept perfect time with her vigorous strokes against Eva's thigh.

"Yes." Eva moaned as the orgasm uncoiled and spiraled out to every nerve in her body. "Yes, my darling, yes."

"You are so beautiful," Greer whispered in Eva's ear before another climax ripped through her. "I feel you coming. Don't stop." Greer's pumping increased as she rode Eva's thigh to another release of her own, then collapsed beside her. "Kiss me, more."

And Eva did. She accepted the sweetness of Greer's mouth, the tenderness of her lips, and the urgency of her tongue with the joyous knowledge that she was receiving something that only one other woman in Greer's life had. Her doubts fully resolved, she hugged Greer closer.

"Again," Greer said.

Eva looked at Greer's red-streaked eyes and half-mast lids and shook her head. "First you rest, then we make love. You haven't slept in over twenty-four hours. When we make love again, I want you to be one hundred percent because I intend to show no mercy."

"But—"

"But nothing, Detective. No excuses." They lay together, cuddling and kissing as Eva stroked Greer's hair, quietly encouraging her to rest. She resisted only slightly before her breathing slowed to the steady cadence of sleep.

As Greer slept in her arms, Eva marveled at this amazing woman. How had she so firmly and seamlessly established herself in Eva's life? Obviously, Greer had come to terms with Clare's death and chosen to take a chance on her. Once she had made her decision, Greer was emotionally forthright and physically engaging, as if full commitment was her only option. But that was Greer—complete and total loyalty. And if Eva was honest, their interaction wasn't simply about sex any longer for her. They had crossed a threshold, and Greer had been brave enough to admit it. But did *she* possess the courage to follow through?

She inched closer to Greer and alternated between taking short naps and thinking about her life. Her career had given her purpose and direction, but it also held her back emotionally and personally. She'd used her job as an excuse to avoid getting close. If she wanted her life to be different, she had to make different choices. Her feelings for Greer were real, she was certain. But how those feelings meshed with her world still puzzled her.

Eva sighed in frustration and Greer stirred beside her. She wanted to wake Greer with kisses, tell her exactly how she felt, and make love to her until they collapsed in exhaustion. But Greer was already fatigued after working nonstop. So instead of another round of sex, Eva watched Greer sleep and counted the minutes until she could wake her lover.

She placed her hand gently on Greer's chest to feel the rise and fall of her breathing. The essence of life itself pounded beneath her hand. She started counting the heartbeats, but her cell phone rang and broke the peaceful calm. Reaching into her handbag beside the bed, she opened it before it woke Greer. "Hold on," she whispered.

Slowly disentangling herself from Greer's embrace, Eva rolled out of bed and quickly dressed. Night had brought a fall chill to the air so she grabbed the quilted comforter from the back of one of the barrel chairs, wrapped it around her, and tiptoed to the bottom of the stairs.

"It's about time," her boss said. She heard him exhale a big puff of cigarette smoke. "Sorry, how are you holding up?" The obligatory concern was so atypical it amused her.

"I'm fine. What's up?"

"I've got an assignment that's right up your alley—Kyrgyzstan, political unrest, the usual. Can you leave in two days?"

"Kyrgyzstan in two days? I'm not sure I can get there that soon." Eva stretched as the muscles along her shoulders tensed. She wasn't ready for a new assignment. Her work here wasn't finished—and neither was her play. But her boss wasn't the type of man you kept waiting. He'd probably had a hard time honoring her family leave and not calling sooner.

"Jesus, Saldana, what's going on? You usually jump at a chance like this. Well, I need an answer tomorrow. If you don't want it, I'll have to pull somebody off another project."

Before Eva could say anything, he hung up. She stared at the phone and shook her head. What should she do now? Paul's case wasn't wrapped up…and whatever was going on with Greer had barely started.

"When do you leave?" Greer's tone made Eva wince. She had no idea how long she'd been standing there or how much she'd overheard. She quickly reviewed what she'd said aloud and knew the conclusion Greer had reached. Eva looked up at her, desperate to explain, and stopped.

Greer stood at the top of the stairs completely nude, hands clenched at her sides and her body trembling. The usual pale pink of her skin was stark white.

"I'm not sure I *am* going."

"You said two days. It's your job. It's what you *do*, isn't it?"

Greer implied that it would be wrong for Eva to take the assignment. She was stable and totally devoted to this place and these people She couldn't understand moving from place to place for the sake of a job. But Eva didn't know anything else. "Yes, it is what I do."

"I don't want you to go."

The statement surprised Eva and her vision blurred with tears. She hadn't expected Greer to say this. But she had been honest all night, so why would this pivotal moment be any different? "I guess I'm not as loyal as you are."

"That's not true." Greer came down stairs and sat next to Eva, covering her shoulders with the edge of the comforter.

"I've never stuck with one thing or one person for very long."

"You stay in touch with your family no matter where you are. You've held a steady job all your adult life. You came halfway around the world to clear your brother's name. What *is* that if it's not loyalty and commitment?"

"I don't know. I'm not sure about anything right now."

"You're every bit as committed as I am, Eva, but you don't believe it. You think your father made the wrong choice and that you're incapable of making a different one. I'm not convinced either of those things is true."

"What do you mean?"

"Your father loved all of you. Why do you think he kept coming back? His family *was* his anchor. It allowed him to rejuvenate and return to the work he enjoyed. And like your father, only you can choose how to live your life."

Greer's words settled comfortably in Eva's mind as she considered their potential. "Maybe you're right. Maybe it is possible to have a job and a life I love."

"I just want you to be happy." Greer raised Eva's hand to her lips and kissed it tenderly. "Come back to bed? I'm freezing out here."

"In a few minutes. You go on."

Greer kissed her and ran back upstairs. "Don't be long. It's lonely without you."

Since that first day, when against her professional judgment Greer offered to help her, Eva had felt a connection. It was as if she'd always belonged here and only now realized it. And Bessie was like a mother and best friend. Eva couldn't remember when she didn't want a life like this. But right now she needed time to think without the distraction of Greer's warm, inviting body just steps away.

She tiptoed back up, placed the comforter inside the apartment, and peeked in at Greer. She appeared to be asleep again. Eva closed the door and left quietly. Maybe she'd go for a drive to clear her head. Walking would be asking for trouble. If Greer were awake, she'd argue that either was too dangerous. But Eva could take care of herself, and she'd be cautious. She'd be observant and head for a public place where she could drink coffee and think—the diner. She needed time to process, and she couldn't while Greer was so close.

At the bottom of the stairs Bessie's old Honda seemed to be waiting patiently. She fished the spare set of keys Bessie had given her from her purse, put the car in neutral, and let it roll out of the garage.

At the bottom of the driveway, she cranked the car and headed toward town. Any other time she would be investigating Paul's death, putting pressure on those who were, or developing informants to help find Baron Wallace. But tonight a more pressing issue demanded her attention. Tonight she had to decide about the rest of her life. Was that the real reason she left Greer's bed? Or was she simply doing what she usually did when someone tried to get too close—running away?

The assignment from her boss would be the perfect out, but it didn't pique her enthusiasm as others had in the past. Perhaps she needed to reconsider her other professional options. CNN had offered her her own show, but she wasn't sure she was ready to give up the excitement and travel. So far this drive wasn't helping her concentration or providing any answers.

She slowed as she approached the first stoplight on the outskirts of New Hope and noticed for the first time how dark it was at this end of town. Either she'd been too preoccupied to notice before, or her recent brushes with death had made her more attentive. She stopped and waited as several cars crossed through the intersection. The last one in the line stalled directly in front of her and the driver got out.

The man wore a pair of torn blue jeans, black sweatshirt, and a ball cap pulled low on his forehead. It concerned Eva that she couldn't see his eyes. Alarm shot through her as he neared her car. She clicked the door-lock button and scanned the area for an escape route. Her years as a foreign correspondent had taught her to trust her instincts.

"I'm sorry about this, ma'am. I'll get it started soon as I can." The man shrugged in apology but still didn't make eye contact.

Eva kept her window rolled up but asked, "Do you need me to call someone for you?"

"That would be real nice, ma'am," he replied as his gaze darted around the area.

Something about this guy was familiar in a scary way. "Okay, I'll make the call," she said as she simultaneously floored the gas pedal, swerved around his vehicle, and left him standing in the middle of the road. Eva turned to retrieve her cell phone and looked in her rearview mirror. As the man was running to his car, she glimpsed his face in the illumination from the streetlight. He resembled the man in the picture Greer had shown her—Baron Wallace. She dialed 911, reported the suspicious activity, and described the man and his vehicle. Eva identified the man as Baron Wallace. She hadn't gotten a good look at him, but the pieces fit. Eva told the dispatcher she'd be at the diner if an officer wanted to talk with her.

When she found a corner seat and ordered coffee, Eva let the fear the encounter elicited surface. She clenched her shaking hands into fists and willed them to be still. The staccato beat of her heart slowed as she regulated her breathing. This was the third time someone, probably Baron Wallace, had tried to harm her since she arrived in New Hope. She didn't worry about being in danger on her job. She assumed she'd be okay. But this was personal, and though it frightened her, she wouldn't back down.

Eva kept her eye on the street out front for the man who'd feigned car trouble. Baron Wallace had probably stalked her, and if he was brazen and desperate enough to accost her in the middle of the street, he wouldn't hesitate to try again. Until Wallace was taken into custody or the nagging feeling in the back of her mind disappeared, Eva was content to wait in a safe public place that served potable coffee. She'd waited out security lockdowns, dust storms, and media blackouts in much worse places.

When the waitress passed with Eva's second cup of coffee, her adrenaline rush had taken a backseat to the caffeine surge. She scribbled the pros and cons of her own CNN show on one side of a napkin and the points for and against a relationship with Greer on the other side. If she ran out of ideas on one topic, she flipped the flimsy paper over and worked on the other.

After cup number three and a couple of hours, Eva's mind was spinning with possibilities and her future seemed more promising. She was ready to talk with Greer about their life. As Eva left a hefty tip to compensate for occupying the table so long, a young police officer entered the diner and headed toward her.

"Ms. Saldana?"

"Yes?"

"Just wanted to let you know that we haven't found your guy yet, but we're still looking. You need a ride somewhere?"

"No, thanks. I have my car out back."

"Let me walk with you. It's pretty secluded out there. If I don't get a call, I'll follow you to the city limits. I'd feel better knowing you're on your way again."

The young man followed Eva to her vehicle, waited until she was safely inside, then returned to his patrol car. As they pulled to the exit, the officer activated his lights and siren and took off in the opposite direction. *So much for the escort*, she thought.

Eva was about to pull out of the lot when her driver's-side window shattered with a tremendous crash. Fragments of flying glass pelted her face and body, stinging and burning as they cut and scratched her. She tried to dial 911 but Baron Wallace stuck a gun to her head.

"Drop the phone and put the car in park. Now!" He punctuated his order by shoving the gun barrel to her temple. Then he opened the door, dragged her from the car, and pushed her onto the uneven ground.

Eva slammed onto the hard surface with a thud. Her knees hit the pavement and her legs went momentarily numb. Her heart raced as she thought about how to defend herself. She had practically no upper-body strength. If she stood, her chances were better. But every self-defense class she'd taken cautioned against resisting an armed subject. Screw that. She'd take her chances fighting.

"Get up and don't try anything stupid," Wallace ordered.

Eva rose slowly and held her arm as if injured. Before she straightened completely, she jabbed her elbow into Wallace's groin in an upward motion and ran toward the diner. Her heart pounded like it might burst out of her chest as fear and adrenaline propelled her forward. She prayed her daily running ritual would finally pay off as she pumped her arms and sprinted at top speed.

But Wallace's superior height gave him the advantage. She heard his footfalls getting closer until he shoved her in the back. She fell forward and the rough asphalt peeled skin from her forearms and elbows. He pressed his foot against the back of her neck and pushed.

"If you try that again, I'll blow your fucking brains out. Do you understand?"

The pressure on her throat made speech difficult. "Yes," she managed to whisper.

"Good, now get up."

Wallace grabbed a fistful of hair and yanked her toward a residential area behind the diner. Why was she still alive? He had the perfect opportunity to kill her when she ran. Did he want to torture and kill her slowly? Rape then kill her? Use her as a hostage for some reason? It could be any of those or none. She wasn't good at thinking like a murderer. Wallace repeatedly jabbed her with the gun muzzle as he walked her into the carport of a house that appeared to be vacant, then pointed to a vehicle covered by a tarpaulin.

"Take it off and get in."

She removed the tarp, slid across the driver's seat of the car, and immediately reached for the door handle. Her heart sank as she realized it had been removed. It wasn't in her nature to give up, but her options were slowly disappearing. She wanted to scream and cry, but she wouldn't give him the satisfaction of seeing one shred of emotion. When her captor got behind the wheel, Eva asked, "Why are you doing this, Baron?"

"I warned you to leave town."

CHAPTER NINETEEN

G reer stretched across the bed and realized that Eva hadn't returned. The covers on her side were cold and the room felt empty. She stared at the ceiling, deciding that Eva had probably gone back to the main house before Bessie woke. The thought filled her with more sadness than she would have anticipated. She'd wanted to wake up with Eva by her side, make love with her, then talk about their future—if there could be one.

Yesterday she'd finally released her tremendous guilt over Clare's death and admitted her feelings for Eva. So much had happened in the past twelve hours and it all seemed right—until she'd overheard Eva's conversation with her boss. Then the questions returned: did Eva have feelings for her, was a life together possible, was it something Eva wanted, and would they have time to explore their options?

Greer could see herself with this woman for years, if they could resolve the differences that kept them apart. But they wouldn't have a chance unless Eva decided that for herself. Greer couldn't influence her choice. One thing was certain—she was falling in love with Eva, and that knowledge frightened her as much as it energized her. She stretched again, buried her face in the pillow Eva had slept on, and inhaled. The familiar fragrance infused her with an immediate desire to see and talk with Eva again.

Greer imagined Eva and Bessie sitting around the kitchen table having their first cup of coffee, allowing her to sleep as long as possible. She'd showered, dressed, and started toward the house when her cell phone rang.

"Ellis."

"Hey, partner." JJ's voice had that cautious tone she associated with bad news.

"What's wrong?"

"Agent Long shared some not-so-good news with me this morning and asked if I'd brief you. The second set of test results came back on the sergeant's clothing. They were the same."

Greer let his statement register. The line was quiet for a few seconds as they both considered the ramifications. "That means he had to have seen who shot him. Why would he lie about that? You don't think—" She didn't want to admit Sergeant Fluharty was somehow involved in Tom's death and the attempt on Eva's life. And if that was possible, by extension, was he also mixed up in Paul's murder?

"I think we have to stay objective, for the moment. But it doesn't look good. Agent Long is briefing the chief this morning and probably bringing the sarge in for questioning. And…"

"There's more?" Greer couldn't imagine how it could get any worse.

"The clerk's office can't find the officer sign-in sheet for the day of the shooting. So Long can't verify whether Breeze was in court like he said."

"Does he think Breeze could've had something to do with this?"

"It makes about as much sense as the sarge being involved. But Breeze did work on the drug task force. It wouldn't be the first time a good cop turned the corner for drugs or money."

"I'm not buying it. Let me know if anything else comes up before I get there. I'm leaving home in about ten minutes." Greer's informant had told her a cop was involved in drugs, but she'd dismissed it at the time. Could it be Breeze or the sergeant? If Baron Wallace was the shooter in Tom's death, was one of them covering for him? The only good connection between a drug dealer and a cop was an arrest. Did Wallace have something on one of them or were they in business together?

"I'll do it." JJ's voice trailed off and Greer heard some chatter on his walkie-talkie in the background. "Hold up, Greer. You need to know about this too."

"What?" When she stepped up on the back deck of the house, Bessie came out with a coffee cup in her hand and a quizzical look on her face.

"Patrol guys have an abandoned vehicle in the diner parking lot. It's Bessie's old Honda. The engine was running, driver's window smashed, and nobody around. Where's Bessie?"

"She's right here." When the other possibility occurred to Greer, her legs threatened to give way. "Don't let them move that car." She disconnected and asked Bessie, "Where's Eva?"

"I have no idea, honey. I thought she was still with you in the apartment." She looked toward the garage. "Is the Honda still here?"

She shook her head. "It's in the diner parking lot. Why would she leave without telling one of us? After all that's happened lately, she should know better. Where the hell is she?" Greer's insides tightened as the list of worst-case scenarios flashed through her mind.

"Don't be negative. She's a firecracker and knows how to talk her way out of just about anything. Give her some credit, but find her, fast." The more Bessie talked, the less certainty Greer heard behind her words of encouragement.

"I have to go. I'll call when I know anything." Greer hugged her and vaulted off the deck toward her bike. What seemed like an interminable ride ended a few minutes later when she pulled alongside the patrol car positioned behind Bessie's Honda.

The beat officer stepped aside as Greer approached and asked, "Is this your aunt's car, Detective?" Greer nodded. "Was she driving it or was it stolen?"

"Neither. She loaned it to a friend, Eva Saldana."

The look of recognition on the officer's face told Greer that he was familiar with the recent events surrounding her arrival in town. "I've called for a crime-scene tech and a wrecker."

Greer hoped the only reason he'd summoned a tech was because Eva was missing, but as she got closer her hopes faded. The driver's window of the vehicle was shattered and Eva's cell phone lay open on the seat. She placed her hands behind her back and stuck her head inside the car. Red stains had dried on several shards of glass scattered across the seat, and the sickly sweet smell of blood made her nauseous. She visually followed a trail of the dark red droplets across the asphalt back toward the diner.

With a sharp intake of breath, Greer realized that Eva had been injured and her heart galloped. She stepped back from the vehicle and drew on all her strength to steady herself. Someone had obviously taken Eva against her will. How badly injured was she, where was she, and who had her? The helplessness of that day two years ago resurfaced, and Greer railed against the improbability and injustice of being unable to prevent the loss of another woman she loved.

"Did anybody see anything?"

"No, ma'am," the officer answered.

"Any sign of a struggle anywhere else in the area?"

"No, ma'am."

"People around here get up pretty early. Have you canvassed the area for possible witnesses?" Greer asked, though she already knew the answer. Her questions were standard procedure and this young officer seemed very capable.

"Yes, ma'am. No witnesses."

As the officer and the crime-scene analyst processed Bessie's car, Greer thought about what she'd give to see Eva again, alive and healthy. If she had to choose between letting Eva go completely and having her returned unharmed, Greer had no doubt she'd choose the former. Having lost one partner, she knew it was possible to love *and* let go. She had done so with Clare after thinking herself incapable for two years. Greer made a silent deal with whatever forces controlled such things, if only she found find Eva unharmed. She could live without love but not without knowing Eva was happy and somewhere safe.

Baron Wallace drove very carefully through the center of town, past the warehouse district, and into a moderate residential area. "Where are you taking me?"

"Shut up. If you attract any attention, I'll kill you right here. I knew if I waited long enough I'd catch you out by yourself."

"Why are you doing this, Baron?" Eva kept her tone even and

matter-of-fact, careful not to betray her terror, which heightened by the minute. He had been watching her and Greer, waiting for an opportunity to attack her again. How could she keep herself safe? Instead of being negative and hopeless, she needed to keep her wits and find a way out of the situation.

"Because you wouldn't leave well enough alone. We dodged the bullet after your brother came snooping around. Then you showed up. I told you to leave, but you wouldn't listen."

"*You* killed my brother?"

Baron shrugged as if he'd made a minor error in judgment. "He got in the way."

She was enraged yet relieved when she realized this man was responsible for her brother's death. She nearly choked as she tried to swallow the anguish that crawled up her throat. She had never been violent, but at this moment she balled her hands into fists so tight her forearms ached. She wanted to hit him, claw his dark eyes, and rip him apart slowly. He had extinguished the bright light that Paul brought to her world, and he needed to pay. She looked around the inside of the vehicle for anything to use as a weapon.

"You'd probably like to kill me right now, wouldn't you?" Baron asked.

"You have no idea." She and Greer had speculated that Baron Wallace was the murderer, but she hadn't allowed herself to accept it without proof. An admission was even better. Eva breathed deeply and forced the rage to settle into a tentative calm.

"Who is *we*?" She desperately wanted to know who else had been involved in Paul's death. Wallace was certainly ruthless enough to commit murder, but he didn't seem like boss material, beyond the brute strength required to maintain order among a band of drug dealers. Whoever was behind this plan was also responsible for Tom's murder, Sergeant Fluharty's shooting, and the attempts on her life.

"You haven't figured that out yet? Not as smart as I thought, then."

"So enlighten me."

"Shut up. I need to think." Baron Wallace peeled the baseball cap off and scrubbed his knuckles across his shaved head. His pale white forehead crinkled and deep frown lines formed on his stubbled face. Careful thought and planning didn't seem to be his strong points. "Need to think," he repeated.

Baron drove around the outskirts and dark places of New Hope until the night sky began to lighten. Eva thought it odd that he didn't immediately take her to some hiding spot and get off the streets. Surely by now the police had located Bessie's vehicle and were looking for her. She swiped at the dried blood that still clung to her face and arms.

As the gray light of dawn filled the vehicle, Eva got a good look at Baron. His black eyes seemed to pop against the pallor of his skin. He was thin, though muscled. His faded black T-shirt had small holes, as did his jeans, and smelled like he'd worn them several days. They rode in silence until Baron pulled in front of a small wood-framed house and cut the engine.

"I'm taking you inside and you better be quiet."

He shoved the weapon in her back as she exited the car and nudged her toward the front of the building. After retrieving a key from above the door frame, he unlocked the door and motioned her inside. Whose house was this and why had they come here? Did the resident know this deranged man? Were they friends or relatives? Maybe Baron's accomplice lived here and she'd finally come face-to-face with the other conspirator.

Though it was a small and sparsely furnished house, it was tidy, as if someone took pride in its upkeep. Baron shoved her past a tiny kitchen that smelled of fried bacon, a bathroom that reeked of liniment, then into a musty corner bedroom. She hadn't seen or heard anyone else, but noted another room with the door closed directly across from the one they entered.

"Sit." Baron pushed her toward a straight-backed chair in the center of the room, with a length of rope on the floor next to it. She was at this man's mercy. Maybe he was the mastermind after all. He had obviously planned to bring her to this place, but she had no idea for how long or for what purpose. She mentally scanned her limited options.

A brief reporters' training session on establishing a connection with your captor if taken hostage offered several suggestions: remain calm, establish rapport, don't talk down to him, avoid appearing hostile, avoid arguments, and maintain eye contact but don't stare. Not much help. The next steps required more restraint, not her forte: be amenable, treat the captor like royalty, comply with instructions, and expect the unexpected.

What could be more unexpected than being abducted from your vehicle in a business parking lot before daybreak in a small town in the United States? The irony was nearly humorous. Why hadn't she been afraid during some of the assignments she'd undertaken in failed states throughout the world, all the times her life was in danger? Maintaining an emotional distance, she had been able to stay objective and to calmly negotiate and troubleshoot with equanimity. But this situation was different. This was personal and Baron's intent filled her with terror.

"Why don't you let me go? This will only get worse for you." So much for the training session. Now was the time for reason and negotiation.

"Can't. I need you for leverage."

Baron secured her ankles to the chair legs and tied her arms to the spindles on the seat back. She had no wiggle room. "These are too tight. They'll cut off my circulation."

"You're lucky if that's all I cut off. Now be quiet. If I hear a sound out of you, it'll be your last." He stuffed a piece of stale fabric in her mouth, tied a gag over that, and left the room.

She strained against the bindings, her wrists and ankles stinging as the coarse ties sawed into raw flesh. She flinched but kept trying to loosen the lengths of rope. The musty rag in her mouth muffled her cries for help, and she gagged on its sour odor and taste. She scanned her surroundings for anything that might help her escape but found nothing.

Except for a single bed and a ramshackle dresser, she saw no other signs of habitation—no clothing or pictures or personal items. The light beige carpet was stained and worn from years of use, and the dark brown curtains blocked the sunlight. Eva felt isolated and her apprehension deepened.

Baron Wallace hadn't bothered to blindfold her—not a good sign. She already knew his identity, and he'd expressed no problem with killing her. But he'd also mentioned leverage. Wallace seemed ambivalent, uncertain about his situation and uncomfortable with the decisions he was making. Their drive around town after her abduction and his concern about waking the occupants of the house didn't indicate a well-thought-out plan. What exactly did he have in mind? Perhaps he had information to exchange for her release.

How did the New Hope Police Department negotiate for the release of hostages? It irritated her to think of herself as a hostage, a victim. She struggled against her restraints with one final surge of anger, then collapsed, exhausted. Her eyes filled with tears and she closed them tight. She refused to show weakness or defeat. As she evaluated her situation again, she thought about Greer.

Eva had left the warmth and comfort of Greer's bed after they made love to answer her phone. What would've happened if she'd stayed in bed a little longer? If she hadn't taken the call, Greer wouldn't have overheard the conversation, they wouldn't have disagreed, and Eva wouldn't have gone for the drive that put her in Baron Wallace's path.

Now she was the center of Wallace's plan, which put him in direct conflict with Greer. She imagined that Greer was feeling helpless and experiencing a bit of déjà vu after what happened to Clare. Greer would find her, and when she did, she would seek revenge. Eva hated having caused Greer so much emotional torment. She wanted to return, apologize for the trouble she'd caused since her arrival in New Hope, and move forward with whatever they might be able to build together.

When Eva was younger her life of constant travel had excited her and provided the sense of purpose and direction she needed. It also protected her from intimacy. But that distance also had kept her isolated from the very thing that made life worth living—deep, meaningful love for another person.

But her job didn't define her. The circumstances of her life from the beginning, her values and beliefs did. Her family had been close despite her father's frequent absences. She and her siblings had enjoyed social and educational opportunities that shaped their paths and provided direction. But most important, their parents had loved and nurtured them. Exciting stories of challenge and survival of spirit filled her father's visits home.

Why had she identified with and held on to the painful aspects of love and not with its abundance or potential? She'd focused on her father's departures but not on his returns. Even those times, bittersweet with parting, had infused her with the possibilities of life. That had been her father's legacy, not the lesson of caution and moderation. Greer was right—their family had grounded her father, been his anchor. They were what brought him back time after time.

She could modify her career to suit her life and curtail her foreign assignments to a more manageable schedule. She'd earned that privilege. And for the first time in her life, she wanted to stay in one place, in *this* place. She would gladly forgo the assignment in Kyrgyzstan for the opportunity to see where her relationship with Greer led.

Maybe now was the time for a change. But as Eva looked around the stark room where she was imprisoned, she didn't see much hope or optimism.

CHAPTER TWENTY

Greer paced the compact basement radio room, looking over the dispatcher's shoulder every time a call came in. She smelled the anxiety and tension in the air. The chief had appeared on television and radio stations appealing for information about Eva's kidnapping.

It was five in the afternoon—twelve hours since Eva was taken—and they hadn't received any reliable leads. Greer and the rest of the force had been looking for her with no luck. Whoever had taken her hadn't called with a ransom demand. Time wasn't necessarily an ally in kidnapping cases. Greer's nerves were on edge but she had no idea what to do next. Her helplessness had nearly debilitated her.

"New Hope nine-one-one, what is your emergency?" the dispatcher asked.

Greer edged forward as if she could hear the caller.

"Yes, ma'am. She's right here. Hold on." The dispatcher handed the headset to Greer. "It's a Brenda Wallace, says she has information for you."

Greer held the headset to her ear and adjusted the mouthpiece. "Yes, Mrs. Wallace, this is Greer Ellis."

"I can help you." The woman's voice was barely a whisper and Greer had to strain to understand her.

"Can you speak up, Mrs. Wallace?"

"Can't, he might hear me. Listen. He brought that woman I saw on TV into my house. God knows what he's doing to her."

Greer's heart raced as she pictured Eva captive in Brenda

Wallace's home with that psychopath Baron. "Have you seen her?"

"I peeped through the keyhole into his bedroom while he was in the shower. I told him not to come back here, ever. I want no part of this."

"Can—" The words stuck in Greer's throat but she had to ask. "Can you tell if Ms. Saldana is injured?"

"I didn't get a good look, but there's some blood on her face and—I got to go. He turned off the shower. Come and get him before he does something awful. But please don't hurt him."

The line went dead. Greer handed the headset back to the dispatcher and gave instructions as she sprinted to the door. "Notify my squad, all the search units, and the patrol watch commander to meet me at our office."

Greer bolted up the two flights of stairs and sketched a floor plan of the Wallace home on the squad blackboard. From Brenda Wallace's information, Eva was being held in Baron's bedroom on the southeast corner of the residence. The shortest distance to her would be through the back door. That's where Greer and JJ would enter. She positioned the other detectives around the residence with reinforcements from patrol. Brenda Wallace had been concerned about Eva's safety, which was enough for entry without a warrant under exigent circumstances. Greer double-checked her plan and pulled her vest on over her T-shirt as the rest of the squad arrived.

"We've got a credible lead. Baron Wallace is holding Eva at his mother's place. She said Eva is injured but she doesn't know how badly. I thought you guys checked his mother's house earlier." She directed her comment to the patrol officers assigned to assist in the search. "I gave you a list of all his hangouts."

"We did, ma'am. But his car wasn't there and it was all quiet," one of the officers said.

"You didn't go in?" The officer shuffled his feet and couldn't meet her gaze. *Why didn't I go myself*, she wondered. *If she's badly injured, I'm to blame, only me.* She shook her head in disbelief and continued the briefing.

"Here's the layout of the house and your assignments." Greer pointed to the blackboard to make each point, then addressed the watch commander. "Lieutenant, can you provide units to back us up on entry?" When he nodded, she indicated where they would be posted. "Let's be ready to move in five minutes."

When the other officers started suiting up, JJ put his hand on Greer's shoulder. For the first time, she realized that she'd taken over what should've been his role with the squad. As acting sergeant, JJ should have reviewed raid plans and authorized warrantless entries. But she saw no sign of reproach in his eyes, only concern.

"Do you want me to take the lead?" he asked.

"No, I've got to do this."

"I'm not asking you to stand down. Just let me give the entry order. We want to be sure we play it by the book."

She considered his suggestion and knew he was right, but somehow relinquishing even a small part of this operation seemed like a failure.

"I'll give the order and we'll go in together, at the closest point. Agreed?"

"All right, but don't get in my way, JJ."

The look he gave her sealed the agreement. "Let's move," he ordered.

As they walked past the sergeant's door, it opened and Sergeant Fluharty walked out. He looked like he'd been sick or drunk for weeks. He'd lost weight and his cheeks were hollow, his eyes lackluster.

Greer stopped, her mind a jumble of confusion about this man whom she'd considered a mentor. He had questions to answer, evidence to account for, but in her heart he was the man who'd saved her life. It would take more than a misunderstanding or a lab mistake to change her feelings about him. "Hey, Sarge, you okay?"

He looked back toward Agent Long, who was seated at his desk. "Sure, kid. Don't worry. Where you going in such a hurry?"

"Baron Wallace has kidnapped Eva."

The news seemed to make Fluharty's appearance degenerate even more. His shoulders hunched forward as he placed a hand on Greer's forearm. "You be careful. He's gone off the deep end."

"Will do, Sarge."

Agent Long spoke from behind Fluharty. "I hate to do this, Greer, but Bastille won't be going on the raid. I need him."

Greer wanted to ask Long about the residue test and about

Fluharty and Breeze's involvement in this mess, but now wasn't the time. She'd get the details and sort it out later. Right now Eva's life was in her hands.

By the time the additional patrol officers joined them at the staging area near the Wallace residence, it was dark and their odds of a surprise approach increased greatly. JJ briefed the uniformed guys on their roles and everyone got into position. "Nobody move until I give the word," JJ said into her earpiece as they snaked to the back of the house.

Greer flattened against the wood-frame building beside the window she'd identified as Baron Wallace's bedroom, and the rough surface scraped her skin. She disregarded the slight pain and listened for any sound from the room. A tiny break in the heavy curtains allowed a dim stream of light to escape, and she edged closer and looked inside.

As Greer's eyes adjusted, her breath caught in her throat. Eva was tied to a chair in the center of the room, her face covered with blood. Baron Wallace stood over her waving a gun like a madman. Greer couldn't hear what he was saying, but she could see his lips move as he spoke to Eva. Then he backed away from her and lay across the bed with the gun on his chest. They needed to move quickly.

If Baron had expected an immediate response to Eva's kidnapping, he was most certainly getting antsy. If he harmed her further, Greer would never forgive herself. She'd failed the woman she loved once before, but it wouldn't happen again.

"JJ, get ready." She raced back to JJ's position at the rear of the house and nodded.

JJ announced, "All units, go, go, go!" Then his size-thirteen shoe shredded the flimsy back door.

Greer was at the bedroom before JJ disentangled his foot from the remnants of the door. Other officers forced their way in the front but she didn't wait. She shouldered into the room, positioned herself between Eva and Baron, and drew down on him. He was still lying across the bed and rose only slightly when she entered, as if he'd been waiting for her. The chair Eva was in had toppled to the floor and she was lying on her side, facing away from the door.

"Drop the gun, Baron," Greer ordered. "Do it!"

"Sure, sure, don't shoot." He eased the gun off his chest and placed it on the floor at his feet. "It's about time you got here."

Officers entered the room behind her and she motioned them toward Baron. "Cuff this piece of crap." When she was certain Baron was under control, she turned toward Eva. She was very still but her eyes were wide. Greer removed the gag and righted the chair.

"Yeah, it's about time you got here, Detective."

Greer sighed with relief. If Eva could still tease her, she was probably okay. "Where are you hurt? You're bleeding. What did he do to you?" she asked as she untied the ropes.

"When he broke the car window, the flying glass scraped my face and hands. It's not serious." Eva stroked the side of Greer's face and her tension eased a bit. "When I heard you come in the back, I turned the chair over so he couldn't use me as a shield. I might've bruised my shoulder, but it'll be okay."

"You're pretty smart for a reporter," Greer said as she helped Eva to her feet and walked her to the door.

"No harm intended, ma'am," Baron said as Eva passed.

Greer turned and charged Baron. She shoved him into the wall and drove her forearm against his throat. *"No harm intended?* You kidnapped her, you sick fuck. How is that not harmful?" Baron's face was bright red and his eyes bulged.

"Greer." Somebody called her name. "Greer, he's handcuffed," JJ said.

At that moment Greer didn't care about excessive force. She wanted to make Baron Wallace pay for touching Eva. He'd crossed the line and Greer had to make an example of him.

But then Eva's soft, calming voice spoke from behind her. "Greer, let him go. I'm all right. He killed Paul and he needs to answer for it."

Greer released her grip and Baron slumped down the wall, choking and sputtering for breath. "He admitted he killed Paul? He said that?"

"Ye—ah," Baron coughed, "and I've got a lot more to say, but only to you."

"We'll see about that," JJ said as he pulled Baron from the floor and escorted him outside.

Greer looped her arm through Eva's, pulled her close, and led her toward the front of the house. "I don't know what I would've done if—"

"I know, darling. I know." She leaned into Greer's side. "We've got a lot to talk about."

The undercurrent of innuendo in Eva's tone ignited a surge of emotional warmth through Greer. She wanted to pull Eva into her arms and kiss her, answering any question in her heart with a resounding physical yes. But this was neither the time nor place.

"Well, I guess you caught yourself a killer, didn't you, Ms. Saldana? You believed that Paul was murdered. Now you have proof and an admission. That's excellent work."

"Don't forget your part. You put yourself on the line to help me and I won't forget that. But we're not finished. Wallace implied that he had an accomplice, as we suspected. We have to find him, Greer. I won't rest until we do. Any ideas?"

Greer didn't want to tell Eva about the unexpected turn in Tom Merritt's murder case—that Sergeant Fluharty or Breeze could be at least withholding information and, at worst, involved. But they'd come too far to keep secrets. "I have an idea. It's not a pleasant one, but I have to look into it."

Before Greer continued, one of the patrol officers called out. "What about her?" Greer turned to see Mrs. Wallace standing between two burly officers.

"We should probably give her a medal. Let her go and see if you can secure her doors before you leave. And file a claim to have them repaired at the city's expense." She waved to Mrs. Wallace and said, "Thank you." When Greer returned her attention to Eva, it looked as if she might faint. The energy she'd displayed earlier had vanished, and the dried blood on her face and arms looked ghastly against her pale skin. "I'm taking you to the hospital."

"I don't need a hospital. Please, tell me about the lead, then we'll go home."

Home? The way Eva said the word made Greer's heart pound with possibility. She hoped Eva meant it exactly the way it sounded— like she considered Greer's home her own. But that seemed too much to wish for. "Bessie would rake me over the coals if I didn't get you checked out first. You know how protective she is."

"But isn't Bessie there? Couldn't she do the honors? She's probably worried sick anyway, waiting to hear from you. Please."

Eva's deep brown eyes pleaded and Greer couldn't say no. She helped Eva into the car and retrieved a first-aid kit from the trunk. "I have to clean you up a bit or you'll scare her to death. She's good with other people's blood, but not when it's someone she cares about." Greer sat on the floorboard in front of Eva and wet a piece of gauze from a bottle of water. She gently wiped around the cuts on Eva's face and flinched each time she saw a new injury. "Bastard," she muttered. "I should've choked him to death."

A smile tugged at the corner of Eva's mouth and her gaze met Greer's. "I'm all right. You don't have to worry anymore. And, by the way, thanks for the rescue."

Greer's skin flushed and she looked away. "It's what I do."

"No, it's who you are." She cupped Greer's cheek. "And I love it. Now tell me about our next move."

"*We* don't have a next move. I'm taking you home, then I'll go back to the station and interview Baron Wallace. He can probably verify my suspicions." The words she was about to say weren't easy. "Sergeant Fluharty or Breeze or both could be involved in this, somehow." The expression on Eva's face froze and she started to speak, but someone came up behind them.

"Sorry to interrupt," JJ said, "but this clown says he's not talking to anybody but you. What do you want to do?"

Greer was torn. She wanted to take Eva home, put her to bed, and stay with her so no one could threaten or harm her again. She and Eva were reaching a tentative understanding, and even the shortest separation could scatter them in opposite directions. But the professional in her wanted the last pieces of this puzzle.

"Let's go," Eva said.

She wanted Eva with her more than anything, but she'd been in jeopardy since she came to New Hope, and Greer wanted her to finally be safe. "Please go home and let Bessie tend to your cuts. I want you out of this. I can't let you come with me."

"You can't stop me, Greer. We've been in this investigation together from the beginning. I have to see it through as much as you do, maybe more because Paul was my brother."

"You're one stubborn woman. Are you sure?"

"I'm positive. *We* have to do this."

Greer tried to be firm, but she lost all willpower where Eva was concerned. "You realize that you can't be in the interview room with me, don't you? But you can watch from a viewing room." Eva nodded and Greer turned to JJ. "You heard her. We're going to the station."

Thirty minutes later, Greer walked into the dingy interview room, having reread the entire Saldana and Merritt files. SBI Agent Long agreed to let Greer handle the questioning in both cases because of the obvious connections. She pulled out a chair across from Baron and placed her notepad on the table between them.

The small room reeked of unclean bodies and stale trash, and its walls displayed the random scratches and smears of many bored suspects. Greer let her gaze roam around the room, in no hurry to engage Baron Wallace. He had something to say, and her apparent lack of interest would only fuel his desire to talk. This man needed to make a deal. She could smell the desperation like sweat seeping from his pores.

Baron's eyes were bloodshot. If her sources were correct, he'd been moving from place to place since the APB was broadcast. Few people could sleep with a bounty on their heads. He constantly scrubbed his knuckles over his shaved head and tried to make eye contact with Greer.

"Ain't you got no questions?" he asked.

"I already have the facts. I know you killed Paul Saldana. Do you have anything to tell me that might help your case?" JJ had already advised Wallace of his rights, so Greer was comfortable letting him speak freely.

"Well, *I* didn't kill him exactly."

Greer felt a momentary rush of panic but it quickly passed. All suspects started out lying about their involvement in a crime, especially one as serious as murder. Baron needed to tell his story his way and then she'd have him cornered. "Why don't you tell me about it?" Greer thought about Eva on the opposite side of the two-way mirror with Agent Long and JJ and wished she didn't have to hear the horrible way her brother died. But she'd insisted on watching the interview, no matter how bad.

"He was at the old warehouse on Lewis Street taking pictures. We couldn't chance that he might've got us in one of his shots. I was told to shut him up and get the camera. I didn't actually kill him. He snorted too much cocaine, that's all. Then I took the camera and left."

"You brought the cocaine?" Baron nodded. "You forced him to snort it?" Again he nodded. "How?"

"I put my gun to his temple and threatened to blow his fucking brains out."

Greer's heart ached as she imagined what Eva must be feeling. "Did anything unusual happen while you were there? Did the man say anything or make any last requests?" Greer wanted to confirm that Baron was in fact in the room, and one minor detail that hadn't been released to the press could do that.

Baron scratched his head as if in deep thought. "He begged a little and he wanted to take his shoes off. I guess his feet were hot or something. He took off his shoes and socks and threw them around the room."

Bingo. She had Paul's killer. A tremendous wave of relief swept through her and she felt almost giddy. All the hours and days of uncertainty about whether Paul had committed suicide or died of an accidental overdose vanished. Eva had been right all along, and Greer was glad she'd agreed to help her, in spite of the challenges her decision had raised. Sometimes justice required a degree of discomfort.

Greer wanted all the tiny bits and pieces of the case before she addressed motive or accomplices. If she led Baron through each event, he would have no bartering kernels. "And you shot Tom Merritt in the warehouse."

Baron looked surprised. "Why would you think that?"

"Because Eva Saldana was snooping around in her brother's death. She wouldn't let it rest. You had to do something. So you called Eva, pretending to be an informant, and set up the meeting. But you're a bad shot. You missed."

"I told her to come alone. That guy wasn't supposed to die. I was aiming for her."

As the callousness of his statement registered, Greer wanted to vault over the table and choke him lifeless. He'd admitted to trying to kill the woman she loved. It took all her restraint to remain professional and continue the interrogation.

Baron kept talking. "I even jumped you that night at the Sunset Motel to get you to back off. Women—jeez, you're a stubborn bunch."

Greer wasn't concerned about her minor assault. She wanted to get to the bottom of Paul's case and everything that had happened since. "And Sergeant Fluharty? Why did you shoot him?" The question registered like a slap on Baron's face. He seemed genuinely surprised and confused. Greer could see the seldom-used wheels turning in his mind.

After several seconds of silence, Baron regained his blank expression and answered simply, "It had to be done."

Baron took too long to come up with an answer. The truth didn't require time for consideration or fabrication. And Baron made no reference to the sergeant trying to shoot him, stop him, or even block his path. Greer was even more convinced that Fluharty was involved in these crimes. She would come back to this line of questioning later.

"And when you botched the first attempt on Eva's life, you kept trying?"

"She wouldn't stop. So I thought a car accident would look natural."

"And when that failed?"

"I watched your house until I found her alone and made my move. But I didn't hurt her."

Greer clenched her fists under the table to keep from attacking him. He'd admitted trying to shoot Eva and run her off the road. Did he expect her to believe the kidnapping was harmless? "I'm having trouble believing that one. If you didn't intend to hurt her, why kidnap her?"

"I knew I was in deep shit and needed something to barter with. I was waiting for you to find me tonight and I'd tell you everything."

"And have you told me everything?" Baron had been cautious about revealing his accomplice. This had to be the piece he hoped to use as leverage for a more lenient sentence. But she didn't intend to let him off lightly. She'd lay the case out in such a manner that

Baron would get absolutely no consideration for cooperation. She owed it to Paul and Eva.

"Not yet. You don't know who the boss behind this whole thing was, and you don't know why we did it."

This was the moment Greer had waited patiently for. This was her opportunity to snatch any chance of a deal out from under his nose. But it was bittersweet. She reviewed the sergeant's recent behavior and appearance. The steady decline after his divorce suddenly made sense. She had to play a hand that she never thought she'd hold. The words tasted sour as she forced them from her mouth.

"Let me tell *you* who the boss is and why you did it. You and Fred Fluharty are in the drug business together. The *why* is simple—greed."

She thought she might have to call a medic for Baron as he paled and his breathing became rapid and irregular. "How—how did you know?" he finally managed to ask.

"I'm a cop, Baron. It's what I do, figure things out. So Fluharty told you about the warehouse meeting and you hid inside until we arrived."

"Yeah, and I had to shoot him to make it look like he wasn't involved. I should've killed that bastard a long time ago."

"So it *was* you and Fluharty in the warehouse the night Paul took the photos."

"That's why I had to get the camera and take care of him."

Greer had all the pieces she needed but one—why would Fred Fluharty resort to dealing drugs? What had gone so terribly wrong in his life? But that was a question she had to ask him face-to-face.

"Well, I think I've heard all I need to from you." She couldn't wait to get away from Baron Wallace, have a shower, and scrub the stench of his evil from her body. Eva would need her now, and she definitely needed Eva. This had been a long and unhappy journey that brought them together. If they were to have a life, it would need to begin with resolution of the past. Greer rose and walked to the door.

"Not so fast, copper." His tone shifted from that of a submissive minion to a man with a purpose. It stopped her cold.

"What?"

"We haven't talked about my deal."

"There won't be any deal, Baron, because you didn't tell me anything I didn't already know. That's how it works." Delivering that message gave Greer more pleasure than she had imagined. But he still wore a determined, smug grin.

"So you're not interested in why your girlfriend died?"

CHAPTER TWENTY-ONE

Greer clutched the door handle to the interview room, afraid she might twist it off. How dared this drug-dealing killer mention Clare, much less try to use her death as a bargaining tool? "I know why she died. Johnny Young, your predecessor, was a desperate bastard who went on a shooting spree and killed her."

"You don't know shit. And if you want the real story, it'll cost you."

The next thing Greer remembered, JJ and Agent Long were restraining her. She was inches from Baron Wallace's face with her fist poised to strike. Her jaws hurt from clenching her teeth so tight and her head pounded with fury. *"You will tell me."* She refused to accept the possibility that any aspect of Clare's death was unresolved or unsettled.

"Greer, stop," JJ whispered in her ear. "He's jerking your chain. He's got nothing."

"Oh, but I do, Detective," Baron answered. "And if you want to know what it is, the name of the game is *Let's Make a Deal*."

Greer struggled to free herself and go after Wallace, but JJ and Long held firm. What could Baron Wallace possibly know about Clare's death? The killer was dead, the case closed. Sergeant Fluharty had prevented the need for a trial.

The last thought drained her. "Let go," she said to JJ. A month ago she would've bet her career that no one could buy Fred Fluharty for any amount of money. But with the recent revelations, anything was possible. What didn't she know about Clare's death? Had that information allowed a co-conspirator to go free for the past two years?

"Talk to the DA." She locked gazes with Agent Long, challenging him to defy her, and left the room. She stumbled into the hall in a daze and backed against the wall for support. She didn't realize Eva was next to her until she spoke.

"Greer, don't let this person get to you. He's desperate." Eva encircled Greer in her arms and pulled her close. "He's playing some sort of sick game."

Raising her head to meet Eva's gaze, Greer asked, "But what if he isn't? I accepted her death as a random act of violence. What if we missed something? I've just come to terms with losing her. But if I failed her in some way, I couldn't forgive myself."

"You couldn't fail anyone, Greer, especially not Clare. It's not in your nature. She certainly knew that and so do I."

"I want to believe that," Greer said as she paced the hallway waiting for Agent Long to return with the district attorney's offer. When she saw his face, she knew Wallace had a deal.

"You want me to question him?" JJ's tone was tentative and gentle. He knew the gravity of this situation and how much it meant to Greer.

"No, I have to do it, but thanks." She wondered if she could.

"If you're sure. You have to be—"

"I know, professional, and not beat the crap out of him. I can handle it, JJ." She gave Eva a smile that she hoped was reassuring and reentered the interview room.

"So, you believe me, huh?" Baron asked with a self-satisfied smirk.

"Not until I hear what you have to say. So start talking." She handed him the DA's offer, which he skimmed and slid back to her. "You realize this *deal* only offers leniency in sentencing, not a full pardon or immunity from prosecution, right?"

"Sure, but every little bit helps. Your girl didn't have to die that day."

Every muscle in Greer's body tensed and her nerves sparked with emotion, but she remained quiet and restrained.

"Johnny Young and Fluharty were in business before I took over. Fluharty stole drugs from your evidence room after the cases were tried and passed them along to Young to sell."

"Why would Sergeant Fluharty suddenly decide to go into the drug business?"

"His old lady left him and he took it pretty hard. I guess he loved her or some bullshit like that. Anyway, she wanted a big alimony check and he couldn't give it to her on a cop's salary."

"How did he and Young connect?" Greer knew a follow-up interview would flesh out all the details of Wallace's statement, but she needed the salient points now.

"Fluharty got drunk in a bar a couple of towns over, got in a fight, and Johnny helped him out. They started talking and it happened a little bit at a time until the business was booming. Fluharty liked the extra cash and it kept the ex off his back."

Greer found it hard to believe someone had lured her sergeant into criminal activity so easily. But she understood the depths of despair that loss and loneliness produced. She'd lost herself after Clare died. "So what happened then?"

"Fluharty was greedy and Johnny got tired of being milked for a bigger cut."

Greer's patience was wearing thin. "What does that have to do with Clare Lansing's murder? Get to the point or your deal is off the table."

"Johnny was willing to risk being locked up to confront Fluharty that day. He intended to turn him over to the chief, blackmail him, or kill him. But somebody tipped Fluharty off that he was coming. The sergeant met him on the steps of the police station and you know the rest. Johnny fired first, hit your girl, then Fluharty shot and killed Johnny. Problem solved and Fluharty looked like a hero."

The churning in Greer's stomach worsened and she fought the urge to vomit. Clare had been caught in an argument between two drug dealers. The senselessness of it ripped at Greer's heart and she wanted to scream. It happened to people every day in cities around the world, but she couldn't imagine that her lover would be the victim of such a tragic act. She'd accepted the idea that Clare's death was an arbitrary act of violence. She wasn't sure which was worse.

"How do you know this?"

"I was Johnny's second. He told me what he planned that day.

And being an industrious businessman, I made an anonymous call to Fluharty. When Johnny didn't come back, I heard what happened on the news. Good and bad for me—I was in charge but I inherited Fluharty. So what does this get me?"

"That's between you and the district attorney." She hoped it got him absolutely nothing. "My concern right now is Fred Fluharty." But *concern* wasn't the right word. She tried to pinpoint an emotion that described her feelings at this moment but couldn't.

"You might be too late."

"What do you mean?"

"All that sugar he drinks in his coffee will kill him someday." Baron laughed and shook his head. "But I'd love to share a cell with him for a few hours. Can you arrange that?"

Greer stood and walked out of the room without answering his question. When JJ and Eva tried to stop her in the hall, she kept walking. "JJ, call Bessie and have her come get Eva." Then she looked at the woman she loved. "Please go home, Eva, and don't argue with me, not this time." She needed answers, and to get them she had to face Fred Fluharty.

The sharp edge of betrayal sliced through Greer like concertina wire as she remembered the many times she'd confided in her sergeant. She'd fallen apart in his office on numerous occasions, and he'd comforted and supported her. He'd arranged for her transfer into the homicide squad "to look after her" for Bessie. She couldn't recall how often he'd covered for her because she was too devastated to come to work. Now she understood the source of his concern—guilt. He was responsible for Clare's death and was trying to make amends. But that was an impossible task. He'd committed the one offense for which Greer could never forgive him, and she needed to tell him.

Agent Long caught up to her in the parking lot. "Ellis, I know you have to confront him, but we're going with you." He motioned behind him to her squad mates. "He denied everything this afternoon, so who knows what he'll do."

"I don't care who comes along, just don't get in my way—not this time."

When they arrived at the rundown hotel, Fluharty's room door was partially open. Greer nudged it wide with her foot and stepped inside, motioning for the others to stay back. "Sarge," she called out, but the room was dark and quiet. She flipped on the table lamp and saw him lying across the bed. "Sarge." No answer.

Greer moved closer and noticed an empty coffee cup and a dark stain on the bedcovers next to his left side. To the right lay a note written on hotel stationery and his service weapon. Fluharty's skin was ashen and cold to the touch, with no apparent signs of injury. Whitish gray froth clung to the corners of his mouth. Greer checked for a pulse but didn't find one. "He's gone," she said to the officers behind her.

With the tips of her fingernails, Greer tweezed the note off the bed and read silently:

Greer,

Forgive me. I never intended to hurt anyone, especially you. Clare's death was a horrible accident. I tried to make it up to you over the past two years, but I know I failed. I've disgraced the department, our profession, and myself. This is the only way out for me.

Fluharty

"I'll notify the state forensics lab and have them process the scene," Agent Long said. "I'm not sure what happened here, but it looks like suicide."

Greer noticed a chalky white residue in the bottom of the overturned coffee cup. "Have your folks check the cup and his sugar container for cocaine. It could be narcotics poisoning. Remember Baron's wisecrack about sugar killing him someday?" That would be apropos, though she wished she'd had a chance to confront him.

She walked to her vehicle and scooted onto the hood. JJ joined her and nudged her in the side. "He fooled us all. It sucks big-time."

"You can say that again, but it clears up a lot of things, doesn't it?"

"Yeah, like why he was so anxious for me to close the Saldana file so fast. He was covering his drug business. He's probably even responsible for the missing hotel guest register, because I know I put a copy in the file. I guess if I was *really* desperate I could understand needing money bad enough to commit a crime, but not murder. I still can't believe he ordered Baron to kill Paul Saldana."

"Yeah, it doesn't jive with the man I thought I knew, the man I considered a friend."

"But once he'd committed himself, he had to keep going. He was in too deep. When Eva came to town she threw a monkey wrench in the works."

"And I was the perfect patsy. He needed somebody on the case review that he could control, somebody he knew would come straight to him with any new leads. And I did. He fed every bit of information I gave him to Baron. I was the one who put Eva and Bessie at risk. Hell, I'm even responsible for Tom's death. How stupid."

"Stop it." JJ's voice was firm. He grabbed her by the shoulders and forced her to look at him. "None of this is your fault, so don't even go there. And in case you've forgotten, you stood up to the entire squad. You even kept investigating after the chief and the SBI told you to stand down. Nobody pulls your strings when it comes to your job, partner, nobody. This is all on Fluharty, so let it go."

"But I trusted him."

"We all did, and he betrayed us. That hurts. I'm beginning to understand how much damage disloyalty can cause. But we'll help each other through it."

Greer nodded and her spirits lifted a bit.

"Good. Now I have to brief the Staties and get going. I've got a date."

"A date? What about Janice?"

"Janice *is* my date. She's agreed to see me. We might be able to work this thing out, but she needs time to trust me again."

Greer patted him on the back as she slid off the hood of her car. "Good for you, Jake. Best of luck. Think I'll go home too. If I'm lucky, a gorgeous reporter's waiting there to throw herself into my arms and pledge her love."

"Yeah." JJ laughed. "Good luck with that."

CHAPTER TWENTY-TWO

E va walked to the edge of the porch and looked again toward the road that led into town. It seemed like hours since Greer had sent her home. She was no good at waiting, pacing didn't calm her, and sitting was impossible.

"Pacing won't get her here any faster, honey." Bessie raised her glass of tea. "Do you know the secret to a great batch of sweet Southern iced tea?"

Eva laughed. The tension in her body demanded release, and screaming wouldn't be polite. Bessie had already cleaned the cuts on her face and arms and listened to her story of being kidnapped by Baron Wallace. The least she could do was indulge Bessie's attempt to entertain and distract her. She returned to her seat. "I can't imagine."

"Some people think it's the sugar. But the secret is in the tea bags. If you don't use the right ones, it's either too bitter or too weak. You can tell who your true friends are if they share their beverage and cooking tips with you." Bessie took a big gulp to prove her point. "Perfect."

"I'm dying to know. What are the best tea bags?"

"Everybody knows they're—" Greer's motorcycle rumbled. They both met her as she pulled into the driveway. "Are you all right?" Bessie asked.

"A little stunned, but no physical harm." Greer hugged Eva and clung to her for several minutes. "How are you?" She held Eva at arm's length and seemed to check every inch of her for signs of injury.

"I'm fine. Bessie fixed me up and I'm good as new."

Greer then turned to Bessie and gave her a prolonged hug. "Fluharty is dead."

Bessie clutched her chest. "Oh, honey, you didn't—"

"No, I didn't kill him. It looks like suicide or an accidental overdose of cocaine. Somebody probably laced his sugar with coke." Greer hung her head, and Eva could tell the guilt had already set in. "He was dirty—drugs." Her voice cracked. "And he's the reason Clare died. If I hadn't trusted him, you two wouldn't have been in danger. I remember what Eva said about having to choose between loyalty and the truth."

"No!" Eva and Bessie said at once. Eva nodded to give Bessie the go-ahead.

"You *will not* take the blame for Fred Fluharty's weakness and deception. I won't allow it. If it hadn't been for you and Eva, none of this would've come to light. God knows how long he might have gotten away with it."

Greer's eyes filled with tears and Eva put her arm around her waist. "Yeah, what she said goes double for me. You can't blame yourself for everything that goes wrong in this crazy world. And what about Breeze?"

"The clerk's office finally found the sign-in sheet. He was in federal court like he said, so he's been cleared. At least we didn't have two rotten apples."

Bessie patted Greer on the back. "I'm glad you're okay and this case is finally solved. Why don't you two go talk or something. I've got reports to do on my wayward nurses. See you later." She herded them in the direction of the garage and walked back toward the house.

When they were alone in the apartment, Eva remembered the last time she'd shared this space with Greer. She'd been conflicted about her life and what she wanted. Her past and her unwillingness to take a chance had clouded her feelings for Greer. As she stood here now, those things seemed small and insignificant. She had no doubt about her feelings for Greer. She wanted to spend her life with her and needed to say those things aloud.

"Greer—"

"Wait." Greer put a finger under Eva's chin and tilted her head up. "I'd like to kiss you. Is that all right?"

Eva stretched on her tiptoes and brought their lips together. Greer's response was tentative at first, but warm and inviting, reverent in appreciation. Eva allowed her to set the pace as her own need rose—the need to be completely and totally joined.

She wasn't ready for Greer to pull away. "Thank you." Her blue eyes lacked some of their usual sparkle and vitality. "I need to take a shower. I feel—"

"I know." Eva understood the film of degradation and distaste that permeated the pores after dealing with the bottom dwellers of life. She'd spent an hour under a hot stream of water to sluice the unpleasantness of the Baron Wallace experience from her body. "I understand."

Greer started to touch her face but stopped. "Are you sure you're okay? Do your cuts still hurt?" A look of pain flashed across her face and she turned away. "I should've kept you safe."

Eva touched Greer's arm and gently urged her to face her again. "It wasn't your fault. You've done everything possible to protect me. I decided to take a drive without telling anyone. What happened after that is my fault. Besides, I'm perfectly fine. Now go shower. I want to be with you, soon."

Without responding, Greer walked toward the bathroom, peeling off clothes as she went. By the time she reached the glass enclosure, she was completely nude and Eva throbbed with the need to touch her. She listened to the steady flow of water from the shower and imagined it running down the length of Greer. She controlled the urge to go to Greer as long as she could, then stripped and sneaked in behind her in the spacious shower.

Greer braced herself against the tiled wall with her arms stretched out shoulder height and her head bowed. Water saturated her thick blond hair, ran down the taut muscles of her torso and over the exquisite swell of her ass. Eva saw the tension along Greer's shoulders, back, and legs. She stepped closer and smoothed her hands up Greer's sides.

"Let me help you, darling." Eva massaged the bunched muscles of Greer's shoulders and felt them relax beneath her touch. She pressed and squeezed her way down Greer's rib cage to the top of her buttocks, paying particular attention to the lumbar section of her back. As she worked some of the tightness away, Greer seemed to unwind and the strong lines that defined her athletic body loosened.

"God, that feels amazing. Your hands are magic." She let go and swayed with the rhythm of Eva's strokes. Greer stood quietly for several minutes as Eva worked her way around her body, kneading and releasing tension in her stiff muscles. "That is great. Would you mind if I hold you for a minute?"

"You can do whatever you want," Eva replied, straightening to make eye contact.

Greer pulled Eva under the shower spray with her. When their bodies merged, Eva thought she might stop breathing. The connection was sensuously gentle and the physical fit perfect. Her breasts rested comfortably under Greer's smaller ones, and the firm ridge of Greer's leg eased naturally between her own.

Eva shifted to accommodate Greer's movements as the slick moisture of arousal coated her sex. She rode up and down Greer's thigh, purposely rubbing against Greer's pubic mound with each rise. Greer responded with deep, guttural moans that shot another current of excitement through her. Eva could come within minutes by rubbing her body against Greer's. But she wanted more than corporeal satisfaction.

Her body ached for the physical touch that would sate her flesh. She craved the release. But the desire to surrender, free from mental and emotional doubt, to give without reservation, consumed her. Greer kissed her and Eva matched Greer's fervor, the hunger growing with each second of contact. Her body tingled with stimulation and her legs weakened.

"Can't stand much longer," she said between kisses.

Greer turned off the shower, wrapped Eva in a bath sheet, and swept her up as though she were weightless. She carried Eva to the bed and placed her gently on the edge. With the corner of the towel, Greer dried Eva's hair and body with light, delicate strokes. "I need you so much, Eva." Her breathing was deep and halting.

"I need to say one thing before we make love."

"Tell me." Greer's touch was excruciatingly tender, the tips of her fingers barely touching skin as she gazed into Eva's eyes, waiting.

"I love you, Greer. I've been afraid to say it. I didn't trust myself."

"And now?"

"It's the only thing I'm completely certain about." As the words gushed from Eva's lips she experienced a sense of peace. The words rang true in her ears and in her heart.

"And I love you, Eva Saldana."

"Are you sure? We have to be sure." Eva searched Greer's face for any sign of reservation but found none. She didn't want to ask about Clare but needed to know if Greer could love her fully while still carrying Clare in her heart.

"If you're concerned about Clare, don't be. She has a special place in my heart, but you're my present and my future…if you want to be."

Eva answered with a kiss, deep and passionate. Their tongues poked and sucked, fueling the heat in Eva's center. Her answer at this moment and forever was yes, and she'd spend her life making sure Greer knew how much she was loved.

Greer reclined on the bed and pulled Eva on top of her, still wrapped in the bath towel. Even with the barrier between them, they still fit perfectly, as if made for one another. Greer kissed her and rocked back and forth, their legs entwined for maximum contact. The firm muscle of Greer's quadriceps rubbed and teased Eva's tender clit through the terry fabric and made her wet with anticipation. Greer inched her hand up Eva's side and cupped a handful of breast, teasing an erect nipple between thumb and forefinger.

The towel between them was like the layers of conflict and resistance they'd overcome to reach this point. With the peeling away of the fabric, Eva imagined their bodies and souls exquisitely revealed to each other. She ached for the sensuous feel of skin on skin again.

"Greer, please touch me."

"With pleasure."

She slowly peeled the bath sheet away from Eva's body. Cool air settled on her heated skin and raised goose bumps. She shivered as her nipples puckered and she stretched toward Greer, begging for her mouth. Greer lightly brushed her fingers down Eva's chest, circling each breast with tantalizing strokes, avoiding the firm contact Eva wanted.

Greer cupped Eva's sex and her hips rose to meet the pressure. Moisture soaked her crotch, and the knowledge that Greer could feel it as well excited her. She wanted Greer to know how ready she was. Greer moved her hand and, again, the cool air against inflamed flesh caused a shudder that rocked Eva with longing.

"Please, baby." Eva sat up and wrapped her legs around Greer's body, rubbing her center against coarse blond pubic hair. She needed more stimulation. Her feelings for Greer magnified the physical sensations and brought her closer to climax. If she didn't come soon, she'd burst. "I want you everywhere. Don't make me wait any longer."

Greer straddled her again and Eva thought she'd never seen a woman more beautiful. Nipples erect with need topped her perky breasts and Eva longed to suck them into her mouth. The patch of blond hair between her legs glistened with arousal. A bolt of excitement shot through Eva as she glided her fingers into Greer's body.

"Don't." Greer grabbed her hand before she made contact. "If you touch me, I'll explode."

Eva tried again. "And what's wrong with a little explosion?"

When Eva finally touched her, Greer's sharp intake of breath was as stimulating as a caress. Her entire body ached and pounded for release. "Please, lie on top of me. I want you inside me when I enter you." Greer's blue eyes shone with emotion, like she was looking into her soul, at the love that radiated from her heart. "I want to come with you."

Greer stretched out on top of Eva and their bodies moved as one in the rhythmic slide and stroke of lovemaking. Their timing was perfect, each moment of contact exquisite in its combination of friction and moisture. Pressure spiraled inside her and discharged bursts of electricity through her system. Soothing warmth became burning heat and demanded attention. She opened her legs wider. "Now, baby, inside me now."

Eva worked her hand between their bodies and curved her fingers into Greer's opening as Greer entered her. "Oh, yesss." She gasped between breaths. "Like that." The simultaneous internal stroking stoked her need and she struggled to maintain her rhythm inside Greer. She wanted to see her lover's face when they came together for the first time. Her body arched to meet Greer's thrusts. She was losing control. "Soon, my darling."

"Tell me when." Greer sucked Eva's breast in time with their cadence. The firm momentum of her hand and the steady pull of her mouth drew Eva's passion from deep inside. She wrapped her legs around Greer and opened herself completely as the coiled pleasure sprang loose. "Now, I'm coming now."

Greer's tempo increased and she answered, "I'm with you." As her climax flowed from her, Eva kissed Greer. She thought she might die from all the sensations. She breathed her orgasm into Greer's mouth as she spilled into her hand. They emptied and filled until they collapsed on top of each other and gasped for breath.

Several minutes passed before either could speak. "Wow," Greer finally said. "That was, well, it was, I mean...you know?"

Eva laughed. "I certainly do." Though words failed her, Eva knew exactly what Greer meant. They were perfect together. This was the woman Eva had dreamed about, hoped for, but had been afraid to find. She represented everything Eva wanted in life—love, excitement, stability, and home—all in one gorgeous package. She couldn't imagine going forward without her by her side.

Greer pulled the bedspread over them and sighed. She couldn't believe how right this moment felt. It had been two years coming and she'd begun to think love wasn't in the cards for her again. But she was wrong. She now understood that love wasn't a one-shot deal. It was possible to fully and truly love more than once in a lifetime. But in order to love someone sometimes you had to let her go. If that's what it took to prove her love for Eva, she would do it no matter how much it hurt. They had things to settle. The desire to resolve those issues tugged at her even at this perfect moment.

Eva snuggled closer and stretched her leg over Greer's. "Mmm, that was awesome, but I can see those wheels spinning in your head, Detective. Spill."

"It can wait. Let me hold you."

"I don't want us to keep things from each other. Please tell me what's bothering you."

"I was wondering what happens now."

Eva rolled on her side and stared into Greer's eyes. "Well, at the risk of sounding like a cliché, we live happily ever after."

Greer thought her heart might pound out of her chest. "And what does that look like?"

"You and me together forever? Could that work?"

"You mean you'd stay here? What about your career? What about the assignment in Kyrgyzstan?"

Eva kissed Greer tenderly and her passion rekindled. "I turned down the job. I've negotiated another position—host of my own show on CNN. The boss has been trying to convince me to change tracks for months."

Greer's breathing increased and she smiled so big it almost hurt. "You'd give up the excitement of traveling all over the world covering the latest-breaking stories for a life here in New Hope?"

"About like you'd give up police work." Her disappointment must've been apparent because Eva hurried to explain. "If I run my own show, I decide what stories I cover. You'd have to accept that as part of what I do—of course, with the understanding that I'd always come back to you."

"I wouldn't stand in the way of your career, no matter what you chose. But I do like that last part." Greer gathered Eva in her arms and hugged her again.

"Besides, I have a story to finish here. I promised Tom a double byline. Who knows how long it could take to wrap that up, maybe months."

"I'd like you to consider something else as well."

"Yes?"

"If things work out, would you consider living in the house at some point? It's my home, after all."

"Living together?" Eva pulled away almost imperceptibly, and the words sounded tentative, as if she was testing how it felt to say them aloud. "I've never lived with anyone."

"The 'if things work out' and 'at some point' parts of the request were for your benefit. Take all the time you need. I want you to be sure about how you feel, about us."

"Oh, darling, my reluctance isn't about my feelings for you. I just don't want to disappoint you."

"That can't happen as long as you're honest with me. It has to be right for both of us. Just let me know when you're ready for the next step."

Eva kissed Greer and nestled against her chest. "Thank you for being patient with me. I love you with everything I am. *You're* my home."

About the Author

VK Powell is a thirty-year veteran of a midsized police department. She was a police officer by necessity (it paid the bills) and a writer by desire (it didn't). Her career spanned numerous positions including beat officer, homicide detective, field sergeant, vice/narcotics lieutenant, district captain, and assistant chief of police. Now retired, she lives in central North Carolina and divides her time between writing, traveling, and amateur interior decorating.

VK is a member of the Golden Crown Literary Society and Romance Writers of America. She is the author of three erotic short stories and one romantic short story published in Bold Strokes Books anthologies. Her novels are *To Protect and Serve*, *Suspect Passions*, and *Fever*.

Books Available From Bold Strokes Books

Breaker's Passion by Julie Cannon. Leaving a trail of broken hearts scattered across the Hawaiian Islands, surf instructor Colby Taylor is running full speed away from her selfish actions years earlier until she collides with Elizabeth Collins, a stuffy, judgmental college professor who changes everything. (978-1-60282-196-5)

Justifiable Risk by V.K. Powell. Work is the only thing that interests homicide detective Greer Ellis until internationally renowned journalist Eva Saldana comes to town looking for answers in her brother's death—then attraction threatens to override duty. (978-1-60282-197-2)

Nothing But the Truth by Carsen Taite. Sparks fly when two top-notch attorneys battle each other in the high-risk arena of the courtroom, but when a strange turn of events turns one of them from advocate to witness, prosecutor Ryan Foster and defense attorney Brett Logan join forces in their search for the truth. (978-1-60282-198-9)

Maye's Request by Clifford Henderson. When Brianna Bell promises her ailing mother she'll heal the rift between her "other two" parents, she discovers how little she knows about those closest to her and the impact family has on the fabric of our lives. (978-1-60282-199-6)

Chasing Love by Ronica Black. Adrian Edwards is looking for love—at girl bars, shady chat rooms, and women's sporting events—but love remains elusive until she looks closer to home. (978-1-60282-192-7)

Rum Spring by Yolanda Wallace. Rebecca Lapp is a devout follower of her Amish faith and a firm believer in the Ordnung, the set of rules that govern her life in the tiny Pennsylvania town she calls home. When she falls in love with a young "English" woman, however, the rules go out the window. (978-1-60282-193-4)

Indelible by Jove Belle. A single mother committed to shielding her son from the parade of transient relationships she endured as a child tries to resist the allure of a tattoo artist who already has a sometimes-girlfriend. (978-1-60282-194-1)

The Straight Shooter by Paul Faraday. With the help of his good pals Beso Tangelo and Jorge Ramirez, Nate Dainty tackles the Case of the Missing Porn Star, none other than his latest heartthrob—Myles Long! (978-1-60282-195-8)

Head Trip by D.L. Line. Shelby Hutchinson, a young computer professional, can't wait to take a virtual trip. She soon learns that chasing spies through Cold War Europe might be a great adventure, but nothing is ever as easy as it seems—especially love. (978-1-60282-187-3)

Desire by Starlight by Radclyffe. The only thing that might possibly save romance author Jenna Hardy from dying of boredom during a summer of forced R&R is a dalliance with Gardner Davis, the local vet—even if Gard is as unimpressed with Jenna's charms as she appears to be with Jenna's fame. (978-1-60282-188-0)

River Walker by Cate Culpepper. Grady Wrenn, a cultural anthropologist, and Elena Montalvo, a spiritual healer, must find a way to end the River Walker's murderous vendetta—and overcome a maze of cultural barriers to find each other. (978-1-60282-189-7)

Blood Sacraments, edited by Todd Gregory. In these tales of the gay vampire, some of today's top erotic writers explore the duality of blood lust coupled with passion and sensuality. (978-1-60282-190-3)

Mesmerized by David-Matthew Barnes. Through her close friendship with Brodie and Lance, Serena Albright learns about the many forms of love and finds comfort for the grief and guilt she feels over the brutal death of her older brother, the victim of a hate crime. (978-1-60282-191-0)

Whatever Gods May Be by Sophia Kell Hagin. Army sniper Jamie Gwynmorgan expects to fight hard for her country and her future. What she never expects is to find love. (978-1-60282-183-5)

nevermore by Nell Stark and Trinity Tam. In this sequel to *everafter*, Vampire Valentine Darrow and Were Alexa Newland confront a mysterious disease that ravages the shifter population of New York City. (978-1-60282-184-2)

Playing the Player by Lea Santos. Grace Obregon is beautiful, vulnerable, and exactly the kind of woman Madeira Pacias usually avoids, but when Madeira rescues Grace from a traffic accident, escape is impossible. (978-1-60282-185-9)

Midnight Whispers: The Blake Danzig Chronicles by Curtis Christopher Comer. Paranormal investigator Blake Danzig, star of the syndicated show *Haunted California* and owner of Danzig Paranormal Investigations, has been able to see and talk to the dead since he was a small boy, but when he gets too close to a psychotic spirit, all hell breaks loose. (978-1-60282-186-6)

The Long Way Home by Rachel Spangler. They say you can't go home again, but Raine St. James doesn't know why anyone would want to. When she is forced to accept a job in the town she's been publicly bashing for the last decade, she has to face down old hurts and the woman she left behind. (978-1-60282-178-1)

Water Mark by J.M. Redmann. PI Micky Knight's professional and personal lives are torn asunder by Katrina and its aftermath. She needs to solve a murder and recapture the woman she lost—while struggling to simply survive in a world gone mad. (978-1-60282-179-8)

Picture Imperfect by Lea Santos. Young love doesn't always stand the test of time, but Deanne is determined to get her marriage to childhood sweetheart Paloma back on the road to happily ever after, by way of Memory Lane—and Lover's Lane. (978-1-60282-180-4)

The Perfect Family by Kathryn Shay. A mother and her gay son stand hand in hand as the storms of change engulf their perfect family and the life they knew. (978-1-60282-181-1)

Raven Mask by Winter Pennington. Preternatural Private Investigator (and closeted werewolf) Kassandra Lyall needs to solve a murder and protect her Vampire lover Lenorre, Countess Vampire of Oklahoma—all while fending off the advances of the local werewolf alpha female. (978-1-60282-182-8)

The Devil be Damned by Ali Vali. The fourth book in the best-selling Cain Casey Devil series. (978-1-60282-159-0)